The Cradle Queen

STEVEN VEERAPEN

First published in 2018 by Sharpe Books.

For my grandmother, Rose
1930 – 2018

CONTENTS

She was walking in the gardens of Joinville, picking her way carefully between the clipped emerald bushes. Sunlight dappled the lighter green of the lawns and cast shadows on the gravel path stretching ahead. Somewhere someone was laughing. Somewhere music was playing. Just out of sight, water splashed happily from a fountain. And then someone was grunting, moaning with alarming intensity. Where? Why? It did not make sense. Nothing was making sense. The greenery began to blur into darkness. No, she thought: please, no, I want to stay here.

Marie of Guise was wrenched from her dream and thrust into darkness. It took a few seconds for reality to etch out her true surroundings, but she was a pragmatic woman. She let it come. She was not in France. She had not been there, not breathed in its mellow perfumes, in years. She was in Scotland, in Stirling Castle, in a tiny, draughty bedchamber above the royal apartments. Next to her, lit only by a handful of candles on the far side of the room, the bedclothes writhed grotesquely, and her husband moaned. He was having the nightmare again.

James V was a poor sort of husband. He could be charming, certainly, when he wanted to be. He could be gregarious, too, putting his arm around his friends and leading dances. Yet he could more often be pensive, moody, sullen, and suspicious. When what she had begun, from the early days of their marriage, to think of as his black-humoured days descended, there was little point in talking to him. The nightmare usually heralded the black mist's descent.

Gently nudging him with a silk-covered arm, she whispered, 'James. My lord. James. Rouse yourself.' She spoke Scots. His French was so poor that he had been nicknamed James the Silent when he visited Paris, because his embarrassment had kept his mouth shut most of the time. Back then she had not considered that she might be thrust into his bed. Then he had come seeking Madeleine de Valois, his short-lived first wife, diseased though she already was. After one last convulsion, he threw back the covers.

In the dimness, it was hard to tell if he was awake. She could hear and feel her heart pulsing. 'James?'

'You woke me,' he grumbled, his voice querulous. A bad sign. His handsome face was indistinct. A Tudor face, they said. To think she had been sought as a bride by his fat, mad uncle. With the thought, the chilly room seemed suddenly welcome. The bride who had been chosen for Henry instead had been hastily rejected before he could even rouse his member to sire a spare.

'You were crying out, as though in pain.' She swallowed. 'You dreamt badly?'

'Aye,' he said, his back stiffening. 'The dream again, Marie. The ghost of Finnart, crying out for my blood.'

No sympathy stirred. Only irritation. It was not the first time he had torn away her own dreams. 'Finnart is dead,' she said without expression. She gave him this assurance every time the nightmare came upon him. James had had his old friend, Hamilton of Finnart, executed in Edinburgh months before. She had never understood the charges, nor been sure if she believed them. But she had kept her mouth shut, letting events happen. It would not to do question him. At present it was her job to give him an heir, and that she had done. More, of course, must follow. Yet when James was undergoing his darker moods Marie half-wondered if he was succumbing to some taint that ran in all those who had Tudor blood. It was a kind of bloodthirst and sang-froid, an ugly lack of humanity.

'I need no ghost from the grave to tell me that, woman,' he snapped, throwing himself back against the cushions with a whump. *Child*, she thought. 'Yet there he was, his sword drawn. He … you know how he does in that dream. He struck off my arms. He rose to strike at my neck, and I could not move. I was refrigerate with horror.'

'It is just a dream, my lord. God give you good sleep.' She let her eyes wander to the glow bouncing crazily off the burnished metal of the prie-dieu opposite.

'Just a dream, only a dream,' he mimicked. 'It is an omen, as you know. Our house will be struck at. It will be struck down. God is showing it all to me. And you say it is only a dream. *Pah*!'

2

Marie settled herself back in the bed. She knew that she should comfort her husband, rouse the servants and call for hot, sweet wine. But what was the point? He would only wring his hands and moan. She had little time for self-pity. It stopped things getting done.

Still, James had planted a seed: a hard, hideous, annoyingly fruitful little seed. Omens, prophecies, forecasts of doom. They were trafficked freely in France. There might be something in them. Well, it was not something good Catholic women ought to meddle with. Time would reveal whether James' dream was a warning from beyond, or the guilt-ridden imaginings of an ill-humoured king. Turning her back on him, she pulled the bedclothes up around her neck and prepared for sleep. A moment later she closed her eyes tightly and bit on the inside of her cheeks. A strong hand had grasped her waist and was beginning to roll her back over.

***

With a year, Marie had seen both of her small sons interred with royal honours, dead within a day of each other. All that she had done in Scotland, her reason for being there – to furnish the royal bedchamber with heirs – had been undone at a stroke. She had not wept. God had laden her with misery, but, she reasoned, that could only prove that He had chosen her for one of His anointed. She firmly believed – she could only believe – that salvation was sweeter to those who endured pain. Her husband, of course, had sunk into horror and self-pity, seeing conspiracy everywhere, poisoners in every kitchen. Almost smugly he had pointed out to her the truth of his dreams. Both arms, the little Dukes of Rothesay and Albany, had been struck off. Her own dreams turned to peaceful French convent cells.

The following year the head too had been severed. As Marie recovered from the birth of a daughter, Mary, King James himself had done the supremely selfish act of dying. She was alone in a strange country, a relict, powerless, with only her daughter to anchor her. At least, though, she might sleep alone.

There, she reflected as she lay in bed again, thankfully alone, in the pleasure palace of Linlithgow: the prophecy, if prophecy it was, had been fulfilled. The nightmare was over.

Or so she thought.

1

Twenty-six. Twenty-seven. Twenty-eight. Simon Danforth counted his steps along the flagstones of Dalkeith Castle, as he had counted them through the courtyard. It steadied his nerves, like playing a game. *Twenty-nine. Thirty.* Ahead of him, the square back of the liveried guard slowed its forward motion and stopped. As the man turned, the crest of the Douglases he wore as a badge caught the torchlight. 'In here,' he grunted, turning to the left and fishing at his belt. *Thirty-six, thirty-seven,* Danforth counted hastily, shrinking his steps. Ending on one of his lucky numbers would be a good sign. As the dull snick of a key turning announced his and his colleague Arnaud Martin's arrival at the cell, nervousness again swept over him. They stepped past the guard, ignoring his sneer, and Danforth laid eyes on Cardinal David Beaton, sitting under a canopy of crimson dulled to claret, for the first time in months.

Prison, Danforth thought, his lip curling, clearly meant something different to the rich and powerful than it did to the poor. Beaton's captors could never be quite sure if or when he'd regain power and they would have to bow before him again. Hence his not-quite-honourable confinement at the Douglas castle of Dalkeith was a study in luxury. On every wall tapestries glimmered with gold thread, and books sat on each table, gilded edging catching the firelight.

Danforth and Martin had been surprised at the number of familiar faces they had passed in the courtyard. Already the cardinal's master of horse was in the stable block alongside the muleteer; his barber, singing boy, and tailor were also playing cards in the courtyard. Even their immediate superior, Mr Lauder, Beaton's chief secretary, was there, piles of paper under each arm. Each had given Martin and Danforth wearied, smiling shrugs and nods as they were shuttled by the frowning Douglas retainer into the cardinal's quarters. It was imprisonment, to be sure, but imprisonment with all the perks of a great household. There was an almost carnival atmosphere to it.

Beaton looked up at they entered, raising a grey eyebrow as the door was unlocked. At sight of Danforth and Martin, his face broke into a smile that did not quite touch his eyes.

Danforth felt his stomach flutter. Both he and Martin had departed from their master on bad terms. In the months following their refusal to help him forge the late King James' will, they had been studiously ignored, their wages delivered, but no demands made on their services. Beaton was unpredictable, one minute the avuncular friend, the next an angry and venom-tongued enemy. The trick, Danforth had learned during his years of service, was to espouse loyalty, and to never, if it could be at all avoided, refuse him anything. Sadly, sometimes it could not be avoided.

'Mr Danforth. Mr Martin,' said Beaton, not rising from his little wooden curule. He was swathed in violet rather than his usual scarlet robes, looking like a jaded Caesar. His face, usually narrow, seemed to have filled out in captivity. He let the silence draw out. It was, felt Danforth, as though he was enjoying their discomfort. Perhaps this was their penance. It was unattractive. In the past, Danforth had never questioned his master's authority, but his treatment of them over the affair of the king's will had done something to him – and, he thought, to Martin too. It was like a small card had been pulled from a house built of them: not a weight-bearing one, not enough to bring it down, but one that made it wobble. He wondered if Beaton could read that on his face, and looked at the carpet, feeling exposed.

On the thought came a wave of guilt. If he could think so critically of the man who had become almost a father to him, then what kind of a son did that make him? But the idea that the man he had transformed into a hero might be otherwise, might even be sometimes wrong, was all the more troubling because it could not be banished.

'My friends,' said Beaton at last, the smile unfeigned, 'it is good to see you. And after such a time, and such disasters. But let's not dwell on the past, eh? You've been well?'

'Yes, your Grace,' they chimed. Danforth looked at Martin, who gave him a nod of encouragement. He cleared his throat before speaking. 'We are both sorry to see you in this state, sir.' They had prearranged the speech. 'And sorry also if ever we have failed you,'

'I said, Mr Danforth, that we shall not dwell on the past. As you can see,' he said, waving an arm around, 'I am quite well kept. A house guest on progress, not a prisoner, they tell me. A house guest without the right to leave – that's the only bugger. You see, that fat wretch King Henry and I now have something in common. We neither of us can pass easily through doorways.'

'Yes, your Grace.' Hobbled, Danforth had nothing else to say. The grovelling apologies could remain unspoken.

'We had your summons,' said Martin. 'It was brought to us in Stirling by your man Fraser.'

'Fraser!' said Beaton. 'Oh, naughty Mr Fraser. He was brought to me just the other day. Come straight from Stirling, he said, and eager for me to learn of your … ah … misbehaviour there.'

Martin reddened and turned to Danforth. They had seen Fraser only a few days before. Martin had pushed the oily, jealous man face-first into a mud pit. Neither had had any time for him: a glorified skivvy with ideas above his station. 'I … your Grace, he … my temper, he – well, you know what he did?'

'Oh, he told me that you would be full of false and slanderous accusations, and I was not to credit them.' A smirk snuck up Beaton's cheek.

'But he did it, your Grace, he grew jealous of Danforth here and spoiled his garden, frightened his servant, a poor old woman.' Martin was rocking on his heels, gesturing wildly. 'Out of spite and malice he acted.'

'And do you say the same, Mr Danforth?'

'I do,' said Danforth, his chin rising. 'Mr Martin speaks the truth.'

'I have no doubt,' said Beaton, thumping a fist on the arm of the chair. 'I made up my mind that Fraser was a liar, a fool and worse some time ago. But needs must when one's honest servants are absent. Och, well, there I go speaking of the past when I forbade it. His protestations of innocence – "don't listen,

7

your Grace", "they will lie, your Grace" – they convinced me that he was as guilty as sin itself. I'll deal with Shug Fraser when I'm out of this place, don't you worry.'

His voice dropped, his eyes flitting to the door. The guard who had brought them had left them alone, closing the door securely; but he was undoubtedly lurking just outside, ears cocked. 'To business. I have had enough of captivity. Enough of being kept from affairs so young Arran can grind his mill. My friends are working towards my freedom. Already I am gathering cash enough to convince the Douglases to make him set me at liberty. Yet in my absence they have, I think, been advancing the English cause. What do you know of it?'

'Very little,' said Danforth, keeping his own voice as quiet as possible. 'We have been in Stirling, your Grace, quite immured.'

'My mother's house was burned down,' volunteered Martin. 'We caught the brute who did it.'

'Jesus,' said the cardinal, concern creasing his forehead as he leant forward. 'Your family, they're all well?' Danforth noted the wrinkle of his brow. It seemed to him genuine. It must be, he decided. Whatever his faults, their master took care of his servants. If that made him sometimes more like one of the protectionist border chieftains than a man of God, then such was the necessity of life.

'Oh, yes, sir,' said Martin. 'Maman's a tough old bird.'

'Thank God for that,' said Beaton, crossing himself. 'Then I've no need to track down the culprits and see them … well … And so in the midst of spoiled gardens and burning houses, you've neither of you been touched by the affairs of the great?'

'Rumours only have reached us that King Henry is making great demands on the lord protector, Arran,' said Danforth. Danforth pictured the protector, the governor, as he called himself: a dough-faced lad in his twenties, full of self-importance, always decked out in silver and, as everyone knew, a master at playing the idiot if it might help line his pockets.

'Ah yes, the governor. My faithful wee cousin. My faithful cousin who keeps me locked away lest I interfere with his attempts to subject the realm to a madman's greed. Moving me to Blackness next, I hear, with Seton to keep me safe. A hard prison with a friendly keeper, eh? Well, young Arran does like to hedge. Yet in putting me away like this, the whelp hopes to strike the sword from the hand of the holy Roman church. Think on why, gentlemen.' The words 'heresy' and 'England' snaked through Danforth's mind, the letters entwined. His cheek jerked. 'Aye, only the new queen's life stands between us and a godless realm ruled by Arran and the Douglases. Henry's imps, all.' Irritation flickered over Beaton's face. 'Do you have something to say, Mr Danforth, or are you having a stroke?'

'Your Grace, I did hear that the governor's party, his friendship with the Douglas brothers, are all a-quiver. King Henry has demanded that Scotland's castles be given over to him. All our defences. And that Scotland is to make no policy abroad without his express command and approval. As though he were this country's true master. He's demanding that this realm finally acknowledge itself as no more than a jewel in his crown.'

'Yes, I had heard. The English king has overreached himself. Even his minions in our nobility balk at the shamefacedness. Is that all?'

'Yes, your Grace,' said Danforth, a little disappointed. He had hoped that might have been news and felt a little foolish that it wasn't. Still, it felt good to be talking politics again, to be back in the thick of it, the swirling of allegiances and the calculation of motives. But he had been outside of the cardinal's sphere for too long to feel confident. For a while, he had felt like quite the private citizen, his mind focused on small-town concerns. The players on the political stage had become just that: players, distant and affected. For a brief spell there had been more to life than work. There had been family, and friends, and even thoughts of women.

'Well, it is a topsy-turvy world indeed. The case is this. The king is dead, the new sovereign a baby, the English king demanding Scotland's subjection. Our daft young governor, having accepted Henry's support and sworn to bow to him, is said to be growing weary of the influence of the Douglas brothers. Well, parliament shall soon confirm his as lord

9

protector. The estates can't fail to do so, as long as he's next in line to the throne. Might even make him full regent. And strengthened by parliament, he might be free of Henry's pair of ancient Douglas puppets.'

'Damned Scotch-English,' said Martin, thudding a fist against his thigh.

'Aye, but even then, Archie Angus and George Douglas have Scottish hearts. Anyway, the governor is finally beginning to grow some bollocks, but neither one is quite hairy enough to tell Henry and his friends to go to the devil. The country needs a firm hand. So does my cousin. They need me, even if they're too damned thick-headed to know it.' Danforth detected a rising note of excitement in the old man's voice, as though active discussion of state affairs was breathing life into him. Even his eyes seemed to sparkle as he spoke. It was infectious. 'Yet I have other work for you, for we have other friends to seek.' Beaton let it hang in the air. Danforth knew his master had a flair for the dramatic. 'I speak, gentlemen, of the queen dowager, mother to our new sovereign lady. Though I dislike women in politics, I will own that she's a sharp one. Too sharp by half. She is one who might be of great use, if we can take her in harness. Her greatest concern, at present, is the safety of her child. They are currently at Linlithgow, but it is a palace, not a fortalice; the dowager wishes against all hope that the little queen be moved to some stronger fastness, safe from the governor or any who might wish her harm. If the baby should die, after all, Arran will likely become King of Scots for lack of a surer heir. The Douglases would certainly support him if he should aim so high.

'It is my will that you court Queen Marie. Mr Danforth, you will turn her against England, if she needs any encouragement in that quarter. Mr Martin, you will incline her to France, remind her of her heritage and my own great love of her old country. Find out how secure her person is, and that of the bairn. Or rather find out how secure they are not and stress my remedy.'

Danforth turned to Martin and both broke out in nervous smiles. The queen dowager, Marie of Guise, loomed tall and smiling in Danforth's mind. He had seen her when she arrived at St Andrews as King James' bride: tall, elegant, bejewelled, smiling and inclining her head seemingly at every individual in the crowd. Had any man there not envied the groom? He shut down that thought quickly. Women of the highest class were like Greek statues – they might be admired for their beauty, but no good servant would ever be low enough to admit to hoping to lay his hands on one. Danforth had time to let the words 'royal service' march proudly through his mind before Beaton spoke again. 'I see this commission pleases you. And it's glad I am of it. I confess I sent Shug Fraser ahead to make your introductions. So, her Grace should know that two men are coming from me, aiming to help her move the queen deeper into the realm. Into safety. I rather liked the idea of shaming that smelly old goat Fraser by having him announce the imminent arrival of his enemies. Aye, when he returns I'll –'

The squeaking of the door silenced Beaton, and all three men turned their heads.

'Beg yer pardon, my lord cardinal,' said the guard, poking his bushy head in. 'I surely hate to disturb your Grace, knowing you enjoy yer solitude and seein' as ye have so *few* bloody visitors, but Ah'm just a humble conveyer of your guests, so it seems.'

'You taunt me, gaoler?' snapped Beaton. 'I'd advise you not to, if you know what's good for you hereafter.' Colour rose in Beaton's cheeks. The guard dropped his sarcasm and turned to someone Danforth couldn't see beyond the door.

'Go in.'

A boy entered, only about twelve but resplendent in royal red-and-yellow. The guard slammed the door after him, staying outside. The child immediately fell to his knees. 'Your Grace, my lord cardinal,' he said, in an affected, piping voice. 'I come from the queen dowager in residence at her palace of Linlithgow with a message from you.' The accent was strange – Scots, but with a barely-there lilt.

'From me?'

'Uh … *for* you,' said the boy, finally looking up.

'That's grand, laddie,' said Beaton. 'Speak softly, now. Speak with care, do you understand me?'

'Aye, your Grace. The queen – the queen dowager I mean –

11

she told me what to say and how to say it.' Canny woman, thought Danforth. 'You sent a man, Fraser, to her at Linlithgow,' he said, his squeaking voice turning to that of a little lecturer as he recited his lines. 'It is her duty to inform you, my lord, that your servant has fallen ill with an accident.' Darting a glance behind him first, the boy drew a finger across his throat to complete his garbled message. 'She bids you get word to her that something must be done for him, and right quickly. Until then she will keep him close. His ... uh, his illness will not be advertised until your own physicians can tend to him.'

Beaton paled, but said nothing. Instead he made a quick sign of the cross. Eventually, he croaked out, 'thank you, boy. My men here will take you down and give you something to eat.' The boy beamed, and Martin reached out and ruffled his hair; he squirmed away, frowning. 'You hear that, gentlemen? You are become my worthy physicians. Though poor Fraser I fear is beyond earthly aid. No family either, no sons to avenge him that I know of. Listen to me, lads, and I say this in all wisdom: you are about to enter upon a stage, on which every person is playing a part. Play yours well, my friends. Find out what has become of Fraser, see if he had any enemies – save yourselves. Then get you both to Linlithgow. Court the dowager. Win her to us. God speed you on your way.'

2

'How did it feel seeing his Grace again, Mr Martin?' asked Danforth. They were in the courtyard. Martin had just returned from seeking the little page a mug of ale and some bread from the kitchen servants at Dalkeith. While he was gone, Danforth had sat down on a low wall by the stable block. Beaton's other servants had left him alone. They knew him, he supposed, as a solitary man, best avoided and only discussed behind his back. There he had let his mind wander. Being back in the cardinal's service is what he had wanted, after all, what he had prayed for. Why did it feel like such a dull climax, even with a potential assassination to investigate? Recently, perhaps, he had come to see that life had value beyond delivering good service.

Martin didn't sit down. Since his mother's house had been burned down, the younger man had seemed constantly alert, eager always to be on the move. They had travelled to Edinburgh before visiting Beaton, to don their liveries and spruce themselves up, and all the time Martin had been desperate to be off.

'How did it feel?' Danforth repeated. It was a question that even a few months before he would never have asked. Then privacy had ruled him, a solid carapace of formality and withdrawal shielding him from the world. Not it seemed natural, almost expected.

'Feel?' asked Martin, kicking at a stone and turning on the spot to watch it skitter away. He shrugged. 'I don't know. Good? Aye, his Grace is a good master. I've had greater things on my mind to be honest.'

'Yes.' Danforth folded his arms and looked up at the sky, a turbid, lowering grey. It was cold, and his breath came out in a funnel of mist. 'Well, is the young page suitably fed and watered?'

'Aye.' Martin brightened. 'He's eating just now. Here, that was some news he brought though. About Fraser.'

'Hmm. Though I confess I did not like the man, it grieves my heart to know that he lies dead. Did the boy say anything? Was it by the hand of some unknown assailant, on the road perhaps?'

'I didn't like to ask him.' Martin jerked his head at the courtyard, where men in the Douglas colours were gathered in groups, sharpening knives and occasionally casting them hostile glances. 'Not in front of these monkeys. Said once he'd stuffed his face to meet us in the stable block. Good boy. He's half-French too, from a good house, sent over when the king was wed. "Before I was a man", he says.'

'Excellent. I should imagine that rogues on the highway have set upon Mr Fraser.' The news across the country was that violence had escalated since the king's death, and that the roads were best avoided unless travelling in a well-armed group. It stood to reason. When the political nation fell into chaos, the rest followed, like water disappearing down a drain.

'Maybe,' Martin said. He had started working his hand at a loose piece of stone in the wall beside Danforth, getting his fingers under it and easing it out.

'Of course, you know, it might be possible that there is some other plot. Something aimed against the new queen, or the old one.'

'Maybe. He was an old shit, but he was one of our old shits, you know? Aye, it's a rotten business, to be honest. Here, have you met the old queen? The dowager? Queen Marie?'

'I have,' said Danforth, unfolding his arms and allowing a smile to tug at the corners of his mouth. 'On her arrival at St Andrews. When she came to the country as a bride. She even spoke to me, when she visited the castle.'

'Oh? What did she say?'

'She said, "are you a scholar or a priest"? In French of course.'

'And what did you say?'

'I said, "A clerk, madam, and pleased you are to be our queen". In Scots. Of course, what I ought to have said was, "With your Grace's leave, I am a servant of the lord bishop". And I should have said it in French, of course. But she did not mind. She smiled and moved on. I suppose she did not understand a word I said, so fresh had she come to these shores.

But smile she did, and one of warmth, too, as I recall it.' As Danforth spoke, he pictured her that day, a winsome smile on her face. He was not naïve enough to think that all high-born men and women had an interest in the lives of servants, but some of them – like Queen Marie – managed to convince people that they did. She had looked around at everyone assembled on a grey, windy day and made each feel like they were the only person in whom she was interested.

'Well, it sounds like you're old friends, then. Maybe she'll remember you.'

Danforth gave Martin a sharp look, hoping to detect sarcasm, but his face was impassive. 'If you think to mock, Mr Martin, I –'

'Peace, here comes the page boy. His name's Mathieu, by the way. Be kind.'

'I am without fail kin –'

'Good morrow to you, gentleman,' said Mathieu, marching towards them and bowing. 'I … uh … thank you for your hospitality.'

'It's not ours,' said Martin. 'It's the Douglases have the run of this place.'

That seemed to throw the boy a little, the affected adulthood faltering. 'Well, mebbe I should go over there and give thanks?' He pointed at the groups in the courtyard.

'I wouldn't,' said Martin. 'Bugger them. Come, let's speak privately.'

Danforth eased himself off the wall, his knee cracking. 'Ouch,' said Martin. 'Would you prefer to be carried in a litter, old bones?' Danforth gave him a sour look, but without much heat in it. It was good to see a bit of humour again.

The stable was dank, dark, and reeked of manure. The door to it was rickety and reached neither floor nor ceiling, but it was better than nothing. Danforth's old plough horse, Woebegone, was stabled alongside Coureur, Martin's sleeker, black mount. Neither paid much attention to the intrusion. Danforth walked the length of the small building and back. 'We are quite alone,' he nodded. 'Now, young …'

'Mathieu,' said Martin.

'I know that, sir. Mathieu, I have some questions regarding your message.'

'I dunno,' said Mathieu, suddenly seeming frightened. 'I was to speak to the cardinal. I didn't get telt I could say anything else.'

'It's all right,' said Martin. 'We're the cardinal's trusted secretaries. You're in the queen dowager's household, is that right?'

'Aye.'

'Well, you're allowed then to speak to her well-trusted servants rather than jetting up and down her palaces, barging into her bedchamber and speaking to her Grace yourself?'

'I … yes. Yes, that's how it works.'

'Well it's the same thing here, Mathieu, exactly the same.'

The boy relaxed, breathing out.

'Now,' Danforth began. 'Are we to understand that the cardinal's servant, one Mr Fraser, is dead?'

'Yes, sir,' said Mathieu, eyes widening. 'Oh, very much dead.'

'Good. Well, not good, but you take my meaning. Was he slain or did he meet with some accident?'

'Most definitely slain, sir.'

'And where did this happen?'

'Just beyond the palace walls, they found him.'

'Who found him?'

'The queen's guard. He was … the night before he was whinging about not feeling well – he was a whinger, Mr Fraser, I thought, though not to speak ill or anything. A … pleurnicheuse, the dowager's women said.'

'Go on, son,' said Martin.

'Yes. He wasn't well, he kept saying. He wanted to leave. Said he would be gone by the morning. And he was, you know, in a way. The guard found him with his arms chopped off, and most of his head, I think. I didn't see him but.'

'Oh shit,' said Martin.

'Kindly do not curse before the lad,' said Danforth, but his own colour had drained. 'Mathieu, was the nature of Mr Fraser's commission known?'

'Eh?'

'Did you know why he was at Linlithgow? Did anyone?'

'Dunno,' shrugged Mathieu. 'The rumours said that he came to tell her Highness to move the queen to safety, to get her deep into the country, you know? But that's what everyone's saying. England will want her. Better to get her into Edinburgh or Stirling. Safe, like, where King Henry can't grab her.'

'I see. The queen's guard, do they have knowledge of who did this evil deed?'

'I dunno. I was just sent out here to get the cardinal's help. The dowager, she's right upset. She looked scared, I thought. Mr Forrest, he'll find the killer –'

'Who?' asked Danforth.

'Forrest, sir. He's head of the queen's guard.'

'I see,' said Danforth. The man might resent any infringement on his jurisdiction. That could be a problem. Some men were touchy about their authority. 'Can you think of anything else, anything at all, about Mr Fraser's visit?'

'Not really. Only that no one liked him much. Not hate, I don't mean, not like any of us wanted to see him all chopped into bits, but he was … not an easy man.'

'That much we knew already,' smiled Martin, taking Mathieu's arm and walking him to the door. He gripped the rusty handle and pulled. 'Well it's us who owe you thanks, young sir. You've been a – urgh!'

Martin, Danforth and Mathieu started in unison at the two men crouched just beyond the stable door. 'Who are you,' shouted Danforth, his voice coming out in a whine. 'What do you mean by listening at doors?' As his eyes adjusted to the light, he could see the Douglas colours and arms emblazoned on their doublets.

The pair got up from their crouch. One of them was taller, his hair curled and styled. He brushed a lock behind his ear before speaking. 'We might listen wherever we bloody well feel the urge to listen,' he said, brushing a speck of dirt off his sleeve. 'This is our land.'

'Who are you?' asked Martin.

'None of your business,' said the tall man. 'But since you ask

17

so nicely, slave, I'm Cam Hardie and my friend here is Geordie Simms. Loyal henchmen of the clan Douglas. Anything said on Douglas land is for our ears. You three are our business. And the Earl of Angus, our master, has a right to know of any whispering in stables.'

'Your master is a paid slave of Henry VIII,' said Danforth, a hand on his hips.

'Oh ho ho,' said Hardie. 'Hark at this long streak of piss with his English sheep's face and English sheep's bleating, slandering our master, a Scotsman born and true.'

'I,' said Danforth, his spine stiffening, 'had the good grace to turn my face from England's heresies.' The accusation of Englishness was so careworn it no longer bothered him – only, perhaps, the laziness of it rankled. 'Unlike your master, who takes King Henry's money and does his bidding here.'

'Watch what you say about the earl,' said the other man, Simms. It was the first time he had spoken, and Danforth drew back a little. Though he was shorter than the foppish Hardie, there was something more menacing about the thin face and the furtive way he kept his hands buried in his pockets. 'Watch it, Englishman.'

'At any rate,' said Hardie, with a swish of cloak. 'We've heard all there is to hear. We know what you know, remember that. Our master will know everything your master knows, and more besides.' What does that mean? wondered Danforth. 'It might be that the earl and the Lord George will have some interest in your dead friend.'

'You're … you're not going to interfere in this matter?' asked Martin.

'We do as we like,' said Hardie. 'You'd do well to remember that. And to keep out of our way.' With that, he tucked the stray lock of hair behind his ear again, turned, and strode away, his cloak billowing. Simms gave Martin, Danforth, and even Mathieu a long, hard look before following him.

'Shit,' said Mathieu, at length.

'You see what you have taught the lad?' snapped Danforth. 'Watch that mouth.'

'Douglases,' Mathieu said. The name came out starkly. In the pearly winter light, the boy looked almost blue. 'The dowager fears Douglases.'

'A slippery breed, right enough,' said Martin. 'Ripe for a bursting, that lot. Here, Mathieu, you shall ride with us.'

'I have to get back. To the palace. I've got duties.' The little chest protruded.

'They can wait another day or two. We'll be going there anyway. You can stay with my mother whilst we see if there's anything to discover about Mr Fraser there. I don't much like the thought of you riding on the road with those ruffians abroad.'

'Ruffians. Aye, they are that, I'll give you. Ruffians, runagates, and scoundrels, all,' shrugged Danforth. Martin had a knack for adopting waifs and strays. He had mentioned once that he had always wished for a little brother. Well, the boy could be his responsibility. 'And I would as soon be out of their clutches. Come, let us – the three of us – make haste. To Edinburgh first, and then with speed to Linlithgow. They cannot touch us there.'

3

They found Fraser's house on the outskirts of Edinburgh, clinging close by the town wall like a wart. It was a meagre affair, partly constructed of timber and partly of wattle and daub. In the street outside the open sewer was clogged, and a variety of flying insects competed for the best scraps, swatted at by the occasional dog or cat. Across the road some shoeless boys were huddled in conversation, casting occasional greedy glances up at them.

'What a place,' said Martin. 'A cardinal's man living like this.'

'He lived well enough in the castle at St Andrews,' said Danforth. 'Perhaps he saw no need to keep his own home up when he could live better at his master's expense.' Stumping through the muck whilst Martin skipped, he chapped on the door. 'Probably we shall find no one. His Grace affirmed that he had no–'

The wooden door sagged inwards. A sallow woman in her fifties stood, a look of fear intensifying her surprisingly delicate features. 'Aye?' she said. 'What is it?' Her gaze fell on their liveries. 'Aw, you must be friends of Shug. Come away ben.' She stood back to let them in.

Danforth and Martin followed, removing their hats. The woman spoke brightly. 'He's no' in. He went to Linlithgow, to the palace there. Well, you'll ken what an important man he is, working for the lord cardinal. For the old queen. I can keep a letter for him if you'd care to write one.'

'Mistress,' began Danforth. He floundered. 'You are housekeeper to Mr Fraser?' He almost said 'the late Mr Fraser'.

'I … aye. I keep house. I'm his wife.'

'What?' asked Martin. 'I didn't know he had a wife.'

She stood with dignity. On the inside, the tiny parlour was extraordinarily well kept. On every surface and hanging on every hook were household tools and furnishings – cheap, but clean and well-kept. With a slight stab of guilt, Danforth realised he had expected Fraser to live in filth. 'We … never according to the church. Never got 'round to that. But we were hand-fasted. So aye, I'm his wife.' A note of challenge rose at the last.

'Then, mistress, I must–' Again, she interrupted him.

'Can I give you a cup of wine, or some bread? I don't – we don't – get visitors. Just the rough men sometimes banging on the wrong door when they're full of ale. Shug'll be right glad to know his friends came for to see him.'

To Danforth's relief, Martin did not take her up on her offer. 'We thank you,' he said, 'but I am afraid we are here on a matter of some … well, I am most sorry to say it is of some delicacy … I – we have been commanded by his Grace to …'

'Your husband, dear lady, has met with an accident,' said Martin. Danforth frowned. The younger man had a frustrating ease with people. It was something he had never mastered. Already he was crossing to take her hand.

'What? What do you mean an accident?'

'He is dead,' said Danforth, regretting it as her eyes widened.

'Pray sit.' Martin guided her to a chair, kneeling by her. 'On behalf of his Grace, we are deeply sorry. All … arrangements will be taken care of, at the cardinal's expense. We shall have him returned to you.'

'What happened?' she asked, looking up at Martin with appeal. 'It wasn't some brawl on the road? He used to carry money for the cardinal, deliver it. I told him not to. I told him to say no. It's a job for two men, that, carrying money.'

'We don't know yet,' said Martin. 'But we shall find out. His Grace has bid us go to Linlithgow and discover what happened.'

'Did your husband have any enemies?' asked Danforth.

'En … he was killed? Someone killed him?' She half rose, and Martin shot up a warning look.

'Ah – as my colleague said, we do not yet know the full nature of the matter. Yet we have been asked to look into every possibility. Do you know of any enemies, mistress?'

'No,' she said, sitting back down. She half-closed her eyes and lowered her head. 'No, Shug was an honourable man. Oh,' she added, letting out a sob, 'I know he talked too much. I know that. And he had a wee bit of a temper – who doesn't? But no man hated him. No, no, no enemies. Oh, Shug.'

'Believe us,' said Danforth, forcing authority into his voice, 'we shall see justice done.'

'Justice,' she echoed, looking up at him. 'Justice. If my man's been slain, sir. If he's been murdered. I want the men who did it slain too. That's justice.'

'We shall see to it,' said Martin.

'By your leave,' Danforth added, bowing, and replacing his hat. Still Martin was kneeling.

'If you need anything, write or … well, if you can't, then come to the lord cardinal. Send someone even. His Grace will look after you.'

'Justice is all I need. I need to know what's happened. Why my husband won't come home. And if you can't deliver it … Shug might not have had much in the way of kin, from a shiftless lot he was … but my folk are his folk. They'll avenge him if you don't.'

Danforth cast one last glance around the little hovel before stepping back out into the street. When Martin joined him, closing the door, he drew a hand over his nose. 'You went rather far there,' he said. 'Promising her the cardinal's favour. All of that about us returning the body to her, at his Grace's expense. Our master is a prisoner still, not a fountain of charity to the poor and downtrodden. She is not even properly the dead man's wife.'

'She is,' said Martin, 'his wife. She believes it. So will his Grace.'

'Well,' said Danforth, after a tut. 'Better she get herself to church and …' he trailed off, remembering that the churches still offered nothing, their services suspended whilst Beaton was kept in thrall. Changing the subject, he added, 'gather the boy. He shall become soft spending his time with your mother. We shall leave for Linlithgow at once.'

'Tomorrow,' said Martin, stretching. 'I want to wash this muck off my boots before riding to that place. One more night in Edinburgh won't hurt. Me, you, or Mathieu. I'm off, Simon. I'll see you in the morning.'

Danforth watched as Martin strode off, leaving him standing alone, sinking to his ankles in other people's filth.

***

'No, Mistress Pollock, I must be on the road again first thing,' he said. His housekeeper, her face stretched tight by the severe bun she wore, shrugged.

'Dalkeith, is it? Seton or Blackness?'

'No,' said Danforth. News seemed to travel fast. He briefly debated whether to tell her of his plans. 'To Linlithgow. There to attend upon the queen dowager.' Though he managed not to smile, he felt a little glow creep across his cheeks. It was sad, he supposed, that he had only a servant to share exciting news with. It was sad that he felt the need to impress.

'Royal service?' she asked. 'Well, there's a good thing. She always looks such a sad woman, I think.'

'Sad?' asked Danforth. 'She has cause to be, having lost a husband.'

'Aye, and with a bairn too.'

'That bairn is the Queen of Scots,' said Danforth. The conversation had gone far enough. 'All I shall require is something small in the morning. Kindly see that my clothes look their best.'

'Aye. Is young Mr Martin going with you.'

Danforth shrugged noncommittally. Then he added, 'Yes.'

'Good. Might do you a bit of good. Still, a woman about the place would be better.' Before he could ask her what she meant, she disappeared out into the yard. The next thing he heard she was barking orders at his stable boy. Scraping back his chair, Danforth rose. He had been sitting at the same chair Fraser had once sat at. Looking around, he compared his own things to what he had seen in Fraser's house. His were of higher quality, undoubtedly – but there was no one else to see them but himself and his servants. He wiped the back of his breeches with his hands, shivering, before going up to his private chamber.

As he sat on the edge of his bed, he looked at the portrait of his wife, Alice Danforth. It was a faded, poorly-done effort,

23

produced by a friend in London. He had, he realised, been looking at the picture for more years than he had ever looked at the living woman. In her arms, a baby was swaddled, its features indistinct, the white of its wrappings faded to sepia. How long had it been now since he had fled England, leaving their bones in their unmarked grave in a London parish graveyard? More than he cared to think about. How many summers had withered? One year seemed to melt into another. Yet something had changed in him recently. Martin, of course, had joined him in friendship. On balance, that was a good thing. But his mind had started to look forward, not back. What waited in his future? Year upon year of service, of fasting and praying and waiting for the grave to welcome him.

He would, he realised with a shiver, leave behind less than Fraser.

Is that what Alice would have wanted for him, he wondered. Is that why God had made him, to love briefly, lose, and then work himself to death? In the past – in the recent past – he would have unthinkingly said yes. He ran his finger over his illuminated Book of Hours. If his mind had changed course and started considering a different path ... well, surely that was alright. Despite what Martin might say, he was a young man yet. It was not too late for him. He looked around his little chamber as though seeing it for the first time. Shuttered and secretive, it was the room of an elderly man.

The mind, he thought wonderingly, was itself like a great palace, full of rooms, hidden chambers, great galleries. Bad memories might be locked away, the key discarded, only to batter at the door crying for release. So might a man confine himself to one room, especially as age beckoned, fearful of getting lost, of what might lie beyond the next door and the next. What a waste, he thought. What weakness it was to let dust gather in all of those halls and chambers, where great treasures might lie. Sometimes all one needed was to be shaken, woken up, handed a key and pushed through those doors.

Tomorrow would be a new day, he thought, slipping off his boots and swinging his legs onto the bed. The first of many new days. The sun had set on one cold, frosty evening, but a new one would rise to melt away the ice and bring up the bluebells.

***

Danforth travelled from Edinburgh with Martin and Mathieu, the three of them making the journey with minimal stops. It was a good thing, he supposed, to be a company of three. It was a lucky number. The roads were surprisingly quiet. Travellers, he reasoned, must have been avoiding them. The threat of armed bands of roving bandits must have grown in the telling, being more a thing of the imagination than reality. Danforth rode at the head, with Danforth and Mathieu riding side by side behind. Along the way Martin bantered ceaselessly with the little page. Danforth had rarely involved himself, content enough with the way the boy seemed to be bringing something light and airy out in his friend. On Mathieu's chest a little tin thistle flashed – a gift, he said, from Alison, Martin's mother.

'We are nearly upon the town,' said Danforth, turning his head as he rode. 'I commend you again on making the journey to Dalkeith alone, Mathieu. Is it not better to ride in company?'

'Aye. Thank you, Mr Danforth.'

'Aye, well done, wee man,' said Martin.

'Wee … I'll be glad to be quit of you, sir, when I'm home. I'm a royal page, not a … not a bairn, not a babe in arms. And you live with your mother, not me. Mr Danforth tell him!'

'Stop teasing the young man, Mr Martin.'

Mathieu smiled at Martin, his jaw jutting in triumph as he bounced along on his little horse. 'Don't make me strike that look from you, laddie.'

'I'd like to see you try, actually. Why didn't you burst those Douglases the other day?'

'Because, you young daftie, if you touch one of them the whole pack descends, like wild dogs.'

'The truth,' said Danforth, turning again, 'is this: that Mr Martin here has a stout mouth and only little courage. It might be measured in a soup spoon.' He waited for the rebuke, but the little troupe kept trotting along. 'Martin, did you hear me?'

As they passed singing fishwives and hucksters, Danforth

noticed that Martin had lost interest in the conversation entirely. He had turned sharp eyes on the crowds of locals, scanning and moving on. 'Arnaud, have you seen something?' Danforth's voice had the edge of a blade. 'What did you see?'

'Huh?' Martin refocused on him, before shaking his head. 'See? No, I ... I was only ... It's nothing. Come on, we're not far from the palace.'

Danforth turned forward, settling again in the saddle as Woebegone picked the way through hard-packed, partly-frozen muck. Odd, he thought.

4

The palace of Linlithgow reared up behind a sculpted loch, a fairy-tale image of polished, yellow-painted sandstone. A great drawbridge led into it from the east but, to Danforth's disappointment, the late king had been a moderniser, and a new gateway had been built in the south range. Instead they had to take the road called the Kirkgate from the burgh, a narrow, cobbled street that led past the Tolbooth and the Song School. As the trio fell into single file, they spotted a figure heading towards them, skirts held up with one hand and a basket over her arm.

As they drew closer, Danforth reined in before the most striking woman he had seen in years. From underneath a white cap, a riot of curly, shimmering black hair curled all-ways, and her skin was not the usual milky white of Scottish women, but a deep golden-brown tan. Not Moorish, like the strange men called Ethiops he had sometimes seen in London, but some mellower hew, neither one thing nor another. He drew off his cap, Martin and Mathieu doing likewise, as she walked sedately towards them.

'Good morrow to you, mistress,' he called down. Woebegone ruined his formal greeting by stepping backwards, making him wobble. The woman jerked in surprise at the sudden movement and then laughed, showing neat, white teeth. She looked directly at Danforth, her gaze penetrating.

'What news, gentlemen? Would you care to buy? For your sweethearts?' She thrust forward her basket, filled with violet and purple shades of heather, and similarly-coloured flowers.

'You are a seller of flowers?' asked Danforth. He wondered where she found them. As they had travelled, he had noticed that winter seemed to have the country in a resolute grip, leaving its shavings across the land despite spring's eagerness.

'You are observant, sir,' she smiled. 'Yes.'

'I – we – have no need of your wares. Do you sell much up yonder?' He had no idea why he felt the urge to keep the woman engaged in conversation. Ah, his mind added: a murder might have occurred, and she was an unknown, and therefore suspect. He had learned to question everyone. One never knew who might reveal something seen or heard, even if an innocent themselves.

'Not so much as I'd like. The queen favours the colours, you see.'

'The queen is barely two months old,' he said, raising his chin. The one-upmanship was automatic.

'The old queen, I mean. Surely that's quite clear.'

'It ... yes, it is. I apologise for my rudeness, mistress. Of course, I shall buy a small sprig of heather, by way of recompense.' He fumbled at his purse, a difficult task with his riding gloves on, and gave her a coin.

'Thank you for your patronage,' she said, an amused look on her face. Her eyes, he noticed, were dark enough to be almost black. She selected the smallest bunch of heather from the basket and handed it over. 'And good day to you.'

'But stay,' he persisted. 'We have business in the palace.'

'I've done with mine.'

'Might I ask you some questions?'

'Are you men of the law? No,' she said, letting her eyes run over his doublet. 'You're ... not royal servants ...'

'We're the cardinal's men,' Martin called out. 'Danforth, let the pretty lady go forth, I'm sure she can tell us nothing and would like to be on her way.'

'Thank you,' she smiled. 'But what is it you want?'

'Is there any talk up there,' asked Danforth, 'of death?'

At this, she tilted her head and gave him a cockeyed look. 'Death? Of the king, you mean? Only what's being said everywhere, that it's a shame a good man went to his grave so suddenly.' Danforth relaxed a bit. The dowager must be keeping news of Fraser's death quiet. That was wise. If it became widely known, she would not be listened to, but hustled about at the command of any man in power. The whole matter, whatever it was and whoever was behind it, should be dealt with quickly and quietly. But she could not keep it covered up forever. Such things always leaked out, and more often than not invited different takes on them over every hearth, the truth getting buried deeper and deeper under layers of nonsense.

'Very good, mistress. Well, then, you are a seller of flowers and herbs. Be about your selling. Not here … walking.'

'Ask her her name,' called Martin.

'Tell your friend my name is Mistress Allen. Rowan Allen.'

'Rowan?' spluttered Danforth. 'That is no name!'

'Oh?' she said, brown flaring over her high cheekbones. 'Perhaps my father was inordinately fond of trees. You have a marvellous way with women, Mr …'

'Danforth. English secretary to his Grace the Lord Cardinal Beaton.' Danforth turned rigid, his back straightening. An antidote to embarrassment. 'We bid you, again, good day, again. Onwards, gentlemen.'

They rode on, Mathieu giving Rowan a wave and Martin giving her a full-toothed grin and a graceful half-bow. Danforth resisted the urge to turn when Martin spoke. 'Mr Danforth, I think you took a liking to that woman. Well, good for you. A pretty one. Bit dark, though. Moorish, almost. Tawny. Seemed to have a ready wit, though.'

'Keep your filthy tongue in your head, Mr Martin. You are … you are corrupting our young friend with your lewd ways. Nonsense.' But his mind was picturing the black eyes, imagining her becoming a blue speck as she disappeared down the Kirkgate to wherever it might be that she lived. She reminded him of another woman he had briefly seen in London: a woman whom he had blamed for all of his misfortunes there.

The path passed a stone arch, above which the chivalric insignia of James V were carved and painted in red, blue, and gold: St Michael, the golden fleece, the garter, and the thistle. Danforth's eyes lingered on the thistle, purple and green. The colours and the carvings would live on, be repainted if necessary, even though the man had gone. Then he was under them, thrust into gloom, and out the other side. The neat parish church of St Michael's stood inside the outer gate to the right. Danforth looked up, to the crown steeple at the top. It was a shame that services were not on. It must be a good sight on the insight. Still, he thought, there was no use in crying over what ought to be. Instead he rode on to the main entrance, where he drew Woebegone to a stop. In a narrow hall to his right a porter stood urinating against the wall, oblivious to the splashing. The reek from the passage announced with a tang that he was not the first.

'Wait there, gonnae,' the man called up, twisting his neck round. 'Nearly there. Takes as long as it takes, for Chrissakes.'

'Indeed I must wait here, or else are we to thrust ourselves into the queen's presence?'

'Hold yer horses,' the man said, fixing his breeches as he turned. 'What are you, more cardinal's men?' He leant forward, looking behind Danforth. 'Och, Mathieu, boy, it's yersel. You've been a time.'

'We,' said Danforth, fighting to keep his voice as imperious as he could, 'are well trusted servants of his Grace the lord cardinal.'

'Aye, well, I'll wish you more luck than the last yin.'

'Precisely that is become our business.' Lax, thought Danforth. The whole place was lax, from the flower-girl wandering out to the porter unconcerned at their sudden appearance. 'Yet we might well have stolen this boy, killed the cardinal's true servants, and come here in their garb to slay the queen, her mother, and the whole rabble here.'

'Two of ye?' asked the porter. 'You'd have a job there, right enough. Stop your jesting, boy. Go on in, get the beasts stabled. Gibb'll take 'em.'

Danforth shook the reins without another word, refusing on principle to acknowledge the man with anything more than an upturned head. He led the party forward onto an open quadrangle, the centre of which was dominated by a varicoloured, circular fountain splashing icy water. At irregular intervals sat flaming braziers, clusters of servants gathered around each of them. The place was, Danforth begrudgingly admitted, impressive: a neat square formed of perfectly aligned ranges, stretching four storeys high. Such places as he had seen in England were sprawling collections of rooms, added to as and when, with little thought of coherence. Here was a carefully sculpted exercise in taste and elegance, tall, neat, and symmetrical. A giant jewel box, stretching heavenward. The word 'graceful' swept serenely through his mind.

Yes, he thought. He would be very comfortable here.

***

Mathieu directed them to the stables in the south-eastern corner; they dismounted, and led the horses in. A man's jovial voice greeted them, but it was aimed elsewhere. He was barking orders at a servant who was polishing a monstrous carriage. A rare sight in Scotland, the few in existence were the property of Marie of Guise. Danforth's heart fluttered at the sight of the great mechanical beast. Here, he thought, was royal splendour, beyond anything even the cardinal took on his cavalcades.

'What's this, fresh meat?' said the man, turning from the carriage.

'Mr Gibb?'

'Aye, call me Rab. Rab Gibb, master of the queen's stable. A pleasure to meet you, gents. Get the last of that dirt out, son,' he added over his shoulder to his underling.

'Good day to you, Mr Gibb,' said Danforth. He became aware suddenly of a tugging at his sleeve. 'What, what is it, Mathieu?'

'Can I go, sir, and tell the queen mother that you two are come? She doesn't like to be kept waiting.'

'Yes, boy, go.' Mathieu scurried off, leaving Danforth and Martin with the stable master. 'Mr Gibb, we are Cardinal Beaton's servants. Would you be so good as to take charge of our horses?'

Gibb gave the horses long looks. 'We're muckle busy at the present, lads.' He gestured around the small space. Almost all of the individual paddocks were occupied. He turned back to Danforth and Martin. 'Her Grace the dowager has ...' He mouthed the word 'spies' silently, before speaking. 'Guests. Hamilton and Douglas kinfolk, watching over her safety and that of the new queen. Yet ... aye, I'm sure those fine guests won't mind their beasts being shunted down into the burgh stables. I doubt they're going anywhere.' He gave a wink.

Danforth's mind worked rapidly as he took in this news. The

Douglas clan, hand in glove with the Hamiltons, were Cardinal Beaton's enemies. They were now the party of England, the minions of Henry VIII. If they were here, that meant … well, he was unsure exactly what it meant. Investigating important people was a hazard. But whether they had anything to do with Fraser's death or not, they would be watching him and Martin, reporting back to their own masters. He would have to tread carefully. This was not some minor domestic case. He was not pitting his wits against a shiftless criminal or a frenzied killer, but perhaps against some organised plotters. And whatever had occurred in the palace, a bevy of high-toned, dagger-wielding adherents of two slippery noble houses was an unwelcome complication. Gibb's voice drew him out of his own head, forcing him to paste on a friendly, returning smile. Already, he thought, the playing had begun.

'So you leave your beasts with me. Though I don't think much of this one, what is it, a plough horse? Shouldn't be riding a plough horse any distance.'

'I …' Danforth began, suddenly ashamed. He had always been proud of only keeping an old beast: there was nothing to be proud of in a horse. Yet in a royal stable it seemed a little mean. Strangely, the thought intruded of what it would mean to be in royal service. Had his wife and child lived, they might have been gentlewomen. He might have been obliged to keep them in furs and jewels. Would they have liked that, Alice or little Margaret? He shut the thought down. 'Just take care of him. We understand his Grace's last servant has met with an accident of some kind.'

'Some accident.'

'So he was slain truly?'

'Unless he struck off his own arms.' Gibb' smiled faded. 'The common voice cries devilry.'

'Mr Gibbs, this is terrible news.'

'Yes,' added Martin. 'What's the security of this place?'

'And where was the body found?' asked Danforth.

'Where is it now?' put in Martin.

'Hold, gents,' said Gibb. 'I'm only in charge of the stables. The body is laid out in the chapel's anteroom, all proper. In bits, right enough. The security, as you call it, is not good. I've served the Stewarts man and boy and I'll tell you, Linlithgow is built for pleasure, not safety.'

'Could a killer from without have got inside this place?' asked Danforth.

'I can't say. Maybe. Or Maybe someone drew him out. If you want particulars, you'll have to talk to the queen mother's depute of the guard.'

'We'll do that,' said Martin.

'I'd get me to the lady herself first, though. Wee Mathieu spoke the truth. Her Grace likes swift action.'

'Where is her master of the household, or a chamberlain?'

'In Holyrood,' said Gibb, frowning for the first time. 'All the great men who held office under the old king have joined the governor's Court since he died. Few know the meaning of loyalty, it's all run with times, run with the times. Give me a Stewart queen over a lord protector any day.'

Danforth nodded his head. There was something tragic about that: a queen, turned dowager, losing her entire household to a wealthy young noble who styled himself first prince of the blood. Gibb was right – there was little loyalty in men. 'Right, I'll have young fella-ma-lad here take your packs to the servants' quarters,' said Gibb, jerking a thumb at the crouching boy tending the carriage. Danforth felt a little stab of anxiety. His things were tucked away in his pack over Woebegone's pack: his cutlery, rosary, pens, even his valuable Book of Hours, a gift from his wife. The thought of some domestic nosing through them was not to be borne. Still, sacrifices had to be made in service.

'You'll have to rely on her usher. He'll like you, will Guthrie. He's hot on religion. Likely as not bend your lugs off about it,' said Gibb.

'You don't mean he's one of these questing reformers, do you?' asked Danforth, his voice suddenly sharp.

'Wounds, no – nothing like that. There is nothing like that here. Believe me, none, if that's what you're after. No, our long-tongued usher is hot on Rome.'

'Very well,' replied Danforth, his arms folding over his chest as he fixed the boy's back with a glare. 'Have a care with them.'

He patted farewell to Woebegone, passing him into the care of the horse master and his boy. Both seemed cheerful enough. There was something odd in that. A man killed, and yet the place seemed to be going on. He stepped on the thought before it could grow into suspicion. Of course life went on, even after a tragedy. It was a sign of good governance of a household that it could.

With the thought came the unbidden one that had plagued him during his last night in his own bed. If he were to be killed, or to die suddenly, the world would go on without him, his hoard of belongings dispersed to charity. He governed his own household, meagre though it was, well. Yet it was governed with no thought to its future, it was governed to be passed on to no one. After his father's death, and the deaths of Alice and Margaret, the Danforth household had simply ceased to be, forgotten, he imagined, by all who remained in England. Would old Mistress Pollock be so cheerful once he had gone, and his own stable boy relieved to be free of him? It was a sobering thought. When he had concluded his business here, then he would have to think seriously about it all. It was a strange thing about thoughts – they were like the evils contained in Pandora's box. He would have to confront them now that they had been released; but not now. For the moment, he retrained his mind. He took one last look at Gibb, at the horses, at the great carriage, and then turned his back on them.

He and Martin left their horses and re-entered the central courtyard. Danforth hadn't heard the church bells of St Michael's and realised he had no idea of the time. The winter day revealed nothing. The scattered servants still seemed to be warming themselves and chatting – that meant that dinner was well over and supper not yet begun.

'Well, Arnaud, are you ready to make this queen's acquaintance?'

'Oh aye,' said Martin. Already he was twirling the feather in his cap with one hand and picking at his teeth with another. Danforth was unsurprised to see that he had already shone up the jewelled buttons he'd had sewn onto his livery. Danforth

looked down at his own regulation wooded ones, as he heard
Martin trill, 'I daresay she'll be impressed with me at least.'

5

'So you've never been to Rome then? That's a shame, I'd like to see Rome. All that work they're doing on the basilica – it's the place to be. You'll be staying just off the hall in the north range. Some of the young wits call it Thieves Row, after a dangerous street in Edinburgh – isn't that wicked of them? Fancy themselves wits, anyway. You'll be quite safe, mind you, and you'll not find any drunken bundles of iniquity there. It's these young ones, they speak with such irreverence, it's no wonder they invite the devil to walk amongst us.' Gibb had spoken true. The usher, Anthony Guthrie, was chattering aimlessly. Danforth took an immediate dislike to him. His own father had been a gentleman usher in Cardinal Wolsey's household, and William Danforth would never have dreamt of making bawdy small talk with visitors. It was the hallmark of a good servant that he kept his thoughts and opinions to himself, no matter how strongly felt. Unless asked, of course. Guthrie had been asked nothing. They went up a flight of stairs, where he briefly paused at a pair of tall doors. 'The king's rooms,' he said, drawing a cross on them. 'God rest his Grace. We have to go up one more to the dowager's apartments.' They followed him, Danforth putting a hand out to the curving wall as the stairs whirled. 'Right, boys, here we are.'

The usher stopped before a large wooden door on the second floor in the southwest tower. A large silver crucifix, which had been bouncing in time with his light steps, settled back against his chest. 'Inside here is the outer chamber. Follow me.' He gave the door three sharp raps with his stave before opening it.

Inside was a large room, about which some women sat playing cards and giggling. They looked up and then immediately back down at their hands, the light streaming down on them from tall, lead-lined glass windows. 'Come on,' said Guthrie, 'look sharp now, eyes front.'

'We're not savages,' said Martin, not bothering to lower his voice. 'We're cardinal's men, we know to how behave.'

'Oh, hark at it. You're not in a clergyman's house now, but a queen's. You listen to me and don't be so saucy. What did I say about you young ones – the things you bring down about our heads.' Their bootsteps echoed on the polished stone floor, patterned in great red and yellow diamonds, as they processed through, watched not only by the waiting women, but by the sightless eyes of the saintly women dominating the room's tapestries.

Across the room was another door, and again Guthrie beat on it before opening it. 'The queen mother may be in here. The inner chamber. Boots clean? Nails clean?' A blush crept into his rosy face. 'Oh, Mr Martin, you might have got your beard trimmed first. Ach, too late for that now. Ready?' He pushed open the door.

The inner chamber was smaller but far more crowded. Instead of the *History of Ladies*, the walls were decorated by silk-and-wool images of Hercules, each panel depicting a different labour. An enormous fireplace roared, and the air was heavy with the good smell of burning wood and the acrid smell of perfume. Even the rushes which lay on the bits of floor not covered by carpets seemed to issue scent. Against the left-hand wall Marie of Guise sat on a wooden throne, embroidery in her lap. Danforth's first glimpse of her was in profile. As he had always thought, she would have been an extraordinary beauty had it not been for the long, fluted nose, which led her instead into the realms of the handsome. If she had gained weight from her multiple pregnancies over the years, the voluminous, shimmering black gown hid it. She turned to them and smiled as Guthrie announced their arrival in an affected, imperious voice. Both fell into deep bows.

'Monsieur Danforth et Monsieur Martin,' she said, and then, in a heavy accent, 'me am most very glad to see you. Me am a great friend to England and to France.'

Danforth kept his eyes down, unsure of himself. They were not there as emissaries of England or France. Had Mathieu garbled another message? Still Marie went on. 'Me would speak … en privé … with youse. The better to share my mind. Please, be to follow me.' She rose from her throne and made her stately progress to the opposite side of the room, the groups of richly-dressed men and women parting for her, a rippling jelly of black, sage, navy, and red. She nodded down her thanks; she towered over all of them. Another door lay ahead of her, this one guarded on either side by armoured men, their halberds held to attention. One of them opened it and she passed through. It was slammed again.

Danforth and Martin looked at each other, before giving sharp nods and picking their own way through the hangers-on. They were less respectful of the interlopers; the pair could feel the eyes on them and hear the low whispers from dozens of mouths. As they reached the far door, the guards crossed their halberds over it. 'State your names' said one. 'And business,' added the other.

'Really?' asked Martin. 'You just heard –'

'They are Mr Danforth and Mr Martin, servants of Cardinal Beaton, and they would speak with her Grace Queen Marie.' Guthrie had trailed them.

Instantly, the halberds were pulled back up. Guthrie did his routine door-beating before pushing it open. Danforth looked at Martin, who was wearing an expression of bemused disbelief. Although he let his own face fall into what he always thought of as his 'service face' – slack, expressionless, neither smiling nor frowning – he was pleased. Here, at last, was some proper order. Martin motioned for him to go first and stepped into a cool cocoon of violet. The door slammed shut behind the two of them.

***

They entered into a haze of cinnamon scent, the air dull with the weight of it. Marie's bed dominated the wood-panelled room, covered in crimson velvet with phoenixes and tears picked out in silver and gold thread. Danforth averted his eyes from it. He knew it was the practice of the Stewarts, like the French kings, to entertain private audiences in their bedchambers. He doubted they even slept in the great beds, likely having some even more private inner sanctum

38

somewhere, but still – the sight of a lady's, of a queen's, bed, even with its red drapes closed, was … discomfiting.

She sat now not on a throne, but on a more comfortable seat on a raised dais, underneath a cloth of estate emblazoned with the arms of Scotland and Lorraine. Flanking her were two women in purple velvet, their faces chalky. Together, the three of them made a tableau: the imperious queen and her ladies, posed fixedly. The light of the smaller fire in the room flashed and danced on them. It was impressive. 'Gentleman,' said Marie, all trace of the heavy French suddenly gone, 'won't you come forward and speak. I can scarcely see you. Come, come, we have much business to discuss.'

Martin led the way this time, and the two stopped before the dais, falling on their knees and removing their hats before looking up at her. 'You will not get uncomfortable like that? I can have Madame LeBoeuf fetch you a cushion. Mr Danforth?'

'You Grace is most kind, but I should be content as I am.' The very thought of lounging on a cushion before the queen affronted him.

'As you like it. Mr Martin?'

'A cushion would be welcome, madam.'

Marie smiled and nodded at the stone-faced woman on her right, who stepped down from the dais and disappeared into the shadows, bringing back a plump pillow and handing it to Martin. 'You like French comfort, Mr Martin,' Marie smiled. 'We shall not judge you for it.'

Danforth's felt sweat pop out in his forehead, indignance at Martin's behaviour pushing it. To think he had seen the worst of the foolish boy's behaviour already – this was a new low. He tried to twist his head and give Martin a quick, angry glare. Marie seemed to spot the tension. 'Mr Danforth, I commend you also on your good manners. But pray turn your mind to more serious matters. Gentlemen, shall we proceed in Scots or French? Oh, pay no mind to my speech out there. I can never be sure who is listening, or to whom they might speak. Better they think me a foolish Frenchwoman with but little understanding.'

The word 'dissimulation' formed in Danforth's mind, and his respect for the elegant woman sitting before him increased. It was hard to believe she was a couple of years younger than him, and he had always thought of himself as grave beyond his days. 'Which language do you prefer?'

'I am comfortable in French, your Highness,' said Martin. 'Yet I think Mr Danforth here might prefer Scots.' Danforth's bottom lip popped out, but he said nothing. Yes, he preferred Scots, his years of immersion bringing 'braw' to his mind and lips more swiftly than 'belle'. But, as befitting his curtailed English education, he spoke reasonable schoolroom French. Admittedly following the spoken language could be a trial, but there was no need for Martin to advertise the slight deficiency.

'Very well. Scots. You know, I think, what has befallen your Mr Fraser?'

'We do, your Highness,' said Danforth, trying to deepen his voice.

'It is terrible, shameless. It is, you understand, an attack on your master. And an attack on the queen my daughter.'

'With respect, madam,' said Martin, 'it might be that Mr Fraser had enemies.'

'Enemies? Know you of any?'

'… No.'

'Enemies who kill him as he was killed, and in such a place, so near to our own presence? No, this is something aimed at us – your master and myself. You are aware I am a captive here? A captive, though I was your sovereign lady six months since, and my daughter is that even now.'

'Now, your Highness,' said Danforth, 'you are surely no captive. My advice is to get you and the queen to some place of greater safety. Take your household further into the realm. This is what the cardinal wills also. It is his advice.'

'My household? Gentlemen,' she said, before giving each of them measuring looks. 'Can I trust you, your master aside?' Danforth was unsure how to react, weighing up loyalty to Beaton with the look of weakened entreaty on Marie's face.

'You can, your Highness,' said Martin. 'Our master's advice was to serve you as best we can.' Her shoulders relaxed, the black material sparkling, and Danforth could see any resolve she might have had to play-act falter and crumble. To her, he dared hope, he and Martin had become islands of rock in turbulent seas. Martin had spoken well, and Danforth felt the urge to make his own contribution. Inspiration struck him.

'Madam,' he said, reaching into the pocket of his outer robe, 'please, accept this small token of our honesty and affection for your estate.' He withdrew the sprig of heather he had bought and held it out, his head still bent. The woman, Madame LeBoeuf, stepped forward and took it, sniffing it with narrowed eyes before handing it to the queen. 'It is fine,' she said. Her voice was deep, almost mannish.

Marie's, when she spoke, was earnest. 'My humble thanks to you both. It is my favourite colour. I welcome you to my service, my friends, and open my mind to you. You spoke of my household? My household has turned to Edinburgh, to serve *that* little man, Arran. Governor of Scotland? Protector? Hah! Protector of himself. I hear how already he empties Scotland's treasury buying his family trinkets.' Danforth again pictured the lord protector, his face still swathed in puppy fat. It was said he was weak and stupid, ruled entirely by Archibald Douglas, the Earl of Angus, and his brother, George. But what if he wasn't? 'And I can do nothing, make no move, but send my things in secret to Stirling. He has commanded that the queen and I stay in this place, this unsafe place. He, that was once my subject, has commanded *me*, until he hears what King Henry's wishes are. The governor of Scotland waiting for the wishes of the English king.'

'Madam, our master has commanded us to take your part. To find out what has become of Mr Fraser and ensure your safety. And the queen's.'

'Safety … We will neither of us be safe as long as we are trapped in this palace.' Marie's voice betrayed no anxiety, but Danforth noticed that the long, slim fingers of one hand drummed volubly on the arm of her chair. Her other hand picked at a piece of thread on the cloth covering it. 'We must move – but to where? Stirling? How? And now that dratted madman in England writes saying he is sending forth an emissary, and I must feign friendship.'

'An English emissary?' asked Danforth. 'Who?'

'I do not yet know. I should imagine that Sadler. He was here before, some years ago. To make discord between my husband and your master – to turn the king's mind from France. He failed. Do you know him?'

Danforth had frozen, a chill running through him at the name. Ralph Sadler. He had not met the man on either of his previous missions to Scotland, but he knew him to be in Thomas Cromwell's service. Or, his mind added, to have been in it. Strange – the politics of England had moved with startling rapidity since he had fled the country, monasteries falling and King Henry racing through wives, and yet a sudden name could overturn the clock. It could bring back the dead. 'I have heard the name,' he said, ignoring the look Martin gave him, half-intrigued, half-impressed. 'I do not know him.' Nor wish to, his mind added with a grimace.

'You know why England sends a man, though? To seek,' Marie went on, not waiting for an answer, her hands growing frantic, 'my daughter. Henry thinks he can win this realm by marriage with his son. The Douglases act as his servants, and bend Monsieur Arran to their will. Cheaper than winning it by the sword.'

'Your Highness would never allow a sovereign princess of Scotland to be given to England,' said Martin. 'France, surely, not England.' Marie drew back a little at the presumption. 'My apologies, your Highness.'

'No, speak your mind. I must only entertain this Sadler. Keeping Henry's hopes alive will keep him from our postern gate. I think. I hope. I –'

A knock made Danforth and Martin jerk, but Marie seemed unmoved. It was followed by another two, and Danforth had time to silently curse Guthrie before the door opened, admitting a pretty little wench in a violet gown and headdress.

'Yes, Mademoiselle Beauterne?' said Marie. 'All is well?'

'Very well, your Grace. The queen has supped of the wet nurse. She is in *perfect* health.' The girl spoke as though scripted, and her smiling gaze was fixed on the kneeling men rather than her mistress. Danforth looked up at her, noting the small features, the stiff, posed way in which she stood.

'And delighted I am to hear it. You may go, mistress.'

Danforth noticed Martin's puzzled gaze as he twisted his neck to see the girl retreating from the bedchamber, but he had realised instantly what was happening. Marie did not entirely trust them yet. The little intrusion had been staged, organised beforehand, undoubtedly, so that they might carry back to the cardinal – or anyone else they might report to – that the infant queen was not a sickly child. Politics, he thought.

'My apologies, gentleman. But before I am a queen mother I am first a mother, and before the queen is Queen of Scots she is my daughter.' Her words had a touching sincerity to them. 'At any cost to myself I will protect my daughter.'

'Madam, do you suggest that the death of Mr Fraser was aimed at the queen, somehow?' asked Martin, his voice a little doubtful. 'Even if someone has killed a lousy old man, that doesn't mean they could take the life of a child. A sovereign child at that.'

'Oh, Mr Martin. I wish that this matter was simple. That your man Fraser had been robbed, or else killed by some creditor. You will soon see that it cannot be so, if you would but inspect his corpse. Before that, though, I must ask you a question, both of you. Gentlemen, do you believe in ghosts?'

6

Silence spun out in the bedchamber. Danforth and Martin both shivered, despite the thick tapestries and the leaping flames in the grate. The light they cast on Marie and her waiting women had now become sinister, making odd shapes on the trio of pale faces. Danforth had a brief image of three witches, beautiful and deadly, wreathed in the light of hellfire. Stupid, of course.

Ghosts. He had considered the question before – having so much time to himself in the past, he had allowed his mind to turn to all kinds of questions, from the scientific to the theological. There were certainly plenty of reports of ghosts through the ages. He had discounted the old notion of spirits which took on corporeal form and wrestled with priests – those were the ignorant imaginings of his great-great-grandfathers. Mouldering corpses did not rise from the grave to terrorise the living. He knew, from experience, that only the memory could play such tricks; the power of the dead lay in the memories of the living, haunting them in dreams.

Yet, he thought, his hand reaching to the medal he wore around his neck, there were reports enough of the spirits of the dead returning to warn of doom. So too were there stories – credible stories, he thought – of the ghosts of the slain visiting relatives and friends to encourage vengeance. Even the pagans recounted them. Pliny told of a spirit which could not rest until its murdered bones had been found and given proper burial. Odysseus was said to have met the ghost of Elpenor in Hades, with Elpenor advising him that he would be trapped there until his undiscovered corpse was found and buried. The Church did not condemn such beliefs, and that was enough to give him pause.

'Ghosts, your Highness? I don't believe in them. But I'm scared of them,' smiled Martin. Marie did not return his smile this time.

'Do you believe that they can do harm to the living? That they can draw our blood and break our bones?'

'I do not, madam,' said Danforth, with finality. 'Men draw blood and break bones. Ghosts – if there are ghosts – seek vengeance through men.'

'And yet this palace – this very palace – is said to be haunted,' said Marie. 'Oh yes, I have heard of it from my first visit. Underneath the paint and the glister there is something rotten. The late king my husband's mother, Queen Margaret, told me she was visited by a blue-robed spirit who warned King James IV not to venture to England. That spirit, if it truly spoke, was right to warn him, and King James wrong not to heed him.'

'That spirit, then, did no harm. It sought to do good.'

'Perhaps. It knew the future.' She trailed off, her eyes looking above them into the ceiling shadows.

'Madam, forgive me, but why this talk of ghosts? We are here, as we understand, to encourage you to move from this place to safety, and to look into the circumstances of our colleague's death.'

'Quite right. Forgive me. You will understand better when you look upon him. Tell me, do either of you recall the late king's traitor, James Hamilton of Finnart? The one they called the bastard of Hamilton?'

Danforth recalled the man, a relative and sometime friend of the cardinal as well as an illegitimate cousin of the king. Together Finnart and Beaton had sat in judgement of heretics … in Linlithgow, as it happened. Yet Beaton had turned his back on him when King James decided to rid himself of his former friend. Did that signify anything? 'Finnart,' he said, 'was half-brother to the governor. Dead these last …'

'Two years, or thereabouts,' finished Marie. 'Dead, but not forgotten after death. You might have heard of my husband's terrors afterwards? His … his dreams.'

Yes, thought Danforth. There had been rumours flying around Scotland about the king waking in the night in fear of Finnart's ghost. But that was as much as he knew. In some versions, Finnart had sliced an 'H' into the King's cheeks; in others, James had been thrown off the battlements of Stirling castle by the ghoulish demon. What the king had actually dreamed, no one really knew. 'The king,' said Marie, 'woke many nights, sometimes abed by me, sometimes alone or with his own servants, having seen Finnart draw his sword and strike off first one arm, and then the other, and then his head. His Grace took it as prophecy that each arm represented the late Princes. My sons.' Her voice grew soft, catching in her throat. She held out a hand and, instantly, the gentlewoman at her side crossed to a side table and poured a cup of wine, passing it over. She sipped at it before continuing. 'The loss of his head, I thought, might mean the end of the king's life. With his Grace now in Heaven, I had thought an end to all danger of prophecy. Yet now I see that the head is my daughter, for it is she who wears this country's crown.

'Gentlemen,' she said clearing her throat and passing the cup back, 'your Mr Fraser's arms were cut clean off, in the manner of my husband's dream. Whatever killed him also cut into the back of his head, not quite severing it, but close to it. I take by this a warning, a message. My sons have been carried off, and my daughter, our queen, is next.'

Danforth and Martin drew their breaths. 'Madam,' said Danforth, 'do not think me a braggart, but I have some experience in cases of murder.'

'It's true, madam,' said Martin. 'He attracts corpses like dunghills attract flies.'

'What? Is this a good thing?'

'My colleague,' said Danforth, side-eyeing Martin, whom he had not yet forgiven for the affront of the cushion, 'means that I have had some occasion to discover murderers. Recently we saw two rogues hang in Stirling for their crimes.'

'What, Stirling? My little Striveling? Pray God, do not tell me that even that place is not safe. I have been sending my chattels there.'

'The castle ought to be, madam,' said Martin. 'And the town a thing safer than it was before us.'

'At any rate, what I have found always to be the case is that men are behind sudden violent death,' said Danforth. 'Always. If there is any to gain by Fraser's death, or even by the death of our little sovereign lady – and God forbid it – then he is our man.'

'And you discount some ghostly or hellish hand?'

'Until I see proof, yes. I do.'

'We shall look into Fraser,' said Martin. 'See if he had any enemies his woman did not know of. And Finnart, too – if he had any friends who would want vengeance on the crown. On your family. The Hamiltons are thick with the Douglases still.'

'The Douglases,' spat Marie. 'That man has stuffed this palace with Hamilton and Douglas kinfolk – all that rabble out there. Spies, all. All working to take my child from my arms and sell her to that old man in England. My child, wed to the English prince, that is what they drive at. And then where am I? Yet ... yet Monsieur Le Lord Protector, that foolish Arran ... he has a little boy also. Hopes might yet be bred in him of his own line as would turn him away from King Henry and his Douglas slaves.'

'Such a thought should keep Arran from giving the little queen to Henry,' said Martin.

'Our master would approve,' added Danforth.

'Yes. I see. Ahh, but sometimes I think my girl would safer in the care of my cousin, le roi de France. To be given in marriage to some great Frenchman.'

'Not France,' spat Danforth. Then, seeing Marie's head draw back imperiously, he quickly added, 'I mean, Queen Mary is our sovereign in Scotland, latest of that noble race of Stewarts. Scotland is her kingdom, and in Scotland she shall be safe. Made safe. Parliament would not allow her to be sent out of the realm.'

'Perhaps.' Marie put a finger on her chin. 'I think that is all, gentlemen. I would that you should deal with the matter, whatever its nature, quickly. Now. Please. I am a patient woman, but this great affront touches me too near. I have given orders already that you be lodged downstairs for the time you are with us. We have increased security around the nursery already. If you think of anything else that might be done, it shall be. For now, I give you leave. And for God's sweet sake, keep this case as quiet as possible. That cursed Arran shall love an excuse to take my daughter into his own custody. For her *protection*.' She raised the hand that had been doing service as a bundle of drumsticks and Danforth crept forward to take it in his and brush his lips over it. His heart thrilled – a royal commission, a royal command. It offset the pain that shot through both knees.

***

Guthrie the usher, to Danforth's vexation, was their courier down to the chapel anteroom. He and Martin trailed the man in silence, each lost in their own thoughts. The king's dream … who would revive that? Was it prophecy or warning, or nothing at all? He would have to revisit any books he might consult on dreams; it had been years since he had done so, and then it had been for his own reasons. Still Guthrie was talking. 'All of this, all of it, I don't know, it's like a curse from on high. I'm doing what I can, laying charms, but without church services, I don't know, and so many young lasses about tempting the lads. Heh. Oh, look up there. See, over the windows – a crown above a thistle. That was the king's work. Well, Finnart's work, too, or James Nicholson, I can't recall who –'

'What?' spluttered Danforth. 'What did you just say, Mr Guthrie?'

'What, weren't you listening? I told you to look at the carving, up there.' He jutted his stave upwards.

'No, after that.'

'I said it was the work of Finnart, the bastard of Hamilton. Or Sir James Nicholson, who worked with him. But I reckon Finnart.'

'What do you know of Finnart?'

'What do I know? Everything – you know he was the king's Master of Works?'

Danforth dimly recalled that. James V had been a prodigious builder; Finnart had been his visionary, designing and organising it all. It had never interested Danforth – to him, it was a silly pastime of the rich, modernising, changing, making everything look like it had been lifted from France and dropped in Scotland. 'How did you come by this knowledge?'

'I dunno,' shrugged Guthrie. 'One hears things. Heh. I've an interest in crafting – what they call construction. I was after asking you about the palaces in England, actually, Mr Danforth. I've heard about King Henry's place, Nonsuch – they say there's none such like it. And take this grand palace – once an old pile of stone, now a great place fit for a queen.'

'All England groans under the bulk of King Henry,' said Danforth primly. 'And the cost of his building work. Or so I hear.'

'True that. For the most part men'll wax weary of a madman's rule. Especially if he's broken with the Holy Father. That's not just inviting the devil in, it's rolling out the carpets for him. They'll grow rich from his purse, but. Heh. Naming no names for who takes that old goat's alms. Still, look around you. A jewel fit for a queen.'

'But not fit for defence,' said Martin. 'Else our Mr Fraser would live still.' Guthrie pouted.

'Tell me,' said Danforth, 'have you heard of the late king's dreams of Finnart, after his execution?'

'Dreams?' asked Guthrie. 'How do you mean, dreams?'

'Never mind,' said Danforth. He didn't want to encourage gossip amongst the staff. 'Do you recall anything of Finnart?'

'Only what was generally said – that he was a bastard in blood and a bastard in habit. Here did you know this: they say he used to cut an 'H' for 'Hamilton' into the faces of those he killed in battle? Tell me that's not true evil. Tell me that's not a sign of the devil working through a man. What do you think of that?' Challenge rose in voice at the last, as though he were daring Danforth and Martin to disagree.

'A charming habit,' said Martin.

'Aye, a holy terror said the common tongue. And a bloody murderer. He was the keeper of this castle until he lost his … well, until Henrysoun got the job, let's just say. A mistress in every town and a victim too. If you want my thoughts, it's his loose living that's tainted this place, left it a dancing hall for dark spirits. They say that, don't they, that a building can be soured by an evil man?

'His *building*, but – that twisted mind was gifted by his dark master. The eye of a … a constructioner. We won't see that like in Scotland again, I'm sorry to say. Heh. Anyway, what's Finnart got to do with the price of fish?' Guthrie's eyes gleamed. 'You don't think your friend Fraser made some enemy of a friend of his? Is that it?'

'I have no idea,' said Danforth. 'Where did Mr Fraser lodge when he was here? Where did he lay his head?'

'Why, he bided with me.' Guthrie gave a triumphant smile, as though savouring the revelation. It faded. 'But, I mean, he slept in my chamber. The chamber you boys will be in. You're forcing me out, you know, of my own room, mean though it is. I'm sleeping in the wine cellar.'

'You lodged with him? What did he say? What was his manner?'

'Och, he was a pain the arse. Not to speak ill of the dead.' He crossed himself. 'For he was a man without God, for all he was a cardinal's man. Asking this and that, "is this all you have? You a gentleman? I have more than this". A prideful goat. Interested in things, not in good discussion about prayer.'

Danforth sighed. Fraser was that. 'And the night he died. What happened?'

'He didn't come to bed that night.'

'And you didn't find that odd?' asked Martin. 'You didn't raise the alarm?'

'Hold on now, why should I? I was grateful for the quiet.' Martin and Danforth cast each other a surreptitious look, eyebrows raised. 'I just thought, you know, that he'd found himself some daft serving lass to wench with for the night. Or a boy.' He shrugged. 'You should know what he favoured more than me. I don't indulge in either loose behaviour – for weak, godless men, that. So, I had me a peaceful sleep and then all hell broke loose the next morning. Well, you recall what I said about inviting the devil in? Someone did, that very night. But whether it was your man casting up devils or just falling prey to them I don't know. But you can't go blaming me for not saying anything. Someone doesn't come to their chamber, you don't think "oh, that'll be another yin in the gardens wi' his bits lopped off". You tuck yourself in and you think no more about it.'

'Is this the room?' asked Danforth.

Through the cavernous chapel, painted a bright blue, its high windows admitting stained light, they had reached a polished oak door. 'Aye,' said Guthrie, as though cheated. 'He's in there. We keep the door locked secure, see, to stop any bad airs from the corpse getting out. Heh. Candles are lit too, to ward off the infection. And I've put some charms about the room to keep the evil spirits away. And the windows draped, that should be a –'

'Pray open the door, Mr Guthrie.'

'Aye, aye. Here,' Guthrie chapped three times with his stave. 'Anybody in?' He cackled, before drawing out keys and unlocking the door. Martin and Danforth looked at one another behind his back, sharing their distaste. 'Well, gents, you're welcome to him.'

'Mr Guthrie,' said Danforth. 'Would you kindly go and summon the depute of the queen's guard. I should like to speak to him.'

'I'm not a page, sir, to be carrying messages. I'm an usher, a gentleman like yourselves. I can't be going upstairs and downstairs, all the time using my feet like a young man. Send Mr Martin here.'

'Just do it,' said Danforth, his patience frayed, 'just do it.'

'Please, Mr Guthrie,' added Martin. 'It would be a great favour.'

Guthrie seemed to weigh up being difficult versus being helpful. After a moment, a tight smile spread across his round face. 'Very well. Seeing as you asked with such grace, Mr Martin. I'll ask him. But I can do no more than ask, mind you, I can't go issuing orders to the queen's depute. You watch him though.'

'Why is that?' asked Danforth.

Guthrie shifted his weight from one foot to another, looking around. His hand wandered to his crucifix, fingers turning white as he gripped it. 'He … the depute. I'm sure he was a good man once.'

'Meaning he is not now?'

'Since last year, when his brother was released as provost of the burgh by the old king … Forrest's changed. Turned towards

51

the heresies, consorts with demons. All the folk in the palace know of it. Her Highness knows. She does nothing about it. And you've heard of the Henry Forrest burned for heresy – oh, must be ten years ago?'

'Aye,' said Martin. 'When I was a pup. I remember my papa talking about it. Said the man went mad in the bottleneck dungeon before he was burnt.'

'Kin to the same Forrests,' said Guthrie. 'I kid you not. Whole clan of devil-worshippers.'

'You're saying the depute is a Lutheran?' asked Martin.

'Aye. A heretic. It's … well that's why it's being whispered that the devil stalks the palace halls. Because the depute invites him in, to dance and sing and slay us all in our beds.'

'Then, as a gentleman usher you should stamp out such superstitions amongst the weak minded,' snapped Danforth. But his own hand had wandered to the St Adelaide medal he wore around his neck, his spine tingling. Guthrie turned on his heel and walked away, crucifix bouncing. 'That is a tiresome fellow.' Something disturbed him about the usher, but he could not put his finger on it. To his irritation, Martin could.

'Aye. He's what you'd have become if we never went to Paisley last year. A God-loving servant more in love with the sound of his own voice. But gabshites have proven useful to us in the past, whether they intended to or not.'

'Hmmm,' said Danforth, frowning and folding his arms. 'Usher, indeed. In my father's day such a man would be working with the women, washing laundry and clucking his tongue.' Danforth saw that Martin wasn't listening. Instead he was staring apprehensively at the door. Disappointment flooded him; he had hoped, by now, that his friend would have lost all aversion to corpses.

'It's the cutting,' Martin offered, as though reading his thoughts, his face pallid. 'The thought of bone sticking out of broken flesh. I can't even … it's rank.'

'It is not very pretty. Like battle wounds. Ugly, jagged. And I am not cold, Mr Martin. You knew this man, worked in his Grace's service with him. Would you prefer to wait out here?'

'No, Simon. Thank you. The last time I saw Fraser I pushed

him into the mud. I'll confess, that weights heavy on my conscious now, knowing the daft old goat went on to get murdered. I … perhaps I owe it to look upon him. Say sorry.'

'And discover his killer.'

'Yes.'

'Well, we shall not do that without seeing what the corpse can tell us.'

'No. No, I suppose not. Only … do you not grow weary of it? Do you not grow weary of seeing death, and corpses … the … all the destruction, the murder?'

'I never grow weary of doing God's will.' Realising how priggish that sounded, Danforth added, 'Only I do wish sometimes His will was less bloody. I do wish He might set me back behind my desk, reading over his Grace's English correspondence. Oh, and Mr Martin?'

'Mmm?'

'Do not ever embarrass me by presuming upon the queen mother's generosity like that again. You're a young man yet. Your knees can cope with a flagstone.' Martin gave him a half-smile.

Danforth pushed open the door, and the pair stepped into the flickering light of a corpse's room.

7

No sheet had been laid over Fraser's body. He lay instead on his back on a wooden board in front of the altar, the board balanced on some stout coffers. Whoever had placed him there had laid out his severed arms, still sleeved, crossed over his chest, in a grotesque parody of a corpse at rest. 'At the very least they have had the good grace to close his eyes,' said Danforth. 'Mr Martin?'

Martin's head was turned to one side, biting on his knuckle. In the guttering light his face was white. 'Do what you must, Simon. Speak to me as you do it. Please.'

Danforth stepped towards the corpse and lifted first one severed arm and then the other, his eyes running over the wounds. 'Little blood here. Neat cuts.' As Martin had worried, bone glinted in the centre of each wound. 'These were cut off at the elbows, all very precisely. I should say with something heavy – an axe, a sword. Likely one hard thrust apiece.'

'What does that mean?'

'I cannot say,' said Danforth. 'Not for sure. My guess would be that they were not the cause of death. The clothing is not very bloody. Oh –'

Martin had crept up behind him, apparently steeled to look at the body. 'Jesus,' he whispered, crossing himself.

'Kindly do not creep about, Arnaud. Do you see? He was not hacked at, did not fight off his attacker. I would wager he was dead before these wounds were inflicted. Help me get him over. Come on, I cannot do it alone.'

With a moue of distaste, Martin helped Danforth roll Fraser's body onto its front. It landed with a soft *whump*. 'There,' said Martin. 'The wounds on his neck. Is this what killed him?'

Danforth leant over the body. The back of the neck had been sliced into, but half-heartedly, as though the killer had been disgusted by the act, or disturbed. 'No,' he said. 'No, there is still not enough blood. The blade has not even bitten far into the flesh. Perhaps it had grown blunt. This did not kill him.'

'Then what did?'

'Arnaud, I am no wizard, plucking knowledge out of the clear blue sky. But … what have we here?' He picked at something stuck to the dead man's clothing and held it up between thumb and forefinger. 'A skelf – just a little wood.' He pressed it, and as it stuck to his finger he held it up. Martin reached out to take it.

'Ow!' he hissed, as the little needle punctured the soft pad of his fingertip. A tiny spot of blood emerged. 'Seriously, Fraser? Is this your revenge? Even in death he irks me.' Danforth rolled his eyes as Martin shook away the skelf and sucked his finger. 'That might have come from anywhere.' But something else had drawn Danforth's attention.

'Look here. Some bruising. The type that comes after death, I should say. And,' he added, running a finger again along the clothing, 'grass stains. Little leaves of grass. Here – they are all over him.' He nudged the body sideways, not quite rolling it back over. 'Look there, on the front too. Twigs.' He picked one off, the leaf still attached, and pocketed it.

'So – Mr Fraser, God rest him, wasn't known for his cleanliness. I saw him once with ale spilled down his jerkin. It was still there a week later.'

'Dirt does not tell us what killed him. It was not these bruises. It was not these wounds. These, I think, were all done to him after his death. I doubt he met that death running wild through a forest. But as to what send him to it – I suspect we should have to open him up to discover it.'

At this, all colour fled Martin's face. 'You're not serious.'

'I wasn't suggesting I do it, Arnaud. I … I confess I would still not know what to look for, even had I the nerve. Yet … you are standing very close to me, very close to Mr Fraser, are you not?'

'Yes.'

'Has it occurred to you that the smell in this room is somewhat foul. Fouler still since we turned over the corpse.'

'But … that's normal, isn't it? Corpses give off foul airs.'

'Yes, but not so quickly, not in a cold room in a cold palace. This reek, I think, is from a voiding of the bowels. Were I to undress the body I think we should find that Mr Fraser had done so.'

'Jesus, Simon, don't.'

'I shall not, no. But I suspect that poor Fraser was overtaken by the need to find easement before his death. Perhaps afterwards as well. Now, what makes us require it?'

'Eating. Drinking.'

'Yes.'

'What are you saying? These sound like riddles.'

'Only this – and it is only a possibility. It may be that Mr Fraser was given – or took – some victuals that were unhealthy. Poisonous. And that afterwards, after his insides were churned enough to kill him, he was carved up. It was done for display.'

'Then there was no ghost here, but a poisoner. That's bad. We're all in danger, then.'

'I fear so. There are some poisons which make the brain sick, make the poor soul flee and the victim run wild before death. Others unbalance the humours entirely, stopping the breath.'

'What do we do, warn the dowager?'

'We must. And we must discover if there are any Italians in service here. Find an Italian, find a poisoner. They are expert in the art. If an Italian is not our killer, at least he will be able to explain the workings.' He leant again over the corpse and slid open the eyelids. 'Yes,' he said. 'The eyes are enlarged. Poison.'

'So what do you think, someone bent on vengeance?'

'Against Fraser? I doubt it, but we shall look into it.' The words of the irritating Guthrie were echoing. He would not make assumptions, though. Information must be stored securely. To his chagrin, Martin had no such qualms.

'This depute of the guard, Forrest – and his brother. If they were kin to a man burned in the past, they might have a grudge against the cardinal. And the late king, if he dismissed the brother from the provostship.'

'It's possible,' said Danforth in irritation. 'You said your father told you of this – when?'

'Dunno. Ten years ago? More?'

'I see. It is probably nothing. Keep your suspicions close until they might be tested.' Privately, he decided to be wary of the queen's depute. If Forrest was a heretic, who knew what twisted thoughts he might harbour. 'To tell you the truth, Arnaud, I cannot see it. Why should a man bear a grudge for years, and strike back only when the king is dead, and the cardinal imprisoned? I doubt Fraser even worked in his Grace's service ten years ago. And to kill for the sake of one little burning. Why, I recall King Henry burning twenty-five anabaptists in a single day!' Martin wrinkled his nose. 'Aye,' smiled Danforth. 'The reek must have been powerful.'

'If not vengeance then what? Madness?'

'Arnaud, think on what we have seen in the past. Those slain for vengeance, yes, and malice. And out of lust, or else some mad desire bred in the evil mind. What we might have here is something else.' Danforth's eyes shone as he spoke, his heart beginning to race. 'A murder of politics.'

As he turned to lead Martin out, Danforth jumped at the hulking figure standing in the doorway. How long had he been there?

'Simon Danforth and Arnaud Martin?' asked the man, his voice gruff. 'Are you the men?'

'We are,' said Danforth, straightening up. The sudden appearance had shaken him, and it would not do to look frightened or nervous. 'You must be the depute of the guard.' The man's shadow had fallen across them, cast by the brighter torchlight of the outer hall.

'I am that.'

'Where's the captain?' asked Martin.

'In Holyrood in charge of the governor's guard. I'm Alexander Forrest. Brother to late provost of this burgh.' By his expression Danforth saw that he was supposed to be impressed. He did not rise to it.

'Then pleased we are to meet you, Mr Forrest. Though we are less pleased with the security of this place.'

'Is that so? Hold on whilst I pull ten fresh soldiers out my arse. Or perhaps *you'd* like to guard all the entrances and exits with a paw-full of men?'

'I meant no criticism,' lied Danforth. 'Forgive me. I mean

only that it is most unfortunate that this … grisly … murder has happened under the roof of our sovereign lady.'

'Under the roof? No murders under this roof,' said Forrest. His hand balled into a fist and he laid it on his hip. Close, Danforth noted, to his sword hilt.

'No?' asked Martin.

'No. Yon corpse was found outside the walls, by the loch.'

'Who found it?' asked Danforth.

'The gardener.'

'I see. Mr Fraser, when he was here – did you have much traffic with him?'

'No.' Forrest's face had turned stony, but his hand had relaxed.

'Did anyone?'

'Not that I know. No more than anyone else. He ate in his room – in the room he lodged. He was only here one day. Mind you …'

'Go on.'

'Well, it's tattle. Nothing, most likely. But on the night before we found him – he was found in the morning – some of the servants said he was a madman. Wandering about. Rambling.'

Danforth turned to Martin, the word 'poison' pulsing through his mind with such force he wondered if the other two men might hear it. Looking back at Forrest, his face as calm as he could make it, he said, 'was this inside the walls?'

'Aye. Since the servants don't wander about outside at night.'

'I see. Mr Fraser, could he have wandered out?'

'He wasn't a prisoner, sir.' The word was delivered with a trace of sarcasm.

'Tell me, do you have any Italians lodged in the palace? In the dowager's service?'

Forrest looked stumped. 'Italians? I don't … aye, there's a gaggle of musicians. From Venice, I think. Bassano is one of them.'

'Do you trust these men, watch them?'

'Why should I watch them? I'm not interested in music. It's not my job to spy on a troupe of good folk who make the dowager merry, for God's sake.'

'We are not your enemies,' sighed Danforth. 'Mr Forrest, we wish only to know what happened to our friend. For his Grace the cardinal's sake as well as the dowager's. And the queen's.'

'Well, friend,' said Forrest. 'Maybe it is that the depute of the queen's guard needs no strangers, no outland men, interfering with his work. I've a job of work to do here, sirs.'

'Then,' said Martin, and Danforth had time to worry as the younger man fixed his own hand on his hip, 'maybe it is that you should be doing it. Else we would not need to involve ourselves. You might start by ensuring that her Grace's food is tasted. And the kitchens watched, however many are in use.'

Danforth expected a rage of abuse from Forrest. He seemed the type. However, instead the big man shrugged. 'You do what you like. You cardinal's imps always do.'

'Perhaps,' said Danforth, trying to sound conciliatory, 'you could show us where the body was discovered? And take us to this gardener? Is he within the palace?'

'He has his own lodge outdoors. And you won't see much tonight.'

'Why is that?'

'Because night has fallen.'

Danforth cursed his own stupidity. Of course it was now dark. Even with a torch there would be little left to see. Another night might not hurt. Then again it might. 'Quite right,' he said. 'We shall retire for the evening then.'

'Guthrie'll show you to your chamber.'

'Excellent,' said Danforth, wincing.

'Here, we've been on the road most of the day,' said Martin. 'Any chance of us getting some supper?'

'You can say to Guthrie,' said Forrest, already beginning to walk away. 'Not my job to entertain guests.' He paused. 'That all, gentlemen? I can't bring you a hot posset later, or tuck you into your feather beds?'

'Not quite all,' said Danforth. 'With your leave – you might let … whoever you let … know that the corpse ought to be sealed in some coffin or chest. It will soon turn, and then even that door will not relieve the palace of the reek. There are, I should imagine, carpenters and joiners here? Or some other appropriate mechanicals? Then, perhaps, he can be conveyed to Edinburgh, when servants are free to take him. His house is near to the Greyfriars. The parish will receive him.' Lamely, he added, 'the cardinal will see to any expenses.'

Forrest gave him a long look but said nothing. Eventually he gave what might have been a nod and strode away. Martin made to follow the depute, but Danforth stayed him with a hand. He waited until he heard the clunking boots soften and disappear. 'Well he's no friend to us,' said Martin, giving the empty space Forrest had occupied a sour look.

'The friendship of some men has to be won. If it is worth winning. Listen, Arnaud: we shall take ourselves to that blasted Guthrie fellow and find our lodgings. Yet I warn you: be wary what passes your lips in this palace. Inwards and outwards.'

***

With much grumbling about having to decamp to other quarters, Guthrie showed them to what was normally his own chamber, on the ground floor in the north range. As he had said, it was just off the corridor they called Thieves' Row, which ran parallel to the top of the quadrangle. Danforth crossed the barren little room and pushed open the wooden shutters with a sigh. No great leaded glass here, he thought. On the wall was the outline of a cross, presumably taken down by Guthrie to be set up in his new quarters. Danforth traced the outline, his finger coming away dirty. Palace living was not quite the luxury it was above stairs. He looked down over the lawns, inhaling the cold evening air and watching it burst outwards in a satisfying funnel. Ahead was the loch, black in the starless sky, but wobbling here and there with pale reflected moonlight.

Martin was speaking. 'Hmmm,' Danforth asked, cracking his back before scraping the shutter closed.

'I said I'll die here myself if I can't eat.'

'I merely suggest we eat only what we see others eat. Out of prudence. For safety's sake.'

Martin had flopped into a hammock suspended from two hooks nailed into the plaster, his travelling pack squashed in at one end. Its twin hung against the other wall, with Danforth's pack – mercifully still tied shut – on the floor beneath it. Danforth eyed the hammock with distaste. It was the stuff of soldiering, not service. 'Royal service, right?' said Martin, rolling from side to side and bouncing off the wall. 'The devil burst it.'

'If you think that service is all feather beds and jewelled fans, you have another think coming, you young fool. Even his Grace does not pamper his servants. If you pamper servants, you will soon find that they would rather lie in their beds all day than get out of them to work.' There, he thought; that might go some way to curing Martin of his fascination with high living.

'Aye, well … it's a sign of a great person if their people live in greatness.'

'Blast it, Martin – why is it always an answer to everything with you?' Martin smiled up, sweetly malevolent, like a naughty child. 'At any rate,' Danforth went on, 'we shall have far too much to occupy us than to spend our days in rest. I daresay that you might sleep on the head of a pin when we have finished working through this business.'

Alertness pulled Martin upright. 'What shall we do tomorrow, then?'

'That,' said Danforth, stepping to his own hammock and unfastening his cloak, 'is for us to decide now. To plan.' He shook the cloak loose and began unbuttoning his doublet. 'One: I wish to inspect where this corpse was found. There might be little to see now, but there might be something of value. Two: I wish to speak to the gardener. The one who discovers a corpse usually has the sight burned into their mind. Three: I wish to visit the town and discover what the common rabble thinks of Hamilton of Finnart.'

'The town?' asked Martin. 'I … well, this sounds like a great deal to do on a short day. I'll go to the town. I mean you know how quickly the days pass in winter, one minute it's the morning then it's afternoon and night again. If you want, that is. I'll do it.' Danforth watched Martin babble, but the younger man didn't seem to want to meet his eye. Instead, he had become interested in ensuring the hooks of his hammock were well fitted.

'Very well,' said Danforth, gingerly sliding into the suspended cloth. 'Since it animates you so much, you might go back into town. Cast about for rumour, for report. That kind of thing.'

'Aye. Aye, I'll do that.' Martin eased up onto his elbows, pushed away from the wall, and blew out the candle that sat on a box in the centre of the little cell.

Danforth closed his eyes, trying to make himself as small and weightless as possible. To his surprise, the body of Fraser did not crowd into his thoughts, the grey face did not loom up at him demanding justice. Instead, he began to wonder what it was that seemed to be drawing his friend to Linlithgow. As Martin did not seem willing to volunteer the information, he could only surmise that it was nothing good.

8

The town of Linlithgow clung to the palace like a suckling child. Martin had walked down after leaving Danforth fussing about in the courtyard, asking the staff of the palace if there was a library which he might commandeer as an office. Privately, Martin had been worried that the older man might make have decided during the night to accompany him, but instead he had sufficed himself with ill-concealed looks of suspicion and a gruff warning to watch himself. They had parted by the fountain, and when Danforth had stalked off, Martin had taken the opportunity to covertly splash and wash his face and neck, before producing a hidden comb and slicking back his hair. He had his own mission to complete.

For what seemed like an age, he had sauntered the market cross, watching the burgh slowly rouse itself. Stalls were set up, tables set out, and children set to work touting for business. Snatches of singing helped waken the place, giving it an air of jollity as shafts of sunlight speared the ground. Martin hummed to himself as he surveyed the faces, none familiar, and fended off questions from the more civic-minded of the burgh folk: 'what news, sir?'; 'what brings you hither?'; and of course, when the livery was spotted, 'is the cardinal free? Might we bury our dead as good Christians?' Above the town, smoke rose from a multitude of chimney holes, rising in columns to be flattened by the wind. The sight brought back the image of his mother's house ablaze, the roofbeams collapsing, the sound of horses screaming in the yard. He turned his face away, looking again to the crowds. His mouth made a little moue and he looked at his shoes as a young married couple sauntered by, their hands clasped. Everyone but him. At the first mention of marriage every lass fled him. It wasn't fair. He looked up again.

None of the faces was the one he sought. As the sunlight intensified, bringing little heat to the chilly air, he began to suspect he might have to do some work. Besides, the mission he was bent on … it was wrong. He knew there was something tainted about it. And yet he could not resist it. The town had pulled on him, the desire to see her face and hear her voice. Perhaps, he smiled to himself, he had been bewitched at the age of eighteen, and the traces still sparked in his veins. As he traced his finger along one of the wooden boards on the cross itself, a soft voice intruded on his disappointment.

'Arnaud? Arnaud Martin?'

He turned, hardly daring to hope. There, within touching distance, stood Marion Muir, the woman he had loved since the autumn of 1539. The woman he had hoped to marry. The woman who had married someone else and been taken as wife to Linlithgow.

'Marion,' he said, his voice husky but his face breaking into a grin. 'I didn't think to see you here.'

***

Danforth stood on partly-frozen ground to the north of the palace, the sun sending just enough light for a thaw. He had turned his back to the pewter spread of the loch and bent to the ground. 'About here?'

'Aye,' said the head gardener, his arms folded. Danforth's eyes scanned the ground, but he could see nothing out of the ordinary. He rose, his eyes trailing up the hill which led to the palace. From here only the north range could be seen, his and Martin's chamber window to the right on the ground floor, peeking out over some sculpted bushes. Directly next to it on the right one of the four corner towers stood proudly. It was a tall building. Above the ground floor was the floor of the king's chambers and great hall; then the queen's apartments; then the royal nursery; and at the top the high guard posts. To leave, the gardener had led him out of the old, disused gatehouse on the eastern range, next to the pool of stinking sludge that marked the open refuse pit. Perhaps Fraser had come out that way. At any rate, where he stood now – where the body had been found – was the back of the building, facing only the loch. No one would be looking out at much here.

'Master Gardener, this part of the place is … somewhat

shielded from view. Do you have much work to occupy you here?' The gardener, his face hidden behind a heavy beard, narrowed his eyes. He raised an arm swathed in the dun of his uniform and pointed. 'The great gardens lie off the western range.' Danforth waited, expecting more. The man had a taciturn air about him. Ordinarily it would be a thing he might have respected, but at present it was an irritant.

'I see. And so you conduct your business there.'

'I direct my men t'attend the gardens there, aye.'

'You have many men?'

'Passing fifteen. Big gardens.'

'And very fine, I am sure.' No response, no smile. 'Where do you keep the tools of your trade?'

'Secure.'

'Yes, I am certain. But where?'

'Over'n the gardener's barn.' He pointed vaguely in the direction from which they had come. 'Under lock and key.'

'Do you have, I take it, some …' Danforth fought for the right words. 'Some large cutting … implement. Such as might have sheared … cleaved Mr Fraser's arms from his body?'

'Hold on, sir,' said the gardener, 'just whit are you accusing me of?'

Danforth sighed, sensing a lost cause. 'I accuse no man. I simply wish to find the weapon which struck off the man's limbs.'

'Well you'll no' find it in my barn. Locked, as I said. I check and check again that barn before I retire. And if any man took anything he'd be the one with his arms chopped off. By me.' His eyes suddenly widened. 'Not that I could … I meant only a jest.'

'I take your meaning,' said Danforth, shaking his head. 'The morning after the death … everything was accounted for, every tool in its usual place? Nothing amiss?'

'Nothing, sir.' The gardener briefly chewed on his inner cheek, the brown thatch quivering. 'No, nothing. I would have remembered special that day, what with the news and the suspicion and the fear and that. I'd remember.'

'Very good, Master Gardener. Well, it is as I thought. After such a time, there is little the ground can tell us. No secret note scribbled in haste, no bloodstains. Was there much blood on the ground?'

'No, sir. You can see, there was so little blood come out of the body that what there was has been taken by the wind and the snow.'

'Yes. I meant to ask you,' said Danforth, reaching into his doublet. 'Can you tell me where this might have come from? Is there anything remarkable about it?' He held up the twig with the little leaf he had taken from Fraser's body, twiddling it between his thumb and forefinger. The gardener leant in, eyebrows knit. Then he sniffed it.

'It looks to me like it might have come from one of the garden's shrubs.' He gestured back towards the palace. 'We plant them all around the place. They keep their leaves during winter. You know, stay green, give some colour. Most of them are in the gardens by the western range. You can't see them from here.'

'Are they poisonous?' asked Danforth, the thought just occurring.

'No. If a man was fool enough to eat them he might puke them up or have a bastard of a gut-rot. But not poisoned.'

'Are there any poisonous leaves or berries or anything such in the gardens here?'

'I …' The gardener fidgeted, looking away. 'Some foxglove, some wolfsbane. Her Grace the dowager is partial to the colours. But you'll no' find them blooming now.'

'I see.' Danforth replaced the twig. He turned with a jolt as some birds rose up, squawking, from hills on the other side of the loch and descended to skim the surface. He felt a blush creeping at the fright. 'It is a pretty place.'

'It is that,' said the gardener, a smile finally threatening.

'Tell me, that gate we came through, in the eastern rooms. Is it guarded?'

'Guarded? I think … well, there's few guards – this is no fast castle. I think those boys have a job of work to do guarding the queens' rooms in the royal apartments. They cannae be everywhere.'

'And so anyone might come and go from that entrance. In the night. In the dark.' An image flashed through Danforth's mind of a shadowy figure, lurking in the darkness under the arched gate, waiting for his moment. A murderer would be much easier to catch if all suspect men were trapped in one place. Life, unfortunately, provided too many entrances and exits. The cardinal's mention of the word 'stage' swam up again.

'I don't want to get anyone into trouble, sir,' said the gardener, removing his hat and scratching his head. 'I don't say anything against any man. The place is well defended enough.'

'That is loyal of you.'

'Aye. Loyal. You … you won't tell the depute I was telling tales, then?'

'Not if you do not wish me to,' said Danforth. The man's manner had changed at the thought of Forrest. Might that signify something? 'Loyalty is a virtue. Tell me, did you work these gardens when Sir James Hamilton of Finnart was the keeper here?'

'Aye.' Danforth noticed his hands tightened on his bonnet, the knuckles whitening.

'He was a good master?'

'He was not our master, sir. Not really. More like an … a colleague, you'd say. A good man for the place – a builder.'

'You regretted his death then?'

'No. Yes. I mean – look, I'm no' daft. I ken the old dream tales, the arms struck off. And I tell you this: it was no phantom left that corpse as I found it, but a man. If it was someone who sought revenge for Finnart's death then it's too late with the old king gone. He'd be after the little queen, his heir, or even your master the cardinal himself. Not some … some … cardinal's servant.'

Danforth watched as the gardener replaced his bonnet in a gesture of defiance. Their gazes locked as a light wind picked at them, ruffling their hair. 'Well, as I thought there is little to be learned here. Perhaps we might return to the palace. Perchance you can find someone who can find me a quiet place.'

Danforth shivered as he hiked back uphill to the palace,

turning his nose away from the seething pool of refuse.

***

'It's good to see you. A true surprise. Are you hungry? I've not had any breakfast – I can't say why. I'm here on the cardinal's business. That's what I do now, work for his Grace.'

Martin had escorted Marion to a tavern, against her protestations that she was a married woman. She had only agreed on the proviso that her serving girl, basket over her arm, would stand sentry outside.

'Good for you. No, I'm not hungry.'

'Are you sure? I'm paying.' Martin shook his purse, drawing several greedy glances from their fellow patrons. The place was busy.

'Aye, I'm sure.'

'So how have you been?' asked Martin. 'I've been blathering on about myself, I should have asked.' He bit his lip. He certainly regretted being so eager to talk, but he didn't want her to know it. He eased back on his stool and looked at her: blue eyes, light brown hair, and gleaming white teeth. She wasn't smiling now, but he hoped to make her so that he might see them again. He wondered if she could read the hunger in his eyes and tried to dim it.

'I've been well,' she said, casting her eyes down to the hands she had clasped on the table. 'I got married, you know.'

'Aye,' said Martin, annoyed. He hadn't wanted her to talk about that. It was an unpleasant reality. 'I did hear.'

'And now I live here.'

'Do you like it here? In Linlithgow I mean.'

'Yes, It's quiet, much quieter than Stirling. Or Edinburgh. How's your ma'?'

'She's well – she's in Edinburgh now. At my house. There was an accident a short time back. The house burned. You know my sister died?'

'Aye, I was sorry to hear that. She was a good lassie. And your mother's … well enough … without her?'

'Aye, well, you remember my mother. A strong lady.'

'Aye.' Marion bent over the table, stifling a laugh. 'She didn't like me.'

'What? She did so.'

'She really didn't.' As she recovered from her giggle, she brushed away a strand of hair with two fingers: a well-remembered gesture that pierced him like a dart.

'My mother likes everyone,' Martin protested. In truth, his mother had said to him on more than one occasion that if Marion Muir were made of marzipan she would eat herself.

'Well she kept it well hidden. She certainly didn't like us going for walks in the woods.'

Martin's heart began to pound as he recalled those walks. The grasses would be knee deep as they strolled, aimlessly, the sunlight glinting in her hair as she picked at flowers. Sometimes they would take a blanket and lie down, talking for hours about people they knew and what they wanted to do with their lives. Kissing occasionally – too occasionally, for his liking.

'Hmm,' he said, returning to the dank tavern with its fishy smells and burble of chatter. 'Here, do you remember that girl we used to know that followed me around everywhere?'

'Meg Robertson?'

'Aye! With the long face and the rat's tail hair. Meg Robertson. What ever happened to her?'

'I think she got married too.'

'Jesus, who would have her!'

Marion laughed then, teeth flashing. 'Oh, you could always be so nasty.'

'You were pretty good at it yourself. Do you remember calling her 'Nutmeg' with the wooden head?' She laughed again.

'Well I wasn't so clever with words as you,' she shrugged, still laughing. 'That's good, though, working with the cardinal. I did hear about that. We all knew you'd do well. Make something of yourself. Wee smart-arse.'

'You did?' Martin's eyes flared. 'You've kept informed about me?'

'I just heard things, that's all.'

'I heard things too. I heard that you'd married. Some fat

merchant who –' Marion's smile vanished, and she began to get up. 'No wait, I'm sorry. I'm sorry, I didn't mean …' Martin trailed off. He knew he had no right to mock her husband. He had never met the man. It was not his fault Marion had chosen him. If he were to admit it to himself, it wasn't Marion's fault for choosing another man either. He had made a mistake trying to see her again.

Slowly, with warning in her eyes, she settled back down. 'I am sorry,' he said. 'I just … I've missed you. I've missed being your friend, I suppose. I just wanted to spend the time of day with you, you know, as we used to do.'

'You … you didn't meet me by chance?' Something like fear crossed her face, replaced swiftly by concern. 'Are you really well, Arnaud? Your health, I mean?'

He barked laughter. 'Sorry. No, I see what you mean. I'm fine, truly. I'm staying at the palace – within the palace. On the cardinal's business, as I said.'

Martin stared at her for a long moment. What had he intended? For her to run off with him, forsaking her husband? Perhaps. But he had not for a moment imagined it was likely. No, he supposed, his eyes following the curve of her cheek, the lines of her throat, he had wanted to see if he still loved her, after years of her just being an image. He had hoped that he could close the book of a story that had no ending but had dragged on for far too long.

'It's good seeing old friends,' she said. 'Sometimes. But I really do have to go. I have eggs to get still, milk. Other things.' Martin nodded. Of course, she had to get the ordinary, boring things of everyday life. His pipe dreams of her falling into his arms splintered and faded, a reflection in a puddle stamped on by a child.

Why did you marry him and not me? I will love you to the grave!

'Of course you must. It was good seeing you, Marion.'

'And you, Arnaud. We might meet each other again. As friends.'

'Yes,' said Martin, hopeful that they wouldn't. If he had taken any lesson from his stupidity, it was that broken things should be left broken, not forced together by a clumsy mender. He stood as she did, and he made to hug her. She let him, stiff in his arms, before stalking through the crowded tables, her head low. Martin watched the door of the tavern close behind her. Before he had time to curse his folly any further, a silky voice interrupted him.

'That must have been a difficult thing to do. It was certainly a difficult thing to watch.'

He turned, anger on his face, and found himself staring into the charcoal eyes of Rowan Allen.

9

Danforth settled himself into a hard, wooden chair in a room in the southern range of the palace, directly above the chapel. The smell of incense had permeated even there. It was comforting, although the room, a library he had been shown to by a slow-footed domestic servant, was almost denuded. He had scanned the shelves, but all that remained were some thin volumes on music, outdated and not worthy of being chained up.

Away from the bustle, he crossed his hands on the desk and closed his eyes. He thought of dreams, visions, and prophecies. His own wife, in an English grave for years, had appeared to him nightly since his coming into Scotland, never ageing, always protesting that her death had been a mistake, a misunderstanding. Why, though? Some overflow of melancholy, an imbalance in his humours. She had revealed no secrets, cast no warnings of what lay ahead of him. Sometimes people he had known in England had appeared to him in dreams: people he never bothered thinking about in his waking life, as though they were annoyed at having been forgotten. Again, their parts were insubstantial, without cause or purpose. And then there was the more recent spate of odd dreams in which his teeth were falling out, but he put that down to Martin's tiresome jabs about his turning thirty in April.

He thought back. When Alice Danforth had haunted his sleeping hours to the point that he had feared to sleep, he had taken himself to the university at St Andrews. Using a fake name – Arthur Arturus or something equally stupid, as he recalled – he had consulted the scholars in St Salvator's about dreaming. His questioning had sparked some debate. What had it been? What had been said?

Yes, thought Danforth. Some had championed the idea that the health of the body governed dreams, which were themselves without rule or reason. Others insisted that the spiritual condition of the dreamer was in control, with God or the devil sending dreams accordingly. Fewer clung to the idea that dreams were predictors of the future, warnings, omens. In the end, there had been no agreement. No one knew why dreams came. To Danforth, it seemed likely that the solution must be some combination of all three. Idly, he took the pen and paper he had brought and began writing, hoping clarity might manifest itself from ink. When he had finished, he was almost surprised to see that he had fashioned a little script.

Arthur Arturus: O great divines, what think you of my dreams?
Scholar 1: Such dreams as come are bred in body only.
Scholar 2: Cry false on him, good sir. For dreams we know
    Are sent from God and faith alone will blow
    All nightly terrors from the cursed mind.
Scholar 3: Yet listen not to my unlearned friends
    For as Cassandra learned unto her cost
    Dreams are no toys but signify the most
    Strange events to come.
Scholar 1: Stop your ears to all such foolish fancies
    For nothing comes of list'ning to such trash.
Scholar 2: Turn instead to God to salve your woes.

(Arthur Arturus knots the scholars' beards together)

Arthur Arturus: I think my friends you will now take advice
    For I have knit you all together close
    Draw your heads as one or be not loosed.

He smiled at his little skit. It summed up his thinking and what he recalled of theirs. King James V might have been moist-brained, suffering distempered thoughts in his waking life that needled him at night. Yet, with an understanding of the body, an interpretation of the dream might be possible. The world knew that James had dreamt of having his arms struck off, with a warning that his head would be next. His arms were his sons, who did indeed die one after the other. The head, it was thought, was the king himself. Yet the royal head could never die – or, at least, every monarch had two of them, one natural and one political. The royal head was now that of the little Queen Mary. If the head was truly to be struck off, the baby would have to–

Something tapped against the door and Danforth started, annoyed at being torn from his thoughts. It opened, and a young woman stepped in, light streaming behind her and highlighting the pale orchid of her gown. She cut it off as she softly drew it closed. Quickly he drew an arm over his scribbling, making a note to burn it later. 'I am sorry,' she said in a light French accent. She slipped forward, little white satin slippers peeking out from under her dress like mice. 'I didn't know there was anyone here.'

'No matter, mistress,' said Danforth, rising and frowning. As his eyes adjusted, he recognised her as the waiting woman who had staged the intervention when he and Martin had met the dowager: the girl who had bragged of the infant Queen Mary's rude health.

'It is … Monsieur Danforth, yes?' A smile touched her eyes.

'Oui, Mistress,' he tried. He didn't like it. 'Aye.'

'I didn't mean to disturb. I'll leave.'

'No, no. You have business here?' He eyed her sharply. What did a scatter-brained lassie want in a near-empty room? Up to no good, perhaps.

'Her Grace sent me to see if there are any, uh, books. Left here, I mean. Most of her books were sent to Stirling.'

'Ah, yes. So I have found. You will find poor pickings.'

She strolled over, her arms demurely clasped over her lower bodice, and bent to peek at the books sitting sideways on the shelves. 'Ach,' she clucked, 'so old and worn. We need books of music to entertain her Grace. She should be entertained with these only if she is cent ans.'

'Santon?'

'Has one-hundred years, I mean. She is a young woman yet.'

'Of course,' grumbled Danforth. If, he thought, the stupid girl did not mix her languages and speak as though speech were going out of fashion, he might have better understood her. 'Well, music is music.' A thought occurred. 'My lady, uh…'

'Beauterne,' she chirped. 'I'm Diane Beauterne. I serve

Madame LeBoeuf, and so the queen.'

'Very good.' He measured her up. She was a pretty thing, the kind of ornament favoured by high-born women. Probably she had little to commend herself beyond some musical skill. Still, such women usually fluttered about palaces, gathering information as bees gather nectar. 'Tell me, Mistress Beauterne, do you have much traffic with the dowager's Italian minstrels?'

'I know them, oui. Pleasant and merry men, those. It is for them I seek books. You should like them to entertain you?'

'Very much,' said Danforth, certain that he would like little less. 'I should first like to speak to them. Do they speak Scots?'

'Not well.'

Damn, thought Danforth. His own Italian was negligible. He had tried, hoping, though he was loath to admit it to himself, that he might be able to take care of any embassies the cardinal might require be sent to the Vatican, but it was a lost cause. 'Yet … if you traffic with these men … do you speak Italian?'

Diane beamed, a blush creeping over her cheek, as she raised a hand and made a wobbly motion with her palm. 'Un peu. Little bit.'

'Where on earth did you learn that?'

'At my mother's lap,' she said. 'My mother attends on Madame la Dauphiness.'

'The Princess Catherine?' asked Danforth. Catherine de' Medici, the barren wife of the French Dauphin. It was said she was an expert in poisons. It was she and her ilk that gave Italians such dark reputations. He suppressed a shudder. 'Then I commend the education given you, mistress. It is a worthy talent to speak many languages.'

'Oh, I've had a talent for it always,' she beamed. 'Talk, talk, talk, as une fille. My mother, she said I was like an … a sponge. I would take in every word.' There was something needy in her voice, something almost childlike.

'Yes, yes. Very good. Would you bring these Italians here, to this room, now? I should like to speak with them.' She gave him a doubtful look and he sighed. 'The dowager should like me to be thorough. Whilst you fetch these fellows, I shall look over these books of music and see if I cannot find something to please the ear.'

With a little bow, Diane left the room and Danforth began picking up the tattered old books at random and looking for something religious and sedate.

***

'No woman wishes to be stalked, like a deer,' smiled Rowan. She eased herself onto the stool Marion had vacated.

'Haul, would you steal her grave as quick?' asked Martin, drumming his fingers on the table. He noticed he had bitten his nails to the quick. He must have been doing so whilst waiting to catch his quarry in the market cross.

'The seat is empty,' said Rowan, shrugging. 'I doubt the lady is for returning. Don't see what you seem to see in Marion Muir – a dull lass, from what I hear.'

'She's the fairest maid in the world!'

'Her? Really? In the whole world? Well, you're a flower of chivalry, to be sure – I'll give you that. Tell me, Mr, what was it?'

'Martin.'

'Oh aye. Have you ever heard of Actaeon?'

'No.' Martin hid his hands under the table, staring moodily past her.

'You should, if you're an educated man. He was a Greek lad who was intent on spying on a goddess. He stalked her through the forest, and then became the prey himself. He was turned into a stag, in the tale I heard.'

Rowan's chatter brought Martin back into the room, chasing out the images of Marion's departing back. 'Greek lads,' he said. 'Where did a flower lassie get Greek tales?'

'My father,' said Rowan, shifting in her seat. 'My dear old da'.' She gestured to a table in shadow further into the tavern, where a skeletal old man sat hunched, his cap pulled low over his face.

'Pray bring him over,' said Martin. 'It's no joy drinking alone.'

'He's proud. Doesn't like to be seen such a shadow of himself.

76

But he was a fine, strong scholar in his day. Old men's wisdom,' she smiled. 'But returning to the case: I think your friend is best left alone. It's sad to see a well-favoured young man pine after a woman who belongs to another. And I reckon it'll tear at your heart.'

'I'm fine,' said Martin, gritting his teeth. 'Thank you.'

'Very well. But if you should take a woman's advice, I'd say find someone new.'

It was Martin's turn to fidget. He gave her an awkward smile. Though she was pretty, there was something disconcerting about her forthright manner, the glinting black eyes and the thick dark hair just about tamed by her bonnet. 'Mistress Allen, you are a ...' he paused. 'Fair' didn't fit. 'You're a remarkably beautiful woman.' He slicked a stray strand of her behind his ear. 'And I think you should make an excellent match for –'

'Oh, ho – becalm yourself there, my young friend. I'm not looking to turn the heads of schoolboys.'

'I am no schoolboy,' said Martin, raising his chin. 'And if you'd let me finish, I was going to say that you should make an excellent match for someone else.'

'Oh?'

'Aye, with your old man's wisdom and that. But never mind.' He sighed, replaced his hands on the table and resuming his tapping. He had wasted time enough. He had promised Danforth that he would get some work done in the town. 'Mistress Allen, you live in the town, yes?'

'Yes,' she said. It was difficult to sustain her gaze. There was something intent and mocking in it. 'I'm afraid so.'

'Do you know anything of James Hamilton of Finnart? He was executed by the king some years back. Keeper of the palace up yonder.'

'Aye, I know who he was,' she said, her voice soft. 'A much-hated man in the town, much-loved up there. He was discovered making some plot to try and shoot the king through a window in the palace. The Douglases were his fellow plotters in it. I don't know – that was the talk of the town when he lost his head, anyway.'

'Why was he hated? Who hated him?'

77

'Who? Anyone who opposed the Hamilton clan. Anyone who he and ... well, who he persecuted for heresy. The bastard of Hamilton they called him. Still do, I suppose.' Martin sensed the good humour fleeing. A little barrier had appeared between them. It had been Cardinal Beaton who had been Finnart's ally in condemning heretics, albeit the cardinal had had the good sense to abandon his old friend when it became clear the king wished to be rid of him.

'I understand that. Men of politics make lots of enemies.'

'Aye, this is the truth. Well, nothing to do with me. One piece of advice my da' gave me: stick to learning and selling. Let the great men of the realm fight amongst themselves. And try and avoid the lightning strikes that sometimes fall upon the rest of us.'

Martin smiled. It was good advice. 'Do you know anything of Finnart's ghost appearing before the king?'

'Ha!' she exclaimed. 'Aye, the old tales of the king haunted by the bastard.'

'What do you make of them?'

She shrugged. 'Nothing. Tales are tales. Like Greek stories.'

'Old men's wisdom,' smiled Martin. She returned it.

'If you want ghosts you've got enough of them up at the palace,' she said. 'Without needing the bastard of Hamilton to haunt your dreams.'

'Aye right – what ghosts?' asked Martin, his smile fading.

'Heaps of them, stacks. My da' used to tell me of the ghost of St Andrew, who appeared in St Michael's to warn James IV against going to Flodden. That's a favourite one in the town. The palace too.'

'Go on.' Martin recalled Queen Marie mentioning the tale. He wanted to hear it for himself.

She leant forward, a smile playing over her lips. 'Let me see. It was a foul night, the winds whipping and the rain lashing. England and France were at war, and James IV was won to France's aid by the pleas of the fair Queen of France. "Help us," said she, "help us, our ancient ally." And King James, being a chivalric sort of soul, raised an army, to make haste to France's aid by invading the old enemy.' She paused, as though for effect. Martin nodded her to go on. She had a lilting way of storytelling. 'King James prayed for his army, for his kingdom, for France, in that great church up by the palace. As he made to leave, out stepped a vision, right into his path. A strange apparition, all clad in blue, its face hidden. "I am St Andrew", it said.' Her voiced deepened. "I am St Andrew, and I come with a warning. Make not for England. Proceed no further. If you do, you will be unfortunate, and will not prosper, nor any of your followers." And then he pulled back his hood.'

'And?'

'And revealed the face of a withered old man, hundreds of years old.'

Martin shivered. The palace, designed for pleasure, was fast becoming a place of secrets and hauntings. He thought of the hammock he'd slumbered in. What might be up and walking the halls and corridors whilst he slept?

As he picked at a stain on the table, a fat man barged past it, jogging it and sending Rowan lurching forward. 'Ho!' she cried. 'Watch yourself!' The man turned, peering down and scowling at her from a pink-flecked face.

'You watch who you're talking to, ya black bitch.'

Martin was on his feet instantly. 'How dare you speak to her like that, you fat-guts? You think you can –'

'Who the hell are you, you daft loon, I'll knock you –'

'Enough,' said Rowan, her voice measured but her eyes flashing. 'Thank you, Mr Martin. I can speak for myself.'

'Saved by a lass. The moor-lass,' chuckled the fat man, staggering away from them and out of the tavern.

'I should have struck that fat beast across the head,' said Martin, teeth bared. 'I won't have a woman spoken to like that.'

'Very noble, my friend,' drawled Rowan. Then her voiced turned friendlier. 'Thank you. I'm used to it. We're all black bitches in Linlithgow. It's another old tale, of a condemned man left to starve on an island in the loch. His wife trained their dog to carry food out to him, and since then it's become the burgh's great symbol: the black bitch.' An edge returned to her voice as she looked down at her sallow hands. 'When they speak of me, though … there is some venom added to it.' She looked up at him again and smiled. 'As I said. Used to it. Moor. Gypsy. Changeling.'

'But ... that's cruel,' he said lamely.

'Ha. I suppose. I used to walk out in the fields to escape it as a child. It's how I came to understand flowers so well. They can't speak or curse. So I'd wander amongst the rowans and my da' would teach me what nature can do.'

'Your name,' said Martin. 'Rowan. It's pretty. But ... why?'

She rocked back on her stool and laughed, light and tinkling. 'Rowan. Aye. My da' over there, he and my ma' found me as a child under a rowan tree.'

'You were a foundling?'

'Aye,' she shrugged, 'no shame in it. It might have been worse. I might have been called "Park" or "Abbey" if I'd been dropped near Holyrood.'

'So, your parents ...'

'My da' is over there.' Martin looked again, but the old man was still hunched. He had not noticed the little affray. 'The folk who bore me ... well ...' Again, she looked down at her hands, stark against the blue of her cuffs. 'You know the old king, the fourth King James, he kept Moorish women back in the day. Musicians, mainly. Black Ellen, Black Margaret. Made much of. Perhaps I was descended from one of them, a granddaughter or something, from the wrong side of the sheets. Moorish blood and Scottish blood mixed, until I'm ... me, I suppose. The Scots do love foreigners. Unless they are mixed breeds.'

'Or English,' smiled Martin.

'Aye, or that,' she said, returning it.

There was something pathetic in her revelation, something sad. Martin wondered at the life she must have had. Mocked, he supposed, slandered. Different. A sudden urge came over him to pat her head, to tell her that she might escape a town in which she was an especial 'black bitch'. However, he sensed she wasn't the type to endure sympathy. 'That was good, then, of the old man and his wife to take you,' he said.

'Good people,' she said, drawing her cheeks in. 'And as they brought me up in the world, so I look after him now my ma's with the angels. The lot of an unmarried woman, eh?'

'You never married?'

'Me? No. Whom should I wish to marry? All the lads in this town are blind fools. Wouldn't know a book from bonfire.' Martin grinned again. He noticed she didn't say 'whom should wish to marry me'. He liked that. Danforth might not, though. 'And I think my da' has probably done with his ale.' Martin chanced a look over at the old man, who seemed to be sleeping. A serving girl obscured his view, and he gave her a smile. 'He doesn't keep well,' Rowan was saying, 'and if he goes, I shall leave this burgh, I hope.'

'Not well? You don't trust him to apothecaries and physicians, do you?'

'Not if I can help it. Too expensive, sure. I treat him myself. I'm skilled enough in it. Old man's wisdom.' She smiled, tapped her nose, and stood. 'You take care, Mr Martin.'

'Please, call me Arnaud.'

'You take care then. No more stalking women. Put one foot in front of the other and never look back.'

10

'Signor Bassano,' said Danforth raising both hands. 'Signor Bassano, *please*.' The Italian minstrels were gathered in the library, huddled and speaking over him in their own language. 'Mistress Beauterne can you now make yourself useful and make them understand?'

The Italians had come en masse. Their presence almost seemed to bother the quiet little room, their agitated movements making the specks of dust in the air dance and whirl wildly in the late-morning light.

'Per favore silenzio,' said Diane, her voice airy. Danforth noticed with distaste that one of the younger musicians appraised her with a leer, which she seemed not to notice. 'Ahh ... questo uomo divertente vuole parlarti.' She turned to him and winked. 'Et voila,' she said whispered.

'Good. Good morrow, gentlemen,' said Danforth. He stood behind the desk, hoping it lent him an air of authority. He paused to see if Diane would translate. When she didn't, he went on. 'I have brought you here because you are strangers in this land and in this place.' He nodded at Diane, who shot him a sour look before speaking softly in Italian. A few of the men frowned at him; some turned to one another, mouthing silent words. 'As you might know, there has been death in this palace. Unnatural death,' he qualified.

He waited whilst Diane translated. 'I fear I must ask if you have any knowledge of it.' At this, an angry gabble of conversation broke out and he thumped a fist on the death. 'Silenzio,' he tried. They quietened, but he sensed a shift in the atmosphere. Already he had turned them against him. Well, he thought, no matter. He had a job to do. 'I must now ask if you have carried into this realm any knowledge of poisons.'

A few of the men began muttering, 'lui dice'; 'veleno? Veleno!' Diane looked at him, her mouth gaping. 'Well?' he said. 'Tell them to go into one of their ill-mannered clannish clusters and give us an answer.'

Something crossed Diane's face – a look between disappointment and disgust. Danforth felt a stab of regret, and instantly damped it down. 'I cannot say this,' she said. 'I ... will be more ...' She left it there, turning against to the assembled musicians. 'Non si offenda. Lui è Inglese.' A few of the men chortled and Danforth allowed Diane to speak rapidly back-and-forth. Then one of the younger ones spoke up.

'I ... Stephano,' he said. 'Son to Bassano. We need know – do you arrest us? My father in service long time. Never complaints before.' There was a hard edge of challenge in his accented voice and his eyes locked on Danforth. His show of confidence brought another welter of excited conversation to his fellows, Diane again waving her hands as though trying to put out a fire. Eventually, she reduced them to black looks and whispered curses.

'They want to know can they go?' she said. 'And are you to hurt them?' She hesitated a moment before adding, 'they ... have heard that King Henry killed his late wife's music man. And one of his other wife's music men. They think you are come from England seeking the blood of musicians. To hurt them.'

'Hurt?' said Danforth. His throat had dried, and he licked his lips. 'No, I ... what did they say?'

'Uh ... they say they hurt no man. They are good servants of the dowager and have her protection. They ... are not happy to be spoken to so, because of their birth.'

Danforth felt very small.

'Let them go. Apologise to them.'

He sat down whilst Diane held the door for the men, who left on a wave of Italian curses. When they had gone, he said, 'I need no Italian to understand what all of that meant.' He rubbed his cheeks before letting his forehead rest on his hand.

'You were very hard, sir, I think. It was not a good thing to do, to accuse so.'

'Mistress, I am not in the habit of handling foreigners.'

'Eh?' She stood before the desk, one hand on her hip. 'Are you not? Yet you are an Englishman living in Scotland.'

Danforth looked up sharply. 'That is different.'

'How so?'

'I am … they are …'

'You English,' she said, 'think every man a foreigner except yourselves. As though you are the only race in the world.'

'I beg your pardon?' said Danforth, feeling his hackles rise. Trust a Frenchwoman to think ill of a man bred in England. What more could be expected from that pampered race but thrice-stewed bile over Agincourt? 'I need no lessons from a French girl, thank you.'

'Ohhh,' she said, her hands grasping at the folds of her skirt. 'You see. It is as I say. You might have better answers from those gentlemen with a little subtilité. Ugh, c'est inutile de discuter.'

'Subtlety,' said Danforth, grasping at the word. 'Italians only know of subtlety in the skill of poisoning.'

'Oh, is it so? And so you accuse the Holy Father of poisoning, oui?'

'What? I did no such … the Pope is … Oh, you are a tiring woman.' Danforth wanted her gone. She had become a female Martin, questioning and mocking, but doubly exhausting by dint of her femininity. It made it impossible for him to mock her back without looking boorish.

'What is this of poisoning? Why do you ask them this?'

'That, I think, is my business.' He gave her a tight smile, which quickly faded. 'Yet … for safety's sake … you might tell the dowager to beware of what she eats in this place.'

'There is some danger them, of poison?'

'I did not say that. I said for safety's sake.'

'But I,' began Diane, her forehead wrinkling. 'Her Grace greatly fears poisons. It will trouble her.'

'But her food is already tasted.'

'Oui, mais … even so. You have heard of Queen Margaret, Margaret of Denmark?'

'Wife to King James III,' said Danforth. He knew his adopted country's history as well as any French girl. 'Of course.'

'Well then you know that she was poisoned by her husband.'

'I know nothing of the sort.' Danforth instinctively looked past her, and then around the room. He was greeted only with the bare shelves and curved ceiling. Still he had a very English suspicion of speaking ill of kings, even dead ones. 'Her death was by God's hand alone.'

'Perhaps,' shrugged Diane. 'Yet the rumours have lasted.'

'Rumours have louder voices than truths.'

Again, she shrugged. 'Still, her Grace has always feared poison since coming into this realm. If one queen might have been done to death,' she mimed eating, 'then so might any other.'

Danforth considered this, and something unpleasant took shape in his mind. Fraser's death was not by the blade – that was for effect – but by poisoning. If Margaret of Denmark had been murdered by poison and by another Stewart king … then it was almost as if the victims of the Jameses were reaching out from their graves, bent on revenge.

'So I do not see how I might speak to her Grace without causing her some alarm,' said Diane, breaking up his thoughts.

'Perhaps you might think of some *subtle* way. Thank you,' he said, pressing as much sarcasm as he could into the words, 'for your aid, mistress. You may go.' Roughly, he slid the hoary books he had located for her across the desk. She took them, not bothering to look down. Then, matching his sarcasm, she curtsied deeply, a whirl of orchid.

She turned to go, paused, made to move again, and then turned. 'Monsieur – Mr Danforth?' she said.

He looked up at her, waiting.

'I don't expect much from people in this world,' she went on. 'No. Not at all. Yet I do expect people to behave with courtesy – bonnes manières. There is never need for hate. Leave hate to those few like the man who hurt your friend. Let us, the rest of us, all be kind. It makes my heart to grieve – it makes me sorrowful – whenever I see a man behave as you did to those poor folks. It reminds me that there is bad feeling in the world, when there should be only love amongst all men. And women. In all our hearts.'

With that, she gave a little embarrassed nod and drifted from the room.

***

The sun was high when Danforth took the turnpike stairs down to the courtyard. Water was burbling from the fountain, the colours of the monument reflecting in a shower of sparkles. Martin was already there, kicking an inflated bladder around with Mathieu, the page boy. The yellow and red of his outsize tabard flailed. 'It is no more time for games,' said Danforth. 'And you, young man, have you not better things to do?' Service, he thought, wasn't what it used to be.

'Is it not then?' asked Martin. 'Well, laddie, the old man's spoken. Off you go.' He stooped to pick up the makeshift ball and threw it to Mathieu.

'Can we play again later?'

'Aye, maybe after dinner. Don't let the queen's ladies catch you at leisure, though.'

'Her Grace has them in the gardens,' protested Mathieu, clutching the ball to his chest, and jutting his bottom lip.

'Then you had best see if they have any need for you,' said Danforth, waving a hand to the western rooms. 'Look sharp, now.'

Mathieu stalked off, dragging his feet. Satisfied that he had gone on to meaningful work, Danforth shook his head at Martin and led him to their room, closing the door. There he looked him up and down. He seemed deflated, somehow. 'You should not lead that child astray. It is poor training.' No response. 'This is a serious matter, Mr Martin. It is not games.' Still Martin did not rise to it. 'We have the queen dowager and our master's orders here. We are not our own men.' Pride crept into Danforth's voice, giving it weight. 'You know, it struck me earlier that this killer might well aim at the queen's life, as the dowager fears.'

'Then why kill Fraser?'

There, thought Danforth. At last some interest. 'To draw the guards away from the nursery, perhaps. To spread them thinly. I cannot say. But if this is truly the case, if there is some design on our sovereign's life … we might well be all that stands between this realm and its destruction.'

Martin let out a whistling breath. 'Think on the rewards of that.'

'Yes. Yes indeed. The glory of God.'

'The glory of our purses, more like. The honours heaped.'

Danforth crossed his arms. 'Turn your mind away from that, sir. It might have escaped your notice, but this country is without spiritual life whilst his Grace is imprisoned. That – it – it makes for a sick realm, apt to infection. If we can salve it, we might be its ...' He was about to say "physicians". Martin would undoubtedly balk at that. Instead, he asked 'did you discover anything in the burgh?'

'Not really,' said Martin, biting at his pinkie nail.

'Well that does us little good, then.' He let silence stretch awhile, before venturing, 'Mr Martin, forgive me if I am pressing upon you. But we are friends, and I think it my place to ask if you had some other purpose in visiting the town. I noted your manner last night. I own I did not like it.'

Martin flopped down onto his bunk, his manner now that of a guilty child. Eventually he looked at Danforth. 'Aye,' he said. 'Aye, I wanted to see Marion Muir.'

'Marion? Marion the girl of your past?'

'Aye, the same.'

Danforth tried on a look of anger, and then let it drop, sighing. He crossed to Martin and put a hand on his shoulder, withdrawing it as quickly. 'She is married, yes?'

'Yes.'

'And you are ...' Danforth tried to think, unsure of what to say but willing the conversation to be over. Friendship was a burden when people insisted on behaving like fools. 'You found what you were looking for, I hope. Now you might go forward as a freer man.'

'Aye, s'pose so.'

'You will not though, will you?' said Danforth tilting his head and pinching the bridge of his nose.

'Likely not. To be honest.'

'We are all of us fools, then, in our fashion.'

'How so,' asked Martin, shaking his head clear. 'What did you do? Discover anything?'

'I questioned those Italian minstrels. With no great subtlety. That infuriating French girl aided me – you recall, the one who intruded on our meeting with the dowager?'

'Oh aye. Mademoiselle Beauterne,' he said, with a flourish. 'Never forget a name,' he winked. 'She was a pretty one. What was she like?'

'Ugh, a little Mistress Peaceweaver. Sunshine, hearts, and flowers. Altogether too much to say for herself, like any Frenchling. You know the cast. Better than anyone, I should think.'

'Flowers … I met the flower girl in Linlithgow.'

'Flower girl?'

'Rowan Allen. She was selling flowers when we came to the palace.'

'Of course,' said Danforth. The purple heather he had given the dowager blossomed in his mind. 'The dark lass. What had she to say? Anything of Finnart?'

'Nothing new. He and our master both made enemies at the heresy trials in the town a few years back.'

'Pfft. Making enemies of heretics and their minions is no bad thing,' said Danforth, swatting his hand at an invisible fly. 'Anything else?'

'Not really,' said Martin. Then something lit up his face. 'Here, she knows her antiquities.' Danforth cocked an eyebrow, which Martin seemed to take as encouragement. 'She was speaking of someone Greek, who turned someone into a stag. Or was turned into a stag. It was something like when you speak – I wasn't truly listen-'

'Actaeon,' said Danforth. 'The tale of Actaeon, who came upon Artemis in the forest.'

'Sounds about right. You would likely find her good company. You could bore each other,' he smiled.

'I have no desire for good company,' said Danforth. 'Quite obviously, since I seem to spend such time with you.'

'Very witty, my friend,' said Martin. 'Tres drôle, indeed. Here – smell that.'

'What?' asked Danforth, sniffing at the air. Was poison detectable in the air, he wondered. He should have asked the

Italians. Or perhaps not.

'I smell cooking. And it's noon or thereabouts.' Danforth looked out the window, judging the sun. Trying to tell the time was a trial without the guiding sound of church bells. It was when they were gone that you missed them. It was like coping with the death of someone close. If only, he felt, he could solve this present crisis, it would go some way to restoring order. To fixing what had become a mad world, a world turned upside down and inside out by the king's death. And there was something else, just as strong. An overriding desire to bow before the queen dowager and have her gratitude. To stand before the cardinal and have him reach out and bless him, the aged eyes kindling as he thanked him for a job well done. Thanked him for being a faithful and reliable son of the Church. Yes, there was that. Perhaps it was sinful but, he reasoned, less so when it turned to good service. There were other types of dream from that which had plagued King James and been recreated in blood. There were the good dreams that men could work to turn to reality.

'Let us pray his Grace is free soon,' he murmured. 'Aye, Martin, I believe I smell victuals. The question is do we dare trust them?'

'I'd rather poisoning than starvation,' grinned Martin, launching himself out of the hammock.

11

To Danforth's silent disappointment, the dining tables were not set up in the great hall in the eastern range, but in the queen dowager's outer chamber – the room that had been populated by card-playing women on their first visit. It had been transformed, a long table running its length, with a higher, shorter table to form a T at the far end. He and Martin were seated by Anthony Guthrie near the entrance to the room, well away from the top table. Closer to the royal end were a jumble of Douglas- and Hamilton-coloured suits. With much bumping of elbows the whole company was seated before Mathieu appeared from the inner chamber, a short horn in his hand. He blew a few notes, and then the doors were opened.

Queen Marie entered, her ladies at her elbows. Everyone rose, waiting to reclaim comfort when she sat on her gilded wooden seat, the stony-faced Madame LeBoeuf at her right hand. Marie nodded for the company to sit and, as they did, a murmur of conversation began, the atmosphere in the room changed suddenly, like air being drained from Martin's inflated pig's bladder.

Directly across from Danforth sat Forrest, the depute of the guard. Danforth chanced occasional glances upwards, to find the man's steel eyes boring into him. Next to Forrest, Guthrie held court, chattering ceaselessly.

'… And so the musicians will have a job, yet it'll please her Grace to have a bit of merry entertainment, you know? What do you think, Mr Forrest?'

The grizzled head turned to Guthrie. 'Of what?'

'Of this wee interlude for the queen dowager?'

'Hmph. Women's games.'

'Och, well I reckon you'd be fancying something a bit more … um … a bit hotter. *A Satire of the Three Estates*, eh? Well, we'll invite no more darkness into this place, I'm pleased to say.'

Danforth's ears pricked up. The *Satire* was an anti-clerical play. 'I'd like,' said Forrest, 'something that brought about some good instruction in the hearers. Not some foolishness that draws the mind from *true* faith.'

'You are a critic of the faith?' asked Danforth. The man had not struck him as religiously-minded, despite what Guthrie had suggested, but perhaps he was. Of the crooked persuasion. Forrest turned to him, eyes narrowed.

'What's it to you?'

Danforth held up his hands, ready to concede. But then he went on. 'I only ask as a cardinal's man.'

'Our Forrest is a right Godly man,' said Guthrie, his voice rich with sarcasm. 'He's no time for those of us that like good cheer. None of his friends do.'

'Hold your tongue, Guthrie,' growled Forrest. Then, under his breath, 'we have a simple faith. No need for baubles.' Guthrie mimed covering his mouth. He couldn't keep it up for long.

'But what's life without baubles, heh? What about you gentlemen,' he said. 'You're faithful men of the Church. The cardinal wouldn't have you otherwise.'

'Oh, Danforth is faithful, to be sure,' said Martin, seated to Danforth's left. 'To a fault,' he added, smiling. 'You'll get on well together.'

'You looking forward to the play then, Mr D?' asked Guthrie.

'What play?'

'Christ, have you fellows been listening at all? The dowager is having a play in the great hall, as soon as. Tomorrow, if she can. Or the day after. A bit of entertainment since the nights are still drawing in.'

'Is that wise?' asked Martin, turning to Danforth. 'With everything?'

'That's for me to say,' snapped Forrest. 'I'll say what's wise and secure in this place. Not youse.'

Danforth shrugged. 'I see no harm in something that might please the ladies. Please all of us, for that matter.' He liked plays, especially the mystery plays that enacted religious scenes, and the morality interludes that showed virtue triumphing over vice. They were good things, simple. They depicted an unfussy religion that even the muddle-headed multitude could understand. They brought people together in condemning evil and championing good. They might even hold a mirror up to people's misbehaviour, encouraging them to reform their ways. Diane's words that morning came back to him. She had said something about bringing people together, about being good. He looked around and spotted her bearing a cup beside Madame LeBeouf, who was, with Queen Marie, laughing at a shaven-headed woman capering about next to the top table.

The food was brought up by teams of domestic servants belonging to the palace rather than the queen dowager's shattered household. As they had to bring it all the way from the kitchens in the north-eastern part of the building, most of it was cold by the time it arrived. Danforth and Martin had agreed beforehand to eat only what they saw others eat first, and they occasionally looked left along the room to make sure that the dowager was being equally careful. Danforth met her eye once and was sure she gave a slight nod. He chose to believe so, at any rate. It relaxed him. Gave him a glow of pride, too. The Queen of Scots, dowager though she might be, acknowledging his wisdom and care. Yes, he was certain she had nodded.

Cold salmon and trout fillets, sauces already congealing, and globules of lard sitting like pearls on the wooden trenchers were placed before them. Danforth picked at the selection, his stomach rumbling, whilst Martin ate even more daintily, occasionally looking up to the queen's table as though hoping to impress with his courtly manners. Throughout, Guthrie kept up a tumult of conversation. It was a fine feeling, despite all, to be part of dinner in a queen's presence. Though her royal husband was dead, Danforth kept reminding himself that she was nevertheless the highest woman in the realm, after her infant daughter. And here he was, taking dinner with her. Yes, it even beat eating in the presence of a prince of the church.

'Gibb's a faithful man, a good man to the queen. You know the horse master. Heh.' Guthrie leant over the table and waved a hand; further down, nearer to the dowager's end, the big horse master was drawing laughter from his neighbours. He ignored Guthrie's salute, pretending not to see it. 'What he needs are good stables, though. Mr D, you've seen the great stables of England? I take it you rode here. Do you favour a great warhorse or a little mare, like old Wolsey?'

Danforth shook his head, unwilling to be drawn into idle conversation. He was sorely tempted to draw a comparison between his own father, who held his peace during dinner, and Guthrie, but refrained. A chunk of bread gave him an excuse not to engage. 'Danforth here prefers a sorry old beast,' offered Martin, drawing a dark look.

'Leave my beast alone.'

'I think it would be best left alone. In a pasture. The sooner you're quit of that poor old brute the better.'

'I would sooner be quit of you,' snapped Danforth. Martin chuckled.

'Christ's body,' laughed Guthrie. 'You pair are worse than an old married couple. Heh. Ach, it's this place. Starting to breed discord in all of us, I reckon. Almost as if someone invited trouble on our heads.' He gave a surreptitious look towards Forrest. 'You ken what they say: the battle rages on against the powers of this dark world and against the spiritual forces of evil. We need to increase our faith towards God, not question it.' Forrest remained impervious, shovelling food grimly.

'Her dowager wants to know if you're enjoying the palace's Lenten fare,' said a voice. Danforth turned to find Mathieu behind him. 'She recommends to you the claret. It's from France.'

'Like you, laddie,' said Martin. 'Working hard?'

'Yes, sir.'

'Good boy. You'll get on.'

'Pray give her Grace our thanks,' said Danforth. 'Tell her that our search for what ails her goes on. We shall find it.'

'I can help you look, sir,' said Mathieu. 'I'd like to help Mr Martin. Whatever you seek, I can help. I know every hidey-hole in this palace. I keep my own things hidden under my bed.'

'Then that's a hidey-hole no longer,' smiled Martin. 'But it is more a man we seek than anything else. What does a young fellow like you need to hide?'

'My books, sir. My book on soldiering.'

'You wish to be a soldier? Me too, when I was a bairn. Scots Guard.'

'Protecting the French king?' asked Mathieu. 'That would be a great honour. Could you get me in to that one day, do you think?'

'Well I never actually became one,' laughed Martin. 'Penning the lord cardinal's letters to France, that's been my calling. That how come I can sit in this fine palace with two queens under the same roof and good salmon on my plate.'

'Oh … well, I will tell her Grace what you say.' The boy bounded off.

'Well,' said Martin, 'bless him for try–'

'Look, look, here comes some good foolery. Look.' Guthrie pointed a knife towards the queen's table.

The shaven-headed fool had ceased her capering and instead squatted down, adopting the manner of a cringing child. She had filled her cheeks with air, her eyes turned piggy. She looked up to her left, as though there were someone next to her, and nodded eagerly. Then she turned to her right, to another invisible person, and performed the same gesture. She repeated this several times. 'Senat,' whispered Guthrie none too quietly. 'The queen's fool. Christ, she's the lord protector. She's Governor Arran. Look, she's cowering beneath Archie Douglas and his brother.'

Senat waved goodbye to her invisible friends, fawning and prostrating herself, and then her eyes turned foxy. She blew out, and a grin spread across her face. She strutted up and down next to the table, attaining her full height again, her chest puffed out. She picked up a napkin, deftly folded it into a crown, placed it on her head, and began shouting, 'go do my bidding. I rule all. And Lord protect ye all!'

A ripple of angry disapproval sounded from the Douglas and Hamilton parties seated close the top table. Danforth could see some hands gripping knives more tightly. But they could do nothing. The fool had license to mock. Taking further advantage of it, she moved away from dowager, who sat with a placid smirk on her face, and began working the room.

'Feed my treasury,' she barked. 'For I spend to my glory. I

mean, to my realm's glory. Give me gold, give, and give some more!' Grudgingly, the courtly members of the dinner table began to thrust coins to be rid of her. She grasped them, stuffing them in a pocket in her dress. She moved her way down the table, on Guthrie and Forrest's side. 'Here,' laughed Guthrie, 'buy yourself some false hair, you japester.'

'I am your governor,' piped Senat. 'Though I've still less hair on my bollocks than on my head.' She moved on to Forrest. 'You, guardsman. Feed my purse.'

'Get you lost, fool,' snarled Forrest. Senat gave him a long look, but said nothing, moving on to the next mark, a man Danforth didn't know. A sudden warmth had overtaken him, creeping up the back of his neck. He hadn't brought his purse to the table, only his cutlery. Bringing a purse was like bringing a weapon, he thought: frowned on, and something one hoped one wouldn't need. He grasped at his wine cup, swilling it to wet his throat, hoping that the foolish woman would move on as she did with Forrest. He considered asking Martin if he had brought anything to pay her off, but didn't want to do so before the whole company.

'You, Monsieur, feed my purse,' she piped, causing him to jump. 'I am your lord and master.'

'I have nothing for you,' he spluttered, trying to make his voice as deep and authoritative as Forrest's. Senat's brow knitted, and she made as though to move on, before stopping. 'Pray speak again and crave pardon from your master,' she said.

'I said I have nothing for you.' Go away, he added silently.

'But peace,' she said. 'You are an Englishman!' Her face suddenly cleared of all expression. 'Oh, oh, forgive me, Master Englishman.' To Danforth's horror, she dropped to her knees so that all he could see by his chair was a stubbly crown inside the ridiculous circlet of linen. She grasped at his sleeve. 'Oh forgive me, England. I am your servant and your vassal. I know my place, master, master, *master.*'

Danforth shook her grip as Guthrie hooted laughter. Through the rushing of blood in his ears Danforth could hear the infuriating usher chirping, 'she's good, is she no'? She's got him marked.' Who the "him" was, himself or Arran, Danforth didn't know.

Mercifully, the fool began retreating from him, still on her knees. She shot one last, vicious look up, rapping the coins in her pocket, before standing and moving to Martin. 'Feed my purse ...'

Danforth turned back to his food, his cheeks flaming, aware that Senat was receiving some coins from his friend. When she had moved along again, Martin laughed. 'She had you there,' he said. Then, with more feeling, 'are you sore, Simon? She's just a fool. She makes sport of everyone. It's her occupation, you know that.'

'And a bootless occupation it is,' snapped Danforth. Then, more in anger than anything else, he added, 'and little surprise to me that you find mirth in it, witless young fool you are.'

'Woah now,' said Guthrie. 'You two behave, else her Grace will have you out. Heh. Devilment at dinner, now, I don't know.'

Out, thought Danforth, is exactly where he wanted to be. He was used to having his Englishness remarked upon, but not mocked before a whole party. Not in the presence of a queen dowager. It made him look ... well, it made look like an exile. Like an English spy. Again, he felt Forrest's eyes on him, this time with malicious amusement. He knew he should meet them with challenge, but he felt unseated.

The dinner ended when the queen dowager rose, giving the assembled men and women another nod. Before she left, Madame LeBoeuf clinked a ring against her silver goblet. 'Her Grace the Queen Dowager Marie of Scotland wishes to thank you all for your company,' she announced in high-accented Scots. With that, the women at the top table retreated back into their cocoon of inner chambers and the swell of discussion rose in pitch. The ordeal, though, was over.

***

'What do we have here?' asked Danforth when they were back in the courtyard. It was late afternoon, the sun creeping over the building. It would, he thought, be shining through the windows of the dowager's rooms. Still it was cold, the shadows sending shafts of ice up his arms. He drew his cloak close around him. 'What we have,' he went on, 'is a man poisoned by known means. Likely drawn from the castle and murdered in mimicry of the death of a traitor. And to what end? Perhaps to lure away the infant queen's guards that she might herself be slain.'

Martin let out a low whistle. 'Killing a child,' he said. 'It's true evil, to be honest.'

'If it is a matter of politics, then perhaps politics is a true evil,' smiled Danforth. It was the first smile that had crossed his face since dinner. 'Yet there is more.' He filled Martin in on what Diane had told him about Margaret of Denmark and the dowager's fears of poison, and his thoughts on the victims of the Stewarts being avenged according to their deaths.

'So what does this mean? Why all this ghostly nonsense? Why dig up the Finnart tale and the story of Queen Margaret at all? If that's what the poisoning was supposed to do.'

'I cannot say for sure. Yet if we are chasing ghosts we are not chasing the killer. Perhaps that is the goal. And if the little Queen Mary should fall prey to a spirit … well, who ever heard of a ghost being tried?'

'But you are sure this Finnart business is – well, a feint? A sleight of hand?'

'Not sure, no. But think on it: Finnart is yesterday's man. His politics are dead. So are Queen Margaret's, God rest her. Times have moved on. We should not be looking for vengeful spirits. Who, this day, would profit from Queen Mary's death?'

'Governor Arran,' suggested Martin, his voice low. 'Lord protector and tutor to her Grace. If she goes, he takes the crown for sure.'

'Aye, and all the Hamilton clan. The Douglases too, as long as they master him.'

'But they are King Henry's creatures,' said Martin. 'King Henry wants the queen alive, for his son. If Arran wants the queen dead, it's without the Douglases. Old Henry wouldn't be pleased if the child dies and he loses the chance of his son gaining Scotland.'

Danforth removed his cap with one hand and ran a hand through his hair with the other. 'What I want is a weapon, some tool that might have struck off Fraser's arms.' It felt good to be talking business, even ghastly business. It felt like forcing movement. It meant forgetting his embarrassment. 'I had hoped the gardener might have revealed some stolen blade.'

'Do you think,' asked Martin, 'a sword might have done it?'

Danforth put his hand on a great unicorn carved on the fountain, drawing it away instantly. 'Cold,' he said. 'A sword. No, I do not think a sword likely. Not unless it were some heavy broadsword.'

'King Henry took off the little Howard lassie's head with a sword,' said Martin. 'It could do it.'

'No, he did not. The cardinal said that Henry called for a sword to slay her when he discovered she had been cuckolding him. Yet she was given the axe.'

'Poor little mite.'

'It was Anne Boleyn's head that was struck off with a sword. A merciful death.' The thought of Anne Boleyn, whom he had glimpsed only briefly on the day of her coronation, brought forth the image of Rowan Allen. It had been the Boleyn woman he had pictured after first meeting the flower seller. They had the same eyes, like deep, cold lochs on a winter night.

'Merciful,' said Martin, barking a shrill laugh. 'What does that fat barrel of pus know about mercy? He had those ladies butchered like they were slabs of meat. So that he might wench elsewhere. Pig.'

'Aye, England suffers as much as they. Both the fools are better out of it, though we might guess at where they fetched – wait!' Something Martin said struck him. 'Butchered like slabs of meat,' he repeated. 'By the saints, I think you might have something. We ought to –'

'Here,' said Martin, 'is our friend the dark lady.'

Walking lightly through the main gate was Rowan Allen. She made straight for them, smiling her knowing smile. 'I was just thinking of you,' said Danforth, without thinking. Instantly he regretted it. 'I mean, something led me to think of you. What brings you hither?'

'Say the devil's name and he shall appear,' laughed Rowan. 'You know, Hecate could be summoned thus at crossroads.'

'And which are you?' asked Danforth. He cursed again. He had wished to follow the thought that had occurred. It would be unwise to speak in front of the girl.

'Just a lass selling flowers.' She shook the basket, this time filled with purples and blues.

'It would take some witchcraft to have such colours at this time of year,' said Danforth.

'You would be surprised. It takes no witch's knowledge to watch the seasons. In this little part of the world we are blessed with sun as winter fades. Blessed to be far enough from both coasts. Of course, they cost more in March than they will next month. The only good thing about this burgh. Anything can grow if you nurture it. Protect it.'

'I care nothing for flowers, mistress,' said Danforth. 'I am sorry, but we will have nothing from you today. You might press your luck with the queen's ladies. Though why they should buy when they might simply wait until the gardens here bloom is beyond me.'

'Ignore him,' said Martin, removing his hat, and giving Danforth a quick, odd look. 'Are you well? How does your father?'

'He's not so well,' she said. 'Thank you for asking, Mr Martin.'

'Arnaud, remember.'

'Yes, I remember. And … it's Mr Danforth, isn't it?'

'That's right. Mr Danforth.'

She smiled, rolling her eyes. 'Are you gentlemen to stay here for some time then? What news of the cardinal and our services?'

'No news,' snapped Danforth, before Martin could reveal too much. His friend was far too trusting. At the rate he was going, he might as well hang Fraser's body up on the entrance arch and invite the people of the town to inspect it.

'Tell me, is it true that a man here was murdered?'

'What?' Danforth cursed. It was almost as if the girl had reached into his mind and plucked out his thoughts. Servants' talk. The lower orders simply couldn't keep their mouths shut. 'No, of course not. This is a palace, not a battlefield.'

She shrugged. 'Sorry. It's only that the burgh is buzzing that some fellow had his legs cut off. Like Procrustes had visited, as my da' would say.'

'Who?' asked Martin.

'A Greek villain,' said Danforth, respect dawning. 'Son of Poseidon. He invited passing travellers to spend the night in his home, and then cut off their legs if they did not fit the bed.'

'Amazing,' smiled Martin, his eyes flitting between Danforth and Rowan. Danforth cleared his throat.

'Where did you learn of that?'

'My father,' shrugged Rowan. 'He studied at St Andrews in his youth. You are a scholar?'

'I studied at Cardinal College,' said Danforth. 'At Oxford. Before it was suppressed and turned to King Henry's college.' He did add that he had not taken his degree.

'He's a proper educated man,' Martin said, patting Danforth's shoulder in an irritating gesture. 'In England, to be fair, but he knows things. More than just schooling, more than just travel and learning from … doing. True books and, uh … pedagogy.'

Danforth frowned at the doltish look on Martin's face before turning back to Rowan. 'But I can assure you there has been nothing of that nature here. No man has had his legs removed, by foul means or fair. Idle gossip,' he sniffed, 'is not to borne. Whether cloaked in a show of learning or otherwise.'

'Well, that's a good thing,' said Rowan. 'I grew fearful on the road. Some men were following me up here.'

'What,' said Martin. 'Not abusing you, I hope.' His hand had flown to his belt, though Danforth assumed he had not taken his dagger up to dinner. 'Not calling you wicked names.'

'No, just a pair of odd-looking men. No so very different from yourselves. They're back there, I think. I hurried on in here to be rid of them.' She pointed behind her, in the direction of the guardhouse.

'Well then,' said Danforth. 'Be about your business, selling. Not standing here talking. Come, Mr Martin.' He grasped Martin by the elbow and propelled him towards the great gate.

'Good day to you, Mistress Allen.'

'Good day,' she said, 'if you should like to speak again, Mr Danforth, just think of me.'

12

Unsurprisingly, the narrow hall that led into the guard chamber stank of urine. Danforth picked his way through on tiptoes, holding the hem of his robes like a girl picking her way through a flowerbed. It opened into the guardhouse, a large room fitted with now-familiar hammocks. He heard the raised voices before he spotted their owners.

'Blast it,' he hissed to Martin, creeping behind him. Before them stood Cam Hardie and Geordie Simms, the Douglas-emblazoned henchmen who had spied on them at Dalkeith. Hardie was speaking to the porter, one hand on his hip and the other brandishing a sealed envelope. Simms was by the wall, stroking a longbow with a hairy finger. At the sound of their entrance, the two men wheeled. A broad grin spread over Hardie's face.

'Ah, the cardinal's slaves,' he said, throwing his head back to set the blonde curls tumbling. He smoothed them with a palm and thrust out his chest. 'Doing the Lord's work, I take it?'

'Who are you calling a slave,' hissed Martin. 'You insult us, sir.'

'And with good reason,' returned Hardie. Danforth clucked his tongue. He was in no mood for a stag-fight between a couple of preening young bucks, even if one of them was his friend. He looked instead at Simms, whom he judged the more dangerous of the two. The man's hand had fixed on the crossbow.

The strangulated voice of the porter cut the atmosphere. 'Please leave that be,' he said to Simms. 'It's … it belongs to the palace.' In response Simms grunted and spat.

'To what do we owe the honour of seeing you fellows again?' asked Danforth. Hardie smiled and held up his envelope.

'Do you wish to know what this is?'

'Not especially,' lied Danforth. He folded his arms and peered down his nose.

'Aye you do. And you'll find out soon enough. We come,' he announced, 'to see her Grace Queen Marie. Not to trade words with you nothings.' He turned to the porter. 'Where is she? Our masters wish the governor's command delivered forthwith. Without delay.'

'Your masters?' asked Martin, his voice turned cloying. 'Your great English-fed puppet men.'

Simms took a step forward. A fist flew at Martin's face, knocking him to the ground. The guard found some strength at last, as Danforth dropped to the stone floor. 'No fighting in the guardhouse!' he cried. 'Get out, all of you, or I'll call the depute.'

'Give me your hand,' whispered Danforth. Martin looked stunned, a spot of blood appearing on his upper lip. Hardie's let out a cackling laugh.

'Bastard struck me,' said Martin, dazed. 'I'll get you for that, you dumb prick, you great ox, you–'

'Not today you won't, son,' said the guard. 'Away and clean yourself up.' Danforth helped him to his feet.

'No, not today,' laughed Hardie. 'Not any day. You dolts need to learn how things work now. The whole machine of the world has turned. The Hamiltons and the Douglases rule in Scotland this day and every day. And the great earl our master has a measure of interest in your work,' he smiled. 'We are lodging in this burgh. You'll be seeing us again.'

Danforth turned a dark look on him. 'You fellows,' he murmured, 'your masters. Both the Earl of Angus and that brother of his. They are like fruit trees grown over a stinking... a *fetid* swamp. Aye, they might be all rich now, their branches all filled with fruit. But only foul insects feed off them. And when they've had their fill they will return to the swamp. And the trees shall tumble.' He turned on his heel, pushing Martin in front of him, the younger man's nose buried in his elbow, leaving Hardie and Simms looking at one another in angry confusion.

'That was well said, Simon,' mumbled Martin through his sleeve.

'Keep walking,' said Danforth.

***

Danforth saw Martin washed at the fountain and, after establishing that his nose wasn't broken, told him to lie down in their room for a while. He was eager to know what message the Douglas men had brought but didn't dare risk another confrontation. Luckily, being punched in the face seemed to have made his friend more amenable. For all the boy spoke with a sharp tongue and a broad mouth, he was for from a fighter. Simms' fist seemed to have brought that reality home, and he retired meekly enough to lick his wounds. Better, thought Danforth, that it was a balled fist. It might have been a dirk, a stiletto, any manner of deadlier weapon.

Danforth warmed his hands by one of the now-lit braziers in the courtyard. He nodded as he saw Rowan Allen leave but made no effort to speak further with her. As he watched her departing back he began to regret that. The girl knew something of the antique myths, a favourite subject of his, and it might have passed the time to match wits with her. Then again, his stern inner voice reminded him, he was not in Linlithgow to bandy words with women, however much they seemed to have been intruding on his thoughts for the past month. It was a useless avenue anyway. His married life was a thing of the past, like his childhood or his university days. His current life was service. If God had wished him to beget children, that is what would have happened. His wife and child would still be alive, he would still be living in London, everything would be different. Their deaths had pushed him in another direction, and that was that.

Or, at least, that was the old charm – the charm which had always worked in the past. As he recited it silently, it felt suddenly hollow. It was, he realised, a shield he had built for himself long ago. Without his realising, it had been gradually chipped away at. The stern voice, the lecturing voice, had lost something of its intensity, now whining at him rather than berating him.

The late afternoon thickened, the flames quivering in a light, cold breeze. Three men left the stable block, their heads bowed in conversation. At they passed a brazier, Danforth identified them: Gibb, the horse master, Forrest, and a figure he did not recognise: a slim, serious-looking man with a neatly trimmed beard and a sedate black suit. He shook hands with Forrest, but Gibb shook his head wearily, trooping back to the stables. Forrest saw the stranger out of the main gate, and then stalked off, his eyes cast downwards. When he had gone, Danforth slinked around the edge of the yard, and entered the stable.

'Good day, Mr Gibb,' he announced, making his voice as airy as possible. Gibb jumped before speaking.

'Good day, sir,' he said. The jocular grin he had wore on their first meeting seemed tempered. 'What can I do for you?'

'I just came to check on the horses.' Danforth made a show of engaging with Woebegone, easing Gibb up with horse talk. Soon enough it seemed to reanimate him, bringing a merry light to his large features. At length, he said, 'I did not notice this beast before. It is, I think, Mr Fraser's?'

'Aye,' said Gibb. 'If you could advise us what's to be done with her. We can't keep her on the dowager's accounts, not if Mr Fraser had family that'll be wanting her.'

'Mr Fraser had no family. A great shame. Perhaps you might tell her Highness that the horse is a gift. Or, leastways, that its value might be used to cover the cost of Mr Fraser's funeral, whenever that might be.'

'When will that be, sir, do you know?'

'I cannot say,' said Danforth. 'As long as the Douglas brothers and our lord protector keep my master in thrall, it cannot be. But tell me, the night Fraser was slain, did you see anyone coming into the palace who was unusual?'

'How do you mean, unusual?'

'Who was … well, not part of the palace, not with the dowager's house or the servants of the place itself.'

'No, sir. It was a usual night. Quiet. Not like now, with everyone closing their doors. The bruit is that the devil has been invited in,' he said, shivering. 'Don't hold with that myself. I can't, or I wouldn't sleep.'

'And so no one required their horse stabled that night?'

'No sir, most definitely not.'

'I see Mr Forrest's visitor had no horse with him.'

'His … oh, he stabled his horse in the burgh.'

'That seems a waste. I could have sworn he had been in here.'

'He was. They were.' Gibb's voice had flattened. 'He's away now.'

'Who was it, I wonder, that Mr Forrest would wish to meet in a stable?'

'You had better ask the depute himself. I'm no clype.'

'It was,' pressed Danforth, 'then someone he would not wish it known that he meets with?'

'I … no,' said Gibb, confidence blooming. 'No, the fellow was a priest, a deacon, a good Catholic schoolmaster. From East Lothian. A friend of Mr Forrest's. Just bringing news, is all.'

'I see. I marvel that he does not show his friend into his own chamber. Or meet with him in the town, in the full glare of the sun.' Danforth shrugged. 'Not my business, of course, I merely wish to ensure that her Highness is kept securely.'

'Mr Forrest can better do that, sir, with his men. And like I said, the man was a priest. Hasn't enough to keep him occupied, I'd reckon, with your master still held and no services. He can visit his friends, can't he?'

Danforth sucked in his cheeks and nodded. The big horse master was an easy mark: good-natured, and therefore willing to have information drawn. But then, a savage internal voice added, it might be that the man was a skilled actor, playing him whilst giving every appearance of being played. 'Naturally, naturally. What was the fellow's name?' At this, Gibb did look more unsure. He peered behind Danforth, then locked his gaze once more, shrugging.

'Knox,' he said. 'Father John, from Haddington.'

'Cannot say as I know him,' said Danforth. 'I shall remember him to the cardinal when matters are more assured. Perhaps his Grace can do something for him. Well, thank you for taking such good care of the horses, Mr Gibb. You are doing a job of work indeed.' He bowed his way out and took up his station next to the far brazier.

He could judge the time passing only by the deepening of shadows. Eventually he saw Hardie and Simms being led out Anthony Guthrie, the usher bending their ears and pointing

106

about the courtyard, at the carved heraldry, at the fountain, at the oriel windows. When the jutting finger turned towards him, Danforth hopped back around the brazier, his head down but his eyes up. The two Douglas men left through the main entrance, and Guthrie turned back towards the royal apartments, skipping up into the southwest tower.

The appearance of the men was unnerving. Not unexpected, but unnerving. For the first time Danforth began to doubt the wisdom of becoming entangled in high politics. It was exciting, to be sure – a vote of confidence from his master – but it gave one the feeling of being a very small creature scampering around the feet of great lions. He shook his head clear, inhaling the scent of clean burning. It was his duty. Scotland had given him purpose when the world he had known in England crumbled. If things were unstable now, he had his part to play in settling them, however minor. To think he had come north all those years ago hoping to either find true faith or to be slain in his boots – whichever came first. Back then he had had no particular preference. How times changed.

The door of the southwest tower opened again, and Danforth stepped out. Not Guthrie this time, but Diane and Mathieu. He stepped out and crossed to them, bowing his head before speaking.

'Mr Danforth,' piped Mathieu. 'Where's Martin?'

'*Mr* Martin,' said Danforth, 'is resting. He was … he was overtired.'

'Aww.' Mathieu kicked at the cobbled ground, as though his ball was there. 'But he'll be about tomorrow?'

'He shall be hard at work tomorrow, as shall you, I trust. Mathieu, would you be so good as to give me and Mistress Beauterne leave to speak privately?'

'Eh? Are you going to ask her to marry you?'

'What?' spat Danforth. 'What nonsense runs through that foolish head, boy? Off you go.'

Mathieu gave them both a measured smirk and then ran off, his tabard tails trailing. 'I apologise, mistress,' said Danforth. 'I have no idea what wild thoughts run through the empty heads of little children.'

'Never mind,' smiled Diane. He noticed the smile seemed a little tight. 'Mathieu thinks every adult must be married. He picks up ideas out of the everywhere.'

'Well, he ought to grow out of foolishness if he hopes to get on. Marriage, indeed.'

'Indeed,' said Diane, and this time her smile seemed less fixed. 'What do you wish of me?'

'Those men, the Douglas creatures. They have been with the dowager?'

'Oui.' She looked towards the castle gateway. 'Have they gone?'

'Aye. The one with the yellow hair had with him some message.'

'The fair one?'

'If you like. Might you know what that message was?'

Diane gave him a hard look. 'Sir, I don't know that I should say. It was for her Grace's ears.'

'I quite understand. But you must know that Martin and I have the dowager's especial trust. It is important that I know what goes on, that I might better serve her.'

She looked up into the gloom, towards the queen's rooms, and then turned to him. Her mouth opened. Closed. And then she said, her voice pitched low, 'the men are fools. They bring news that her Grace is forbidden from leaving this place. She may not go to Stirling, as she has long wished, but stay in this place until she knows the governor's further pleasure. She is truly trapped.'

'Was she told why?'

'She believes it to be King Henry's pleasure, advertised by the Douglases. The governor does not think the English king would like the little queen safe behind Stirling's stout walls. He wishes to be seen before the whole world to be Henry's man in Scotland.'

That damned Arran, thought Danforth. Governor and protector of Scotland, but dancing to the tune of England's king. 'Is the dowager greatly troubled?' he asked.

'I think ...' again, she cast a look around the courtyard. Danforth followed her gaze. Only a few domestic servants moved about, none of them interested in the man and woman talking by the brazier. 'I think her Grace is saddened by remaining in this place. Now it is so unsafe. Yet … well, I say those two men are fools. They think their masters the Douglas brothers control the governor, but the queen has let it be known that she might let her daughter marry Arran's son and heir. And so our lord governor wants the little queen taken to Edinburgh, to his possession. The Douglas men are so busy cheering their puppet, they forget they are puppets of King Henry. Arran thinks to play them now, as they have long been playing him. Exactly as Queen Marie has hoped.'

'Yes,' said Danforth, understanding. 'Her Grace is turning Arran away from the Douglases, though they are too blind to see it. If Arran thinks the child might be bride to his heir, he will not countenance Henry taking charge of her. He is now feigning to do the Douglases and their master Henry's bidding, whilst pursuing his own ambitions.'

'Her Grace is a wise woman,' smiled Diane.

'She is that.'

'But her troubles are more pressing.' A little frown creased her brow. 'I wished to let her know of what you said, sir. Of the danger of poison.'

'But that is good. It shall keep her safer in her mind.'

'No,' she said, shaking her head. 'I was a fool. I told the usher, Mr Guthrie, to take the news to her.'

'What?' asked Danforth. 'You must know that man is an inveterate rumour-monger. A – a monster of verbosity! What were you thinking, woman?'

'I thought only that it might come better from a man than a frail woman,' she said, holding up her hands. They were very white, very small. 'But he has terrified the queen so, she is all agog. Like you say, at sixes and sevens, from his chatter.' Danforth stared. She looked ready for tears. A sudden suspicion of her came upon him and he brushed it aside. She was guileless, her face open and innocent. 'In her present mood, she is so terrified she might be willing to send her daughter anywhere but here.'

'There, there,' he tutted. 'There is no harm done. Her Grace is a woman of rare sense. Not,' he added, by way of admonition, 'like some.'

'Still, she would have this killer caught. She desires more than anything the sure safety of her child.'

'Naturally. If nothing is done soon, she might have to give up the little queen to Arran.'

Danforth pictured the baby girl, sent to Holyrood to be brought up under the governor's tutelage. It would separate the mother from the daughter, likely. But it would also separate the Douglases from Arran; the Earl of Angus and his brother would surely lose King Henry's favour. 'So Stirling is scrubbed out, and Holyrood is Queen Mary's fate. Poor Queen Marie. She wishes her daughter safe, but not sold in marriage to Governor Arran's whelp.' It must, he thought, to be an unpleasant thing to be parent to a royal child. During his own daughter's brief life, he had thought only to have her married when the time came to some wealthy son of a good family. He thought of holding her, of owning a life. Then came the inevitable remembrance of plague-ridden London, banks of smoke choking the breath from the body whenever one stepped outside. He screwed his eyes shut.

Another thought struck. If Arran wanted Mary for his son, he would do nothing to harm her. He needed her alive. Similarly, if the Douglases wanted her for King Henry, they would not be out to hurt her. So who might aim at her life? Why? It was an ugly puzzle.

'Well,' he said at length, 'the dowager might grumble, but there are worse places to be than Edinburgh.'

'You will find this murderer, though? You will make this place safe for our young sovereign?'

'I vow it shall be so,' said Danforth, hoping that saying the words would forge them into reality. Full darkness had come on. He glanced upwards and around. The four ranges of the palace, studded with countless blazing windows, stared back. He wondered who might be watching him.

13

Shame and embarrassment seemed to have ignited a fighting spirit in Martin. Danforth did not like it. Early the next morning he insisted that the pair visit the church of St Michael's, immediately inside the decorated palace entrance arch, but before the building proper. Services were still suspended, but the atmosphere, he hoped, would breed calm in his friend. As they bustled through the courtyard, Rab Gibb strode out of the stables. 'Are you off, lads?' he bellowed. 'I can saddle your beasts now.'

'No, Mr Gibb,' said Danforth. 'We are just going for a walk.'

'As you like. Your fellow was taken off this morning. Some servants took him. I spared good horses and one of the dowager's own chariots.'

'What? What fellow?'

'Mr Fraser,' said Gibb, one hand on the doorway of the stable. 'Taken off to Edinburgh. He can lie there until he can be buried.'

'Oh,' said Danforth. 'I see.' He had virtually forgotten about Fraser. The man was nothing but an empty shell now. It was a shameful thought, just how quickly the dead can become nothing, their physical remains either puzzles to be solved or nuisances. Fraser had become both. 'Thank you.' Gibb waved a hand and disappeared back into his stable, leaving Danforth to lead Martin out of the front entrance and towards the church.

'It irks me, Simon,' he said. 'That ox – it was – it was bad form. Dishonourable. To hit a man without warning. It wasn't the behaviour of a gentleman, but a common street brute. That's what he is, a common street brute. They both are.'

Danforth let him babble, not breaking his stride. The church was made of the same pale sandstone as the palace, but it had not been washed in king's gold. Instead, it was cast in a more sedate hew, its tower rising to form an elaborate crown steeple. He tried the iron handle of the door. Locked. He hissed in irritation, turning to Martin. He winced, seeing the purple bruise around his eye given fresh lividity by the sullen grey sky. 'It seems our priest has flown the nest.'

'Probably off wenching,' said Martin, scuffing at the stone steps. 'Nothing else for him to do.'

'Bite your tongue. I shall have none of this ugly talk, just because you are sore.' He looked back towards the palace, then downhill towards the town, hesitation stalling him. 'Perhaps a walk in to the churchyard. We can speak freely there.' Martin only shrugged.

They walked around the side of the building. A low stone wall separated the graveyard from the palace grounds. 'A fair place to be laid to rest,' said Danforth. The laws were all clipped. Here and there were some ancient oaks, stately, barren sentinels amongst the wasteland of the dead.

'I'd like to put that Simms ox in the grave.'

'Vengeance again, eh?'

'Whatever you wish to call it.'

'You remind me of what I wish to discuss,' said Danforth. Martin had been sleeping when he'd left Diane the night before. He had felt an almost superstitious disinclination to talk inside the palace walls earlier in the morning. 'I spoke again with the lass Mistress Beauterne last night.'

'Oh?' asked Martin, something kindling. 'Did you, aye?'

'Yes. After you fell into Mr Simms' hand.' Martin threw him an angry look, his fist balling and striking his thigh. 'I discovered what the Douglas lads were here about.' He paused, letting Martin digest this, before telling him of the queen dowager's confinement in the palace, and the progress of her attempts to lure Governor Arran into believing the infant Queen Mary might be wed to his son.

'So … if Arran wants the little queen alive. And if the Hamiltons need her alive too … then who is it might want her dead?'

'I cannot say,' frowned Danforth. The question had kept him up most of the night. A motive was what he needed – but with that need brought the danger of inventing one. And if the intended victim was a queen, and queen of a European nation, then there might be more potential motives than there were hairs on the infant's head. 'We are back to vengeance again. Or the ghosts of the past. It none of it makes a whit of sense. Arran might stand to gain the crown from her death, but it would be a great risk. Far safer to have her alive and wed to his son. All done in good order, no scandal. And the Douglases too – they are King Henry's men, working to control Arran, but only to gain delivery of the child into England. If she dies – hell, even if she is promised to Arran – their credit with Henry falls.'

'Wait,' said Martin. 'Hold on. Look – we know this now. Those two came from the Earl of Arran and George Douglas only yesterday, to inform the queen. Neither Arran nor the Douglas brothers could have known that the dowager would hold out promise of her child's hand to the son of Arran when Fraser was killed.'

Danforth's eyebrows rose. 'By Jupiter, Arnaud, you are right. Of course, you are right.' It was so obvious he had not even considered it. He had been so engrossed in the ever-changing nature of events that he had not stopped to consider that their killer must have been acting at a specific moment, unaware of what might happen next. He might have planned to bring about the baby's death only to discover he needed her alive. 'So, Arran, with or without the Douglases, might have wished for the child to die yesterday and found he needs her alive today.'

'Aye,' said Martin, grinning. On his bruised face the smile appeared almost comical. 'It doesn't reveal the killer, but at least we don't close our minds to his identity.' He stepped past Danforth and stood before one of the big oaks.

'Perhaps Arran wished the death of the little queen. Then he would be nearest heir and take the throne for himself. As nearest prince of the blood – you know, second person of the realm – it would be his with or without Henry of England. But now it is clear she might marry England's Prince Edward *or* Arran's little lad, and so she must live.'

'Yes,' agreed Martin. 'Aye, better he takes power through his son's great marriage than through bloodshed. Lord protector or not, all Scotland would rise against him if it were ever suspected he had had their child queen murdered.'

'Ah,' said Danforth. 'It might be so. Still it might be that an *enemy* of Arran might be the killer, wishing to set him up.'

Martin, who had been raising a finger to illustrate his own point, paused it in mid-air. As Danforth's word sank in, he lowered it. 'Jesus how can we be expected to follow any of this? We are arguing round and about in circles.'

'We cannot. We can only hope that the simplest solution thus far is true. Arran sought the queen's death last week, and planned for it, sending some agent of his – any of those Hamilton men at dinner – to find means of exposing the child to attack. This week, the governor wishes the child to live, since Queen Marie has offered her daughter's hand to his son.'

'Do you believe that, Simon?'

'For the present, I must. So must you.'

'And so we close the book? We let Fraser's killer go free, hoping that his job of work has been cancelled? I don't like that. He was still one of us.'

'No. No, of course not. But we must put aside the politics and find Fraser's killer as we have found others. We are being drawn into a maze otherwise. Only he can reveal the truth of this tangled web. We shall not find it from chasing the mysteries of politics. No more than from chasing ghosts.'

'And if this is the true case,' Danforth went on, 'then our killer has shot his mark, missed, and the quarry is now something he must preserve. We can, then, expect no attempt on the child's life. We can only be grateful that the first step of his plan was all that he carried forth. He sought to draw protection away from the queen, failed, and now has no reason to get at her anyway. The cause, the motive – it has been removed.'

'And so it's over?' asked Martin. 'Before it truly began?'

'Let us pray so.' He let his own image of God smile into his mind, a figure not unlike his father, bearded, and benevolent. Let there be no more death, he asked. 'Although I should be far happier knowing who killed Fraser and hearing that this was the way of it from his own lips.' Danforth looked up into the clouds, a haphazard mixture of greys and white. 'We can tell the dowager of our thinking. It might yet be worth imposing some manner of – of confinement – on the palace and servants. Whilst her Grace is here, I mean. Everyone to keep to their rooms now, save the guards patrolling. That manner of thing.'

'Perhaps he's flown now,' said Martin. 'And you can turn your eyes elsewhere. You might be getting on in years, but I reckon the lusts bloom again when you near thirty. If I were – uuaagghhh.'

Danforth's head jerked back from the sky and his mouth fell open. He leapt towards Martin. His friend was pinned to the oak tree, an arrow jutting from his body.

***

'Martin! Arnaud!' Danforth reached out for Martin's shoulders. On instinct, he grasped at the arrow, making to yank it out. He paused, not sure what to do. His hands shook wildly as he saw that Martin's eyes had closed. A physician – an apothecary – that is what he needed. But who had done it? Why?

He pivoted, his robes flying. 'You!' he called, anger, fear, and shock colouring his tone. Cam Hardie was standing in the churchyard. 'You bastard! You've shot him!'

Hardie looked between Martin and Danforth, the usual smugness wiped from his face. He shook his head, his mouth working silently. 'It wasn't me,' he said eventually 'No, no.'. He turned. 'Simms? Simms? Where are you?'

Danforth watched as Hardie began skipping away, back towards the church. 'Get back here! You can't run!'

Hardie disappeared around to the right of the church, leaving Danforth unsure whether to give chase or stay with his friend. Before he could decide, he heard Hardie's screams. With an anguished look at Martin, he began running towards the sound.

As he turned the corner, his hands grasping the stone for speed, he drew up short. Only a few steps ahead of him, Hardie was hunched over Simms, who was lying on his back. 'Help him,' shouted Hardie, turning. Danforth peered down, his heart thundering. Simms was alive, but he had been slashed at. He was grasping up at Hardie's coat with bloody hands.

'A fine show,' said Danforth.

'What?' barked Hardie.

'You will both of you hang. You have shot my friend and

115

think to hide it by some wounds done by your own hands?'

'What the fuck are you talking about, you bloody madman? He's been stabbed.'

Danforth stood his ground, but a little more doubtfully. He chanced a look towards the churchyard, but all was silent. 'Can you speak, Simms?'

The man on the ground grunted. 'Who did this to you?' persisted Danforth.

'The devil,' croaked Simms. 'A devil. In a blue cloak. He … bastard stabbed me … tried to stop him running.'

His words hung in the air as Danforth roughly dragged Hardie to his feet. 'You can plead for your lives later,' he said. 'The pair of you. And you can explain then what you meant by following cardinal's men on the dowager's business. Get you gone now. Find help.' Hardie gave him an angry look, not moving. 'Go and find help,' hissed Danforth. 'Go into the palace. Go now!' He shoved at Hardie, which seemed to bring back some of his bravado.

'Don't you push me.'

'Go!' Danforth shouted. And then, 'I shall keep an eye on your friend.'

Hardie ran, and Danforth turned back towards Martin, abandoning the groaning Simms.

He was half slumped against the tree, neither standing nor sitting. The arrow, he saw, had gone in under his left shoulder. It didn't look like it had pierced the heart. No blood spurted. With luck, it would be a slight wound. Painful, but not life-threatening. The pages of a book he had seen in London opened in his mind: a book on anatomy, with the image of a man who had undergone all the wounds one might receive in battle. It was a hideous thing, the figure having a spear clean through his thigh and a sword in through the ribcage and out through the back. He tried to banish it.

'You'll live, my friend,' he whispered. 'As God stands above us, you will live.'

Danforth produced a handkerchief from inside the folds of his robe and wiped gingerly at Martin's forehead. It was a pointless gesture, but it felt like something. A light wind started up, making the bare branches above them sway.

He shivered. It was not over before it had begun.

14

The hubbub in the small guardhouse only died down with the arrival of Depute Forrest, his hands on his hips. 'You will all,' he said, his voice low but carrying, 'be silent in the presence of the depute.' Danforth, Hardie, and the quailing porter ceased. 'Now what the hell is all this? Don't you dare all speak at once.'

The assembled men looked at one another, and the porter spoke first. 'It's all been wild, Alexan–'

'Forrest,' snapped the Depute.

'Sorry.' The porter shrank. 'It's a' been wild. These lads were oot in the churchyard wi' their friends. Fightin' last night, there were, in here. I threw them oot, o'course. Noo they've been duellin' on hallowed ground. Shameless knaves, the lot.'

Hardie started to protest, but Forrest silenced him, his arm cutting the air. 'Was that the way of it?'

'No, indeed,' said Danforth. 'My colleague, Mr Martin, was pierced with an arrow. This man,' he gestured at Hardie, 'and his friend were following us. He claims his colleague, Mr Simms, was stabbed.'

'Claim nothing,' snapped Hardie. 'He was stabbed to be sure, sir. You might go and take a look at him yourself. He has been carried down to our lodgings in the burgh, bleeding like a butchered hog.'

Forrest looked at them both through lowered brows. 'A strange tale. A tale I don't like.'

'Nevertheless,' said Danforth. 'That seems to be the way of it. You might look upon Mr Martin too. He is lodged in our room in the palace.'

Hardie had returned with a stream of palace and household servants, all eager to see what the commotion was. Between them, the wounded men had been removed to their beds. Both, judged the dowager's physician, were likely to live. If infection did not rot the broken flesh.

'And who, pray, did these foul deeds?' asked Forrest, crossing his arms and leaning back. 'Who have you fellows upset? Who have you feuded with?'

'I feud with no man,' said Danforth, lowering his head. 'And Mr Martin and Simms have nothing to bind them.'

'Simms saw him,' said Hardie. 'Aye, he saw the bastard.' Forrest only raised an eyebrow. 'A devil, he said, in a blue cloak.'

'Blue cloak?' The depute looked sceptical. 'What foolish fancy is this, a devil in a blue cloak? Danforth, are you of this mind?' Danforth shrugged. 'If you expect me to believe the ghost of St Andrew is haunting the churchyard, shooting men in their boots ...'

'Ghost?' asked Danforth, a weight forming in his gut. 'Mr Forrest, what do you mean, the ghost of St Andrew?'

Forrest waved a hand in the air. 'Pfft. Daft old legend for bairns.'

'Please,' Danforth insisted.

'The old church is said to be haunted by the ghost of St Andrew. He appeared before King James IV, warning him not to go to Flodden.'

'He should have listened,' put in Hardie. Forrest turned a scowl on him.

'It's a bootless tale. One of the palace's scare stories. Likely it was some man in disguise, working for the old king's wife.'

'And this fellow, then?' asked Danforth. 'The man who shot Martin and stabbed Hardie. A man in disguise?'

'If there was such a man. If you pair aren't trying to hide your friends' fight. Me, I think you're a pair of goddamn liars. I think this whole tale a steaming puddle of pish.'

'Uh, sir?' said the porter, clearing his throat. 'I think ye're right.' Craven little rat, thought Danforth. 'But ... well, one of them stole a crossbow from here.'

'What?'

'A crossbow is missing. One of them must have took it. A gun too. You ken, one of the old wheellocks.' He cowered.

'What? Those things are damned expensive. And where the hell were you?' The porter pressed himself against a wall. 'I ... I was oot, sir, by the auld gatehouse.' His voice turned querulous and Forrest's bearded face darkened. 'Well you were

119

the one who said no more pissin' in the hallway there, so I had–'

'Enough!' The depute began kneading his forehead with a knuckle. 'Hell damn and blast it.'

'We must have a search,' said Danforth, slamming a fist into his palm. 'This whole palace must be searched, from its lowest stone to its highest.'

'Don't be a fool,' snapped Forrest. 'Do you know how many rooms there are in this place? How few men to search?'

'We might work in earnest, every man paired–'

'A bootless endeavour. Too many places to it. There was a maid here once, some years back.' Forrest paused to rub his eyes. 'Stole some jewellery, little trinkets. Hung her parcel from a hook dug in under her chamber window, on the outside. One of the gardeners only found it in summer, trimming the hedges. When it caught the sun.'

'Still, we must do something. This fellow has a gun. He must mean to use it.'

'Goddammit, get out of my sight, all of you,' roared Forrest. 'Now.'

The three filed out. The porter drew his eyes off of Danforth and Hardie theatrically before marching away, scratching at his backside as though fighting to dislodge trapped breeches.

'Well,' said Danforth. 'Do you care to explain why you were following us?'

'I don't have to explain anything to you.'

'Our friends have each been hurt here. What have you to hide? Unless, that is, what I thought out there was true. You shot Martin and stabbed at Hardie to draw away guilt. I feel certain I could argue that case very well before any court the dowager wished to call.'

Hardie bared his teeth. 'You bastard, if we hadn't been following you you'd both be dead. It was us coming upon you that frightened that blue devil. And for our pains you dare make threats?' Then he stepped back, brushed at his front, and straightened his hat. 'You have a care, sir. We are great men. Working with and for men of great power and fame. You don't frighten me, nor your whoremongering master either.'

Danforth let the insult pass. 'I have no wish to scare you. I only wish the truth.'

'Is that so?' Hardie seemed to be thinking. He threw his head back and put a hand nonchalantly on his hip. 'Aye, we were following you. Archibald Douglas, the esteemed Earl of Angus, has every right to know what you know, as long as you meddle in the affairs of the great. The lord protector will pay well for any news,' he added, tapping at his purse. 'But now ... well, sir, now this thing has become a matter of personal honour to the House of Douglas. One of our own has been nearly slain. An injury to one of us is an injury to all.'

'The fellow who did this,' said Danforth. 'He is likely the one who slew our colleague, Mr Fraser. We had hoped his diabolical scheme was at an end. Oh, but then, why am I telling you this? You heard us in the churchyard as you heard us at Dalkeith, your noses pressed against the door like schoolboys.'

It was Hardie's turn to ignore provocation. He shrugged, bobbing his head to let the feather in his hat flounce. 'As you have been too stupid to catch this bastard, perhaps it is up to me.'

'You cannot be serious. You think you can discover the fellow where I have ...' he hesitated to say 'failed'. 'Where I have not yet done so?'

Again, Hardie shrugged. 'I have no doubt of it.'

'I have no need or wish for a new colleague,' said Danforth, his nose rising in the air. 'And certainly not one of your–'

'Ha! I have no intention of *helping* you, you fool.' Hardie drew a loose strand of blonde behind his ear. 'Only ... perhaps we might agree like gentleman to stay out of one another's way. For now.' With that, he turned and strolled out of the courtyard, leaving Danforth gaping in his wake.

***

Martin sat up in his cot. The hammock had been wrenched down, and a grumbling Guthrie had ordered a proper bed, with a wafer-thin mattress, brought in its place. 'Much better than I've ever had,' he had muttered, 'and me a gentleman-born'.

'Ahh,' said Martin. 'This is more the kind of thing for which I was meant. He prodded the pillow – a rare luxury – with his elbow. The one on the good side. Still, the movement sent a jolt of pain running through him, and he felt pearls of sweat pop out on his forehead and run down his face.

'Cease moving,' said Rowan.

Although Danforth had insisted that the queen's physician was an honourable and trustworthy man, Martin had insisted on the services of Rowan Allen as soon as he had come to. The physician had stamped off, ignoring Danforth's apologies, cursing 'Scotch ruffians, thieves and ingrates', and swearing in French. Martin had returned the curses in kind. Rowan Allen had, he recalled, said that she was skilled enough to care for her father in his dotage, and Martin trusted to the instincts of a girl who worked with flowers, herbs, and possets more than a man who looked to cutting and bleeding.

'You know,' said Rowan, 'the apothecary in the burgh says that everything can be cured by the right diet. If you have a stomach ache, eat this. If you cut off your thumb butchering meat, eat that.' Martin laughed. 'What did I say about moving?'

'Understood.' He chewed on his lip.

'What on earth happened to your face?'

'My … is it bad?' Martin's right hand brushed his cheek. 'Is it really bad?'

'Pretty bad.'

'I was in a fight.'

'Fight, ha!' Danforth's voice barked from across the room. 'He was struck in the chops by the fellow who was stabbed. Yesterday.'

Rowan laughed. 'Well, that at least will fade. Your wound there, that will close up soon enough. I'll fashion a bandage for your arm. It'll keep it raised. Stop you from using it and tearing the hole. You have rare luck, Arnaud – it passed through you.'

'He has rare luck that the man was a weak shot,' sniped Danforth.

'A hunting accident, I thought you said.' Rowan turned sharp eyes on him. 'It was *poor* luck, surely, that the man was a weak shot.'

'So it was. I misspoke.'

'And the man carried out, swearing and cursing, as I came in. Was he in the same accident?'

'Yes.'

Martin looked away, whilst Danforth clasped his hands behind his back and looked down. 'What were you hunting this time, the Calydonian Boar?'

'Eh?' Still Martin was looking at his chest, suddenly interested in the bloodstains on his shirt.

'A great boar which ravaged Calydon,' offered Danforth. 'As I recall, it was shot by a woman in the end. That did not please the men.' Martin looked up, to find Danforth looking at Rowan. His stare was somewhere between suspicion and, perhaps, attraction.

'Atalanta,' she said. 'Who killed also two ravening centaurs. But she did not kill the boar, sir, only took the first shot and claimed its hide.'

'Look, will this bandage stop the pain?' asked Martin, ignoring the strange atmosphere between the pair.

'It'll stop it getting worse,' said Rowan, drawing her gaze from Danforth.

'Can't you do something for it now?' He lowered his voice for the last, conscious of Danforth's presence whilst Rowan ran hands over his chest.

'With a basket of heather? I think not. The arrow entered just under your armpit, a tender spot. It will sting and trouble you for some days yet.'

'Then some other natural remedy, then? You must have your garden, where you … grow things?'

'I'm not,' Rowan sighed, 'a cunning woman. My father's garden grows some hardy flowers and herbs. For cooking. I know what can dull pain yes – I've had the knowledge from books. I visit the apothecary for what's needed like everyone else.'

Martin slid down again, disappointed. 'Fine,' he said.

'What's that?'

'*Fine*. Go to the damned apothecary. But please, only ask of him what you trust.'

'Very well. You are a truly ungrateful patient, you know.' She smiled first at him, and then Danforth. 'Would you care, sir, to accompany me into the burgh? We can talk Hippocrates on the road, if you like.' She held up an arm, for Danforth to help her rise from the low stool by the cot.

'I cannot, mistress. I cannot leave the lad alone in case … in case he … falls from the bed.'

'Really?'

'I won't fall, Simon,' smiled Martin. 'I can look after myself. I'll be safe enough in here.'

Danforth took her hand. Martin grinned.

15

Danforth stood in the bustling market cross, Rowan at his arm. Being outside of the palace brought a sense of relief. It was as though he were suddenly engaged in some great, gladiatorial battle, and leaving the place was stepping out of the arena to catch breath. She raised a finger towards a well-kept wooden building, its door painted. 'That's our Master Apothecary,' she said. 'He knows me, so I should speak.' Danforth nodded, a little put out. It ill became a woman to take charge. It was a trait peculiar to Scotswomen, he thought. Some men, perhaps, found it attractive enough. They must, or there would be no more Scots.

'Very well. Wait. Here is a friend of mine. Mistress Beauterne,' he cried, 'ho, mistress. What news?'

Diane started at the sight of him, and then she smiled an impish grin. 'You've caught me. I am come into the burgh to pick up some cloths,' she said, skipping towards him, a length of purple draped over one arm. 'For the dowager's entertainments. Her tailor went off to the governor, so we must shift for ourselves, get what we can from the burgh. Mind, I enquired of books?'

'Ah, yes. They were useful?'

'Uh … Signor Bassano can turn his fellows' lutes to anything, really.'

'An entertainment?' whispered Rowan. Her eyes had clouded. Danforth thought he saw something like longing in them.

'Oui,' said Diane. 'What brings you to town, monsieur? And good day to you, Mistress Allen.'

'Good day, Diane,' said Rowan.

'Are you to walk back up to the palace? I should be glad of the company.'

'You came down here by yourself?' asked Danforth.

'Yes, sir. I hoped to be here and gone before the rain comes. You can feel it in the air.'

'It is unwise to go jetting about alone,' warned Danforth.

'Mistress Allen here does so,' chirped Diane.

'It is hardly the same,' said Danforth. Diane was a gentlewoman. Rowan Allen was … he was unsure what she was. 'Mistress Allen belongs to the burgh. She knows it. You do not.'

'It is but a short walk. Mr Guthrie offered to walk me, but I couldn't bear listening to his chattering about God and so I sneaked out before he could come.' She tinkled laughter, reached out and lightly touched Danforth's arm. Rowan, he noticed, fixed her eyes on the gesture, her smile frozen in place. The politics of women, he thought, resisting the urge to roll his eyes. 'Besides, I like taking the air. Especially now, shut up in the palace.' She shivered. 'Shall you both come back with me?'

'Not yet. Perhaps Mistress Allen can take you. I can see to the business which brings me alone.'

'No, no,' said Diane. 'I did not mean to break you up. Have you much to do?'

'Not very much,' said Rowan. 'We must pick up some stuff from the apothecary over there. *Excuse* me,' she barked at a woman who had nudged her elbow with a basket as she passed. The woman gave her a dirty look but kept moving. 'Aye,' called Rowan, 'you keep walking, sweetheart. Sorry.' Her attention returned to Diane. 'We shan't be a minute. Please wait on us.'

They parted, Diane going off to look at some stallholders' goods whilst Danforth and Rowan visited the apothecary. Inside the place was scrubbed clean, free of the usual bric-a-brac held by the conmen of the profession. No jars of exotic-looking organs or strangely-carved talismans sat on the shelves; no skulls hung from ropes suspended from the ceiling. There was not even a speck of dust drifting in the air, and the whole place smelled like mint. Behind the counter, a clean-shaven man of about forty stood measuring out powders, a pair of spectacles pinched to his nose. He was well built, thought Danforth, although slightly anaemic-looking. He did not look up but held up a finger on his free hand. 'Won't be a moment.'

Rowan and Danforth waited until he had finished. 'Good Mistress Allen,' he said. 'And a friend.' He looked at Danforth through the spectacles, up and down, before removing them.

'What can I do for you?'

Danforth opened his mouth to speak, but Rowan got in first. 'This is Mr Danforth, a gentleman of the lord cardinal.'

'Aye,' said the apothecary. 'The livery. Good day to you, sir. I'm Mr Dunn.'

'A pleasure to meet you.'

'Mr Danforth's friend has been pierced with an arrow.'

Dunn blew a low whistle. 'Nasty. Where?'

'Through the armpit,' said Danforth, the words tumbling out. 'Clean through.'

'Have you washed and dressed the wound, mistress?' Rowan pouted, one black eyebrow arched. 'Of course. Well, what do you need?'

'He wants something for the pain,' said Danforth. It was an irritating feeling, being part of a conversation in which he was the only stranger. 'Something to ease it.'

'Well I didn't think he'd want something to increase it,' laughed Dunn. His teeth were prominent, all there, all white. 'Tell me, what does your lad eat?'

'Eat?'

'Aye. I need to know his constitution.'

'He eats anything he can get his hands on,' said Danforth. 'And living at the palace … salmon, rich sauces, cheese, bread – good manchet, not the cheap stuff – some–'

'That'll do. He's a rich liver, then?'

'He tries to be.'

'Tell him to stop trying to be.' Dunn had a no-nonsense manner, abrupt, but not intentionally rude. 'Was the food served hot?'

'Not especially.'

Dunn tutted. 'That's the worst of places like yon palace. Food that ought to be eaten hot, eaten cold. It leads to melancholy, an excess of black bile and phlegm. You get some hot food in him.'

'And for the pain?' asked Danforth.

Dunn disappeared under the counter, popping up with some thin vials held between his fingers. 'Get these on his wound. He can rub them in himself.' He held them out, the muscles on his arms flexing.

'They will dull his pains? What are they?'

'Honey. And powdered ore of antimony. Tell him to use the honey first. They won't ease his pain, but they will do much more. They will clean out the wound, stop infection getting in from the bad airs you have living amongst such a crowd.'

'But it is pain he asked to be dulled,' pressed Danforth. Dunn tutted, apparently irritated that his solution had not been met with praise. He reached under the counter and produced another stoppered vial. 'He might try this. Mostly pure water, but there is a touch of hemlock and henbane in it. He should drink it.'

'This will work?' asked Danforth.

'It will if you tell him it will. And if you get some hot food in him to get the body working as it should.'

Danforth considered this as he slid the vials inside his robes and fetched out his purse. As he paid, he let his voice turn casual. 'That is a rare thing, hemlock. Henbane too.'

'Aye. Don't care for it myself. It's all a lot of trash.'

'Come on now,' said Rowan. 'Mr Dunn, really – the ancients knew the properties of these things. They act on the body.'

'The ancients,' sniffed Dunn, 'were a lot of pagans who walked around without shoes, amongst the weeds, like the heathens they were.'

'Yet they founded the civilised world. Isn't that right, Mr Danforth?'

Danforth gave a tight little nod, unwilling to be drawn into a pointless argument. 'I cannot say,' he said. 'Perhaps. Forget it. Master Apothecary, I … I should like to ask you something else.' He cleared his throat, putting a finger to his lips.

'Of course,' said Dunn. 'Ask away.'

'It is of a private nature, personal.' He cast an apologetic look at Rowan. 'Mistress, would you leave us?'

'God's wounds,' she said. 'You are a sensitive soul.'

'Please.'

Appearing to hold back laughter, Rowan shrugged, easing her basket into the crook of her elbow. 'Suit yourself. I'll go and find Diane. We shall await your escort back to the palace. I can help Martin with his medicines.'

When the door at shut behind her, Danforth let the

sheepishness fall away. He congratulated himself silently on his acting prowess. 'Now, Master Apothecary, to business, and quickly.'

'I understand,' said Dunn, winking. 'You wish something for your master the lord cardinal. Don't worry, the priest at St Michael's sends his boys down for pox treatments for his baths, and I've –'

'What? No! How dare you speak of his Grace thus. I have a good mind to report your slanders!'

'Peace, sir. I meant no offence. It's for yourself then? Forgive me, but you didn't seem the type to let nether parts wither from–'

'It is not the pox, nothing like that,' snapped Danforth, crossing his arms. 'No, sir. I have no need of medicines but information. What I seek to know is whether there Is there much call,' he asked, 'for these items, these dangerous items. In quantities enough to kill.'

The word hung in the air, Dunn's face paling. 'Kill?' he asked. 'What do you mean?'

'I mean do you ever have people coming in here looking for enough of such stuff to kill?'

'I … I don't hold enough dangerous stuff.' The man was hiding something. 'Folk can ask, but if they know me they know better.'

'Who asked, Mr Dunn?'

Dunn sighed, before coming around from behind the counter. He went to the door and opened it, looking out. Seemingly satisfied, he closed it again. 'Look, Mr Danforth. In this profession, yes, of course there are sometimes folk who think to fool me into giving them dangerous medicines. But I am nobody's fool. I send them away, fleas in their ears.'

'Was there one such in recently? Last week, or around that time?'

Dunn went back behind the counter, as though it were a defensive barrier. 'Christ, someone's died, haven't they? Someone's been bloody murdered.' Danforth stared, saying nothing. 'I didn't … it was such a foolish moment, I thought it someone at a caper.' He bent forward before collapsing on a stool and leaning on the counter, his head in his hands. Was it genuine, wondered Danforth, that distress of his? It seemed so.

'What happened?' asked Danforth, keeping his voice low and level.

'Last week,' said Dunn, looking up. 'Some foolish creature came in here, all swathed in a blue cloak. Hooded. I couldn't see their face.' Danforth frowned. 'It happens often. A goodwife in looking for something to revive her husband's member, but not wishing her identity known. Young men and women in looking for love potions but hiding their faces. I tell them, I say just mind what you eat – there's no surer enemy to love than foul breath. And aye, sometimes they ask for poisons. Och, never to kill, oh no. To take care of rats or cats. To help them sleep. To *dull pain*.'

'Who was this person, a man or a woman? What did they say?' asked Danforth.

'As I said, they were wearing a cloak. I should say it was a man, but of course the voice was disguised, false. Asking for unhealthy doses of hemlock or anything like it. To put a sick man to sleep. Oh aye, I get that too. The relatives of the dying asking for something to speed them to God. To put an end to the pain. I … I thought it was that. And so I said … I told them that they'd have nothing by me. But that if they needed aught of that nature, they could find it themselves.'

'But you did not say what to pick, nor where to find it?' asked Danforth.

'No, sir. Of course not. I simply said that they might find the knowledge themselves. Either by a man with such knowledge who wasn't me, or from a book. And some luck they would need finding either. Look, you won't say anything, will you? I didn't report it – but I never do. I would be run out of the burgh if I went around reporting every person who behaved oddly or asked for odd things.'

Danforth grunted, but more in assent than anger. His mind had turned elsewhere: to the denuded library at Linlithgow. Every royal library was bound to have one – likely more – volumes on herbs and medicines, for the household physician to consult when necessary. Diane had told him that the bulk of the books had been packed up and shipped to Stirling, when Marie had still harboured hopes of escaping there. It would have been a simple thing for someone in the household – or even a palace domestic – to lift one of those books.

***

Danforth found Diane with Rowan, still in the market cross. To her arm she had added some pink and blue cloth, all of it neatly folded. 'Merci, monsieur,' she said, thrusting the material at Danforth.

'What?' he said, holding it as though it were toxic. 'What do I want with such a load?'

'You are a gentleman,' said Rowan, grinning, 'to carry a gentlewoman's things for her.' She and Diane dissolved in laughter, and Danforth frowned, his cheeks blazing as he walked out of the market cross, his arms a confusion of purple, pink, and blue, flanked by women. Someone in the crowd wolf-whistled. Danforth turned, furious, to see that it was Cam Hardie. He looked away, his chin high.

They climbed up the hill, past the Song School and Tolbooth, the palace looming in front of them. As Danforth felt his calves stretch, Rowan and Diane chattered. He let them prattle, eager to be free. That was funny – previously, freedom had meant getting out of the gilded cage, not into it. After only a few minutes he noticed, however, that Rowan trailed off from whatever nonsense she was spouting. 'Something is wrong, Mistress Allen?'

'No, no. It's just. Well, I'm being followed again. We all are.'

'Here,' said Danforth, thrusting the bundle of cloth at Diane. He turned, expecting to see Cam Hardie again. Instead, tottering a good distance behind them was a blue-cloaked figure. His blood froze. 'You ladies go on in. Take yourselves to the queen's apartments with these things. And here,' he added, after a moment's hesitation. 'Take these to Martin afterwards.' He dug out the vials and passed them to Rowan. She and Diane looked at one another before hurrying past St Michael's and through the gate. Danforth followed, walking backwards. There was something odd about the creature shambling after them, its gait awkward and ungainly. When he reached the hall to the porter's little guardhouse, he stuck his head in.

The room had undergone a change. The usual porter seemed to have been stripped of his authority, Forrest himself making his mark. He sat on a stool, sharpening a dagger. Weapons had been lined up everywhere, in ordered rows. Absurdly, Danforth's gaze landed on a little mounted wooden sword. His surprise must have shown on his face. 'My son's first sword,' said Forrest without expression. 'What do you want, Mr Danforth?'

'There is someone entering the palace,' he said, a tremor rising in his throat. 'A fellow has followed me up from the burgh. All cloaked in blue.'

Forrest was on his feet.

'You've paid some urchin to play your ghost, have you?' he smirked. He stepped past Danforth as the figure appeared outside. 'State your business,' he snapped. 'Who are you?'

The figure turned towards Forrest's voice and rasped something. 'What did he say?' asked Danforth. Forrest ignored him. The figure croaked again, and this time the meaning was clearer.

'I have a message for the queen's wet nurse.'

'What the hell? Are you a friend of hers?' barked Forrest. 'Uncover yourself.'

'Only … for the queen's nurse. I must give her …' he stopped to wheeze. 'A warning. From France. Remember … Queen Madeleine.'

'I said show yourself, you wretch.' Forrest leant forward and jerked the hood back. Then both he and Danforth jolted away from the figure. The face was mostly eaten away, a mass of sores and running phlegm. Some foul disease seemed to be leaking out from each pore. 'Jesus, Mary, and Joseph,' said Forrest. He had raised one sleeve to his face, as Martin had done to stem his nosebleed. His other arm became flash of brown, steel flashing briefly at its end. To Danforth's horror, he stabbed the dying man through the heart.

16

'Sweet Mary, mother of God! What are you about, woman, sneaking around like that? I just saw … I thought for a moment you were the demon, haunting the halls! Have a care! Heh. Are you well? What in God's own name's happened out there? All this noise, it's like a hellish choir.'

'No, I'm quite well. I don't know – I was going to ask you. I'm sorry to have frightened you.'

'Och, och … no harm done, lass. Well I'll go sniff it out. If you need anything, you come to me. Anything. Heh. Without church services in the town, we might pray together. Does no good for a young lass like yourself to be without God's love.'

The voices drifted into Martin's semi-slumber, one soft and mocking, the other querulous. He tried to push them away. But they were replaced by a *skreeeeing* sound. His eyes flew open. Someone was forcing their way in.

'Thank God you're alive,' said Rowan, looking down before stepping around the dislodged barrier. Before going to sleep, Martin had pushed the little box that served as the room's table against the door. He had reasoned that it was better than nothing. It was, but not by much.

'Eh?' asked Martin. He had been dozing. It was strange – the more sleep he got, the more his body seemed to crave. He started at the sight of the dark skin and the cloud of hair escaping its cap.

'I came down from the dowager's rooms just now and there was a great tumult, as though the Greeks were storming the walls.'

'What's happening?' His voice was thick still.

'I don't know. Mr Danforth and I – Mistress Beauterne too – we all came up from the town. Some strange creature was following us, and Mr Danforth said to come in. So we did. Then when I came down I saw someone being carried out on a board, a sheet over them. I thought it might be you.'

'No, I'm fine. Mr Danforth?' His eyes widened, and he began

to rise.

'Stay,' she said. 'I just saw him, but I couldn't speak. He forced himself right past me, with the depute of the guard. Up into the dowager's rooms. A face like Furor, both of them.'

'Well, as long as he's unhurt,' said Martin. 'Have you spoken with anyone since you saw all that?'

'Only that old goat Guthrie, but he's useless.'

'I don't know. Mr Danforth taught me that gossips might sometimes be goldmines. If you're willing to dig.'

'Then let's leave Mr Danforth to turn out his pick.'

Martin laughed. Rowan had wit, as well learning. If only he could get Danforth to see that. He tested him arm, bending it at the elbow. 'Tssss,' he hissed through clenched teeth. 'Did you get anything to relieve the pain?'

'Aye. So hold your tongue and let me work.'

She gave him the medicine, rubbing in the ointments before bandaging him up. 'You have a tender touch, mistress,' he said when she had finished.

'Don't get any ideas, sonny,' she said, and he blushed.

'I wasn't thinking of me.'

'Oh?'

'No.' He took a deep breath. 'Look here, you're a clever woman.' She gave him a tight smile. 'You should belong to someone – to someone like Mr Danforth.' He drew back in the cot to see the effect, expecting some cutting remark. Instead she looked sad. 'Don't you like him?'

'He seems pleasant enough.'

'He *is* pleasant enough. Uh, what I mean – I mean he–'

'Does Mr Danforth have any especial liking for me?' she cut in.

'He will. Like I said, he's a clever man, full of wisdom. Grave in his judgements.'

'He's made no mark of his favour, shown no sign.'

'Well, he's also an idiot.'

They laughed, the sound rising to meet the cracked plaster ceiling. When it died down, they sat awhile in silence. When Rowan spoke again, he voice was low. The usual bravado seemed to have been damped, and she looked down. 'Who'd want the black bitch of Linlithgow? Who'd want a clever wife, full of her da's tales of the ancients?'

'A clever man. A brave man. A man like old Danforth,' said Martin, eagerness lending him animation. 'He is a man who would protect a woman's name, guard her against vile tongues.'

'Then he might show it.'

'Have you shown him?'

'Shown him what?' she asked, humour returning to her face – a mock aggrieved look.

'That you might be willing to take him. He's ... Mr Danforth is a strange one. He's loyal, he values good order and service.'

'Yet he never married?'

'He was married in England. She died. His child too.'

'Oh. I didn't know that.' Again, the humour faded. 'That's sad.'

'He was a sad man. For a long time, to be honest. But he's coming around. I've been helping him. For friendship's sake. And I reckon it's time he joined the world as an honest man. A married one.'

'Well I shan't force anything.'

'But you are interested? If he knew that, maybe he'd find courage.'

'A stout heart needs no assurances. I want no faint-hearted Paris.'

'Aye,' mused Martin, yawning. 'Keep that up. You'll get him.'

'You assume I want him.'

'I say what I see.' Martin shrugged, before letting out another stifled yelp.

'And what you feel,' said Rowan. They both laughed again.

***

Queen Marie sat scratching the arms of her chair. Dark pouches bulged under her eyes and, as Danforth spoke, she rhythmically whacked the back of her head off of the gilded wood that rose up behind her. He revealed all that he knew, confirming his belief that she had been right: there was a plot against her daughter. The true aim of all that had happened – all that was happening – was the end and overthrow of the House of Stewart.

'Mr Martin, though – he shall live?'

'He shall, your Highness.' Danforth was on bended knee again. At his side was Forrest. He had been reluctant at first to speak so openly in front of the depute but could think of no way of asking to speak with Marie alone. How did one tell a queen that she might not trust the man in charge of her and her child's safety? Besides, he reasoned, Forrest had touched the infected man, grasping at his hood. He would not have done so had he known the danger that lurked beneath.

'An arrow,' said Marie. She was not flanked by Madame LeBoeuf, nor any other women. She saw Danforth and Forrest alone in the bedchamber. It was, whether she intended or not, a mark of high favour and trust. Still, her face was ashen in the menacing firelight. 'It happens again.'

'What happens, madam?' asked Forrest.

'The past, it torments us. You say this creature wears a blue robe?'

'Aye,' said Danforth. 'As was said to be worn by the spirit of St Andrew when he appeared to James IV in the churchyard where Mr Martin fell.' Marie nodded impatiently. Danforth recalled it had been her who first recounted the story.

'Yes, yes. But there is still more. Queen Margaret Tudor herself claimed visions before Flodden. Of the body of her husband, pierced with arrows. You have heard this?'

'No,' said Danforth.

'Aye,' said Forrest.

'Well, it is a story known to many. An old tale. I have collected many of the like. Every castle, every palace, every church has its own tales of the visions and hauntings of the great who once walked within its walls. But until now they have been only stories. Now it seems the line is being crossed. Between this life and the one hereafter. And this message brought by a walking corpse: a message from France. Remember Madeleine. You know who that is?'

Danforth stared at the carpet in silence, tracing the patterns made by passing feet. Queen Madeleine had been Marie's predecessor, a daughter of the French king who had married James V only to die within weeks of setting foot in Scotland. Danforth had known a woman some weeks before who had adopted the name. She had been killed too. People cast long shadows.

'Queen Madeleine died in Holyrood, madam,' said Forrest. 'Not here.'

'Yes, and so I am warned that my child will not be safe in Holyrood. Nor even France. Madeleine carried her illness from there, born in her father's guts, it was whispered. This dead spirit is reminding me that my daughter is safe nowhere, not in Holyrood with Arran, nor in the disease-pit of France's court. Queen Madeleine's death was blamed on her father by my husband, and on my husband by her father. Another death at the hands of a Stewart king. Another ghost crying for vengeance against my daughter's line.'

'No, madam,' Forrest rumbled. 'No spirit. If it kills, if it wounds, it can be killed and wounded. It's a man. Playing on your terrors.'

'I agree,' said Danforth. 'I think it passing likely that our killer is using the stories of old to distract us. We cannot hunt and capture a spirit, but we can do a man. Yet if the palace and its people are hiding from shadows, locked in fear, he might move unseen. And if he is seen, dressed in his evil garb, people might only cry ghost. They might cower away, run from him.'

Marie took her hand from the arm of her chair and kneaded her temple. 'Then who is he? Why is he doing this? This, Mr Danforth, is what I asked you to discover. Thus far you have only told me that which I might suspect.'

Danforth felt himself redden. It was true. He had accomplished little. From the start, the dowager had suspected that the murderer sought her daughter's life. He had come around to her way of thinking, but that buttered no parsnips. Nor did it make her daughter any safer.

'My men now surround the queen day and night. In her nursery, in her outer rooms. Madam, I have a man even in your oratory. She could not be got at even by one passing through here. Believe me, that thing downstairs never had the smallest hope of getting at the queen's wet nurse, still less the lass herself.'

'Yes, Forrest. You do well.'

Danforth pouted, his head lowered again. It was true; in coming to the dowager's bedchamber, he had not even had to go through the performance of admittance by halberd-wielding guards. He and Forrest had simply marched through the queen's apartments after seeing some domestic servants, their faces shrouded in linens, carry the body of the infected man out for burning, or to be dumped in the loch. 'It might have been better had I been allowed to question the fellow,' he said. There had been something maniacal in the speed with which Forrest had slaughtered the diseased man, something horrific in his quickness to kill. It was his job, naturally, to protect the palace and its people, but still. To see a man die, his blood spurting in a red jet as the dagger was withdrawn. It was callous. 'Mr Forrest here slew him before he could scarce take breath.'

'And a good thing too,' snapped Forrest. 'What, you'd have had him bringing his vile vapours right inside the walls? Infecting us all, killing us all?'

'I should have taken him outside,' Danforth protested. 'Found out what he was about. It is a strange method of assassination – weak. More like a warning. Yet with his tongue stopped we might never know!'

'Do not both of you argue here. It is bootless. The man is dead,' said Marie. As she spoke, the door opened behind Danforth and she looked past them.

Closing it, Mathieu entered, bowed, and then smiled up. 'I'm back, your Highness. Je reviens.'

'Scots, Mathieu,' said Marie, smiling back. 'In front of the gentlemen. You wish to speak both languages in their places if you hope to work well in either realm.'

'Aye, madam. Sorry.'

'You have been to the place?' Forrest had ordered Mathieu to the lazar house of St Magdalene near the burgh. Underneath the blue cloak, the dead man had been wearing the smock of one of the place's inmates. The boy nodded, holding out a letter. Marie nodded for Danforth to take it. 'What did the masters of the hospital say?'

'Only that one of their patients ran away,' said Mathieu.

'They gave you this letter?'

'No, madam. They found it in his cell. They all have cells there, they said, because the folk there would swive each other otherwise and make sick babies. Mad ones.' The dowager crossed herself.

'And so they did not know who had spirited the poor creature away, brought him to the palace?'

'No, madam.' Mathieu beamed, the scrubbed face shining. He had no idea, thought Danforth, of the severity of the situation.

'Pray read the letter, Mr Danforth.'

Danforth cleared his throat. It was difficult to make out the writing. It was oddly written, certainly, as though the writer had used the wrong hand, but the light from the fire was also poor. He bowed his head, stood, and moved closer to the grate. 'Sir. With this letter is a cloak. Disguise yourself in it well and gain access to the queen's wet nurse at the palace of Linlithgow, there to deliver to her this message: I CARRY A WARNING FROM FRANCE. REMEMBER QUEEN MADELEINE AND ALL WHO HAVE DIED AT THE HANDS OF THIS REALM'S JAMESES. A PLAGUE ON THE STEWARTS ALL.' There was a space beneath the message, filled in with some strangely-careful doodling of the gate of the palace. Beneath that, Danforth read on. 'Seal this message to the nurse with a kiss and your own kin will be rewarded still further than that which I have already given you. St Andrew.'

Danforth looked up. Marie had remained expressionless throughout, but Forrest's face had turned thunderous. His hands were balled. Mathieu simply looked confused. 'Did they,' asked Marie, 'find anything else in the man's cell?'

'Some money,' said Mathieu. 'Coins. But they wouldn't give me those. I asked. Said the man should have had no money – said he must have stolen it from them. They were evil-looking people, madam, all in masks.'

'I see. The letter states that the poor creature had kin.'

'Yes,' said Danforth. 'Your own kin will be rewarded still

further. Who delivered this letter, boy? Did they say?'

'No, sir. They didn't know. They said they didn't know he could read even.'

'Mathieu,' said Marie, 'go back to the place find out who the man's kinfolk are. It is not their fault. We shall give them something.' A faint smile passed her face. 'Perhaps one day my daughter might need the loyalty of her subjects.'

But Mathieu had turned pale. Without warning, he began sobbing. 'What is it, mon petit chou? Why tears?'

'I don't want to go back there, madam. There's folk dying there.' And then, as though realisation dawned, he turned wide eyes on the letter quivering in Danforth's hands. 'And I touched it, madam, I touched it. I touched the sick man's letter. Am … am I to die?'

Stirred by the boy's hysteria, Danforth looked down himself. Before he could speak, Marie had launched herself out of her seat and stepped over. She took the letter from his hand, touched it to her face, and then cast it in the fire. 'You see?' she said. 'Gone. Nothing. Dry your tears, my boy. He cannot harm you, and neither can that place. Tomorrow you shall have merriment, what say you?' She looked around at Danforth and Forrest. 'We shall finally have our interlude tomorrow. We shall all be lighter and take our pleasure in the great hall. Go now, Mathieu. Be brave, as befits a royal servant.'

Still the boy sniffled, dragging his feet as he made to leave.

'I'll go,' said Forrest. 'The lad's traipsed around enough today. I'll go.'

'No,' Danforth interjected. 'I shall go and speak to these people. Mr Forrest, I imagine you are required in the palace.'

'So … I don't have to?' asked Mathieu, one hand on the door's iron ring.

Marie's voice carried over all. 'For the love of … No, Mathieu. Go off and find something else to do.' He scooted from the room, apparently eager to be gone before the dowager changed her mind. 'Mr Danforth, you go and discover what has gone on in that lazar house. Be safe.'

Danforth resisted the urge to smirk. Instead, he said, 'do you think it wise, your Highness, to have a company assembled in the great hall tomorrow, at such a time as this? If you must stay here, at King Henry's pleasure – or the governor's, you must be kept in sure safety. We all must.'

'I think it necessary. I am weary, Mr Danforth. Weary of gloom. Weary of troubles. Mr Forrest here shall see to our safety.' At this, Forrest turned a smirk on Danforth.

'I pray you again to discover this murderer and put an end to all our troubles. He has used a poor diseased creature as a weapon. And a bow. And a dagger. And whatever he used on poor Mr Fraser. Have you discovered even that?'

'No,' began Danforth. 'But I have some idea–'

'I wish more than some idea, sir.' A white hand, long-fingered, was held out as Marie regained her seat. Danforth and Forrest took turns hovering over it before following Mathieu outside.

Together they began progressing through the inner chamber, the usual conglomeration of heads rising to watch them. Someone had set up a hopscotch game, and the man playing paused, one leg in red breeches held in the air. Forrest tutted. Under his breath he whispered, 'foolish games. Foolish thoughts. Foolish superstitions. Damned popery.'

'What was that?' asked Danforth, from between gritted teeth.

'None of yours.'

As they neared the door to the outer chamber, Guthrie appeared, grasping at Danforth's elbow. He gave Forrest a strange look, half-scared, half-irritated. 'Mr Danforth, sir, might I have a word with you? It won't take long, but it might be important. Heh.' Danforth shook him off, not even bothering to turn. He had no interest in the warbling of the irritating usher and was still less in the mood to tolerate the annoying little laugh the man sounded after every sentence.

'Not now. Some other time, perhaps.'

'As you wish,' said Guthrie, stepping back.

Danforth and Forrest continued walking together, taking the spiral stairs downwards. Danforth pressed on about security arrangements for the dowager's play, about the number of guards that might be sacrificed from watching the queen. Forrest returned only one-word answers and the occasional grunt of approbation. Still, Danforth kept it up. He did not yet know where Forrest slept, and so followed him back to his chamber, on the same floor and in the same suite as his and Martin's. Forrest stopped and turned when he reached the door, one hand on the iron handle.

'If that's all, sir, you might be off and doing her Grace's bidding. I can order my own guards without your suggestions.'

'As you wish. Well, then, I shall bid you good day.' His stomach growled. The northeast tower was ahead. 'Perhaps I shall fetch something to eat and drink. For me and Mr Martin. Where is the kitchen?'

'Up the turnpike,' said Forrest, motioning towards the tower. 'First floor. Goodbye.'

As he opened the door and slid inside, Danforth saw something gleaming on the floor. Before he could make it out clearly, the door slammed shut. Though he could not swear to it, he thought it looked very much like a crossbow.

17

'Butchered like slabs of meat,' Martin had said. He had been talking about Anne Boleyn and Katherine Howard, but he might have been talking about Sir James Hamilton of Finnart, or Thomas Cromwell, or, thought Danforth, crossing himself, the blessed Sir Thomas More or Bishop Fisher.

He moved away from Forrest's door and opened that of his and Martin's chamber, intending to tell him what he had seen. However, he found himself intruding on laughter. Rowan was standing by his cot, lining up the vials they had procured from the apothecary. Martin was still lying down.

'Good day again, Mr Danforth,' she said. 'What news? There was such a tumult, and no one knows what has happened. Who was that fellow chasing us?'

'A wandering beggar seeking alms,' said Danforth. 'He fell ill and died.'

'That was sudden.' There was no smile on Rowan's face, only a look of weariness. 'Well I must return to my da'.'

'Quite. I only come to ask if Mr Martin would like anything from the kitchen?'

'Aye,' said Martin, propping himself up. 'Anything. Everything.'

'Recall what the apothecary said about his diet,' said Rowan.

'I shall.' He turned to leave.

'Perhaps we can speak later?' she said. Martin coughed. 'At your convenience, I mean?'

'Aye. Perhaps.'

He closed the door on them, disappointed and annoyed. Trust Martin to be laughing at some stupid thing or other with a woman. As he moved down the hall, Forrest pushed past him without a word, his head down. 'Mr Forrest, I,' he began, but the man ignored him, striding out of the servant's hall. Danforth watched until he was gone.

He had decided to speak openly in front of no one but Martin and had hoped to share his thoughts on the murder weapon, on

143

the possibilities opened by Martin's references to King Henry's butchered queens. He pictured the parade of headless figures as he clambered up the stairs. Before he reached the first floor, he had left them behind. Instead he began cursing the palace's towers. The way the staircases in each of the wound in circles was disorientating. When one finally emerged at any floor, it took time to work out the direction. The whole place was a big, golden puzzle.

The door to the first floor opened onto a short corridor, the doors to the great hall on the right and the kitchen on the left. The great hall doors were closed, but the latter stood open, the smell of fish strong, a sourer tang undercutting it. Stepping in was like stepping into an inferno, choking heat gusting outwards as though trying to escape.

The kitchen was surprisingly small, a rectangular room dominated by a thick, weather-beaten table. It looked, to Danforth, almost like carved waves, the wood warped and cracking. Leaning on it on his elbow was a tall, stout bald man. 'Master cook,' he asked. Already beads of sweat were bursting on his forehead, his armpits beginning to feel damp and warm.

'Aye?'

'I am Mr Danforth, secretary to the lord cardinal.'

'Oh aye? The cardinal's no' free is he? Is he here?'

'No, no. Nothing like that. I have some questions.'

'We can give you something to eat, but you're better taking dinner with the rest at the right time or it's just bread and cheese.'

'Bread and cheese would be welcome.' The thought of another dinner was anathema. Martin's injury was a good reason for them to eat in their rooms, avoiding pointless chatter and the mockery of fools. 'But that is not why I come.'

'Oh? Well, come in then, out of the cold. Leave the door.' The cook stepped from round behind the desk. His white clothes were clean. Danforth had expected powdery arms, splashes of sauce. Perhaps the job of a master cook was more instructive than participatory. As he moved towards Danforth, the cook stepped around something. Danforth moved to see what it was and was surprised to see two boys lying on the floor on their stomachs, stripped to the waist. Propped on their elbows, they were rolling dice between one another. Beside them the huge fireplace blazed. 'Mind yourselves, you lazy whelps,' snapped the cook. 'You're supposed to be practising your lines for the dowager. Do you wish to make bloody fools of yerselves? Sorry, sir. My boys haven't enough to do during Lent. No spit, no meats.' He wiped his hands on his shirt front and held one out to Danforth. 'I'm Marshall. What's the matter?'

'You know of my colleague's death?'

'That Fraser fella? Aye. Servants' gossip,' he shrugged. 'A bad business.'

'It was that.'

'But what's it to do with me?'

'I seek a weapon. Something that might be used to cleave.'

'We've no weapons here. You want the armoury. Downstairs. In the guardhouse.'

'I think not.' Danforth opened his robe, loosening his collar. It was difficult to breathe. How anyone could work in the tiny smokehouse was a mystery in itself. 'Have you any blades in the kitchen, any stout blades.' He mimed the swing of an axe. 'For cutting meat.'

'Aye. Look here.' The cook stepped back over the lounging spit-boys, Danforth following him. Against the far wall, a huge wooden cabinet sat against the yellowed plaster. In one gesture, Marshall threw it open. Inside, on a series of hooks, were blades and cleavers of all sizes. 'Plenty. All accounted for.' The cabinet was arranged so that the tools each fit neatly, the smallest at the bottom and the biggest at the top. On either side of the resultant triangle were smaller knives and ladles.

'And none has been taken? None was unaccounted for on the night of Mr Fraser's death?'

'None. All there. Although ...'

'Yes?'

'Well, the day he was found – the day everyone was talking of it. I thought this yin was a wee thing clatty. Probably nothing. One of the domestics probably hadn't cleaned it right, ye ken? Shiftless lot, with most of the court no' here.'

Danforth sensed some frenzied whispering at his heels, the

voices pitched just below the crackling grumble of the fire. He trained his ears to it. 'Naw, shhh'; 'he'll fun' oot'; 'haud yer clack, 'sake.' He wheeled, as much as the small space would allow.

'Your spit-boys,' said Danforth, 'have something for us, I think. What are you saying? Tell me or I shall instruct Mr Marshall here to have it from you by surer means.'

'I'll no' lay a hand on my boys,' said Marshall. 'But tell me, lads. What is it?'

The two boys got to their feet, nudging one another and hissing oaths under their breaths. Their ribs showed, but their upper arms and chests were grotesquely muscular. One had a sallow brown tan down the left side of his face and body; the other, paler, was burnt red and flaking down his right.

'Cease muttering,' snapped Danforth. They stopped speaking but continued to fidget. 'What do you know of this blade?'

'Ghost took it!' spat the reddened boy. His fellow elbowed him in the ribs and he turned. 'Go tae the devil!'

'Clype,' spat the tawny boy. 'I'm tellin' everyone you're a clype.'

'Enough,' said Marshall. 'What is this nonsense?'

'Go on,' urged Danforth. 'What is this about a ghost?'

Sighing theatrically, the first boy spoke again. 'The other night. Ghost went intae the cupboard. Took it and then put it back.'

'Which night?' asked Danforth. As he spoke, his stomach audibly revolted at the thought of the bloodied cleaver being used to prepare food. Thank God, he thought, for Lent. 'Describe this ghost.'

'It was St Andrew his' sel'. Frae the stories. All in blue, hidin' his face. At night. We were scared stiff. We couldnae stop him.'

'When? When was this?'

'The night before the old man died.'

'Mr Fraser? You mean the night before he was discovered.'

The boy shrugged. His friend had lapsed into sullen silence, arms crossed against his strong chest and eyes downcast.

'Why,' barked Marshall, 'did you not tell me of this?'

'We were gonnae, we were gonnae! But he brought it back.

So we thought it was a'right.'

'I have told you and told you, you whelps tell me of everything that goes on in this kitchen.' He turned to Danforth. 'I'm sorry, sir. I let the lads sleep on the floor in here at night rather than in the old nether kitchen wi' the rest. For the heat. Only when it's cold.'

'And where do you sleep, sir?'

'In my pantry.' Marshall gestured to a tiny doorway that led into the wall by the fire. 'It's warm in behind the fireplace, but not too warm, you know? But I never saw any ghost. A lot of nonsense. They've been listening to daft stories from the servants' weans.'

'Describe this spirit to me,' said Danforth, his gaze still on the boys. He focused as much consternation into his voice as he could manage. Children, he supposed, would respond only to discipline. Mr Marshall was a soft master.

'He was all in blue, like I said, sir. Like St Andrew in the stories.'

'He floated,' offered the angrier boy. His expression had muted, softening to awe. 'He had no feet.'

'I saw feet,' said the first.

'Naw ye didnae. He floated.'

'He had hooves,' answered the red-boy, not to be outdone. 'And claws for hands.' He folded his own fingers. 'And his eyes were bright red, sir, they glowed. I saw them frae underneath the hood.'

'Enough of this,' said Danforth. 'You little fools have had your minds turned to fancy. I think you saw only a man in blue. Nothing more.'

'It's their age, sir,' said Marshall. 'And this not havin' enough to do. It breeds strange fancies in the mind.'

'But we saw him,' said the half-sallow boy, seemingly now fully committed. He took the blade and made it disappear, just like that.' He snapped a finger. 'Over there.' His finger pointed over the table, at the far wall. 'We were both scared, and wondering whether Tom–'

'Mr Marshall,' said the cook, looking at Danforth.

'Mr Marshall, sorry. Whether he'd have words in the mornin'' when he saw it was away.'

'But then it came back. The creature came back with it, put it away, so we thought it was all just some trick.'

Danforth turned his back on the boys and wound his way around the cook, past the cabinet, to where the boy had said the blade disappeared. On the wall was a wooden hatch, the black paint on its iron handle worn away in places. 'What is this, Mr Marshall?' But before he could answer, Danforth realised. From around the edges, a foul smell felt its way into the kitchen. 'A refuse hatch,' he said under his breath.

'Don't open that, sir,' said Marshall. 'Please. It's a double hatch, but the smell still gets through.'

Danforth ignored the cook, who had appeared at his shoulder. Instead he quickly calculatedly where he was facing: the west of the building. On the day he had visited the place were Fraser's body was found, he had passed the great, stinking rubbish pile. Our man, he thought, likes to cast objects through ports.

He turned on his heel. 'Thank you, Mr Marshall. This has been instructive. I recommend you take greater care of these boys. More discipline. Skelp them if need be. Perhaps they can find needful employment in carrying light dinners down to my chamber, for my injured colleague and myself. And,' he added, 'pray see that is carefully prepared. You lads, let no one else touch anything that reaches our lips.'

'Aye,' said Marshall, frowning. 'Aye, mebbe they can do just that. Here, I'll fetch you some food.'

***

Fifteen minutes later, Danforth and Martin were standing at the edge of the rubbish pile, armed with long sticks. They took turns watching the woods a short distance away, and the windows of the palace, alert to the glimmer of metal that might indicate a gun trained on them.

Martin prodded gingerly using his good arm. 'Christ,' he said. 'I can't even bury my nose in my elbow. What are we even looking for?'

'It will do your body good to be in action,' said Danforth. 'It shall help it heal the quicker.' Despite the cold, the pool of sludge seemed to cast up a hot, clinging stink. It had corrupted the ground. The gardeners had not even attempted to grow bushes here.

'But you said the blade was back in its place,' protested Martin. 'Here, look!'

'What? You have something?'

'No, look at this gallus fellow. Get away from me!'

Martin brandished his stick like it was a rapier, attempting to dislodge an enormous seagull that had landed on the rubbish pile and was inching ever closer. It stopped, flapped its wings without rising, and then squawked. 'Away with you!' shrieked Martin. The gull cocked its head and then flew a few feet away, sending some magpies crying into the air. 'There's nothing here but birds and shit,' said Martin, wrinkling his nose and throwing away his stick. 'I wasn't made to wade through shit looking for the Holy Grail. There's nothing here, Simon.'

'No,' said Danforth. He looked at his own stick and then tossed it. 'No. In truth, I wanted to see where the hatch let out.'

'You could see that from above. Without touching it.'

'Perhaps. I wanted to see how one might recover something.'

'Very easily, if it had just been thrown. Not many days later when a week of filth has rained on it.'

'Hmm. Yet I think I see how this was done, if not why.'

'Go on.'

'It might be this way,' said Danforth, stepping away from the filth. Martin skipped after him. The birds who had been chased off began to regroup. 'Mr Fraser, we know was drugged. He was lured outside or went. Probably he was lured. Our killer, not content with drugging him, but keen to make a spectacle of his death, donned a disguise to frighten the spit-boys. At night. When he knew they were alone. That tells us that he is someone who knows the order of this place – who sleeps where.'

'Not necessarily,' said Martin. 'Perhaps he reasoned his disguise would frighten off anyone. Or if he knew who slept where, he might've learned it from one who knows.'

'Well, whatever,' said Danforth, shrugging in irritation. 'He
149

took a blade from the cabinet upstairs, threw it out the little window, and retrieved it later. Then he cut apart Mr Fraser and put the blade back. It would be safer to do so later, safer to carry it on his person when his gory deed was done. When the household would assuredly be in bed.'

'But that blade didn't shoot me,' said Martin, raising his arm in its sling.

'No. No, that was a crossbow.' He chanced another look around. It was clear. 'Arnaud, I think I saw a crossbow on the floor of Forrest's chamber earlier.'

'You sure?' Martin's eyes widened.

'Pretty sure. Though I could not swear to it. What do you make of him?'

'I dunno,' said Martin, looking downhill towards the loch. 'Does the dowager trust him?'

'I think so. Most assuredly.'

'He might have one in there for any reason. He is depute of the guard.'

'And a blasted heretic, I fancy. I heard him speak against the pope, under his breath. And tell me, have you ever heard of a Knox? A John Knox? Calls himself a priest and a schoolmaster.'

'I don't think so. Knox … I think there are Knoxes serve the Hepburn Earl of Bothwell.' He shrugged, wincing. 'I *think*. Should I have? Who is he?'

'I do not know, as yet. Only I spied a man coming out of the stable with Gibb and Forrest. He took Forrest by the hand. I did not like the look they shared. It had the look of secrecy. And the fellow's eyes. They were … dark.'

'It's no crime to have dark eyes.'

'I am not saying it is,' said Danforth tartly. 'Only I did not like the look of the thing. Gibb told me the man was a priest, but I cannot be sure of it until we speak to the cardinal.'

'What do you think?'

'Perhaps he is. Perhaps he isn't. But their secret counsel looked to me like the meetings the hot reformers used to have in London. In taverns, in hidden rooms, in stables and other such filthy places. They kept their heresies hidden. But still they would meet, hopeful of sharing their madness, opening their minds to one another. My ... my father always said that the true Church was too big to fail. We none of us foresaw a king who was bigger still, who would lend an ear to the cringing madmen in their privy places.'

'Well ... with this parliament giving them hope that Arran might push reform,' said Martin, kicking at the ground, 'perhaps that is what was happening. Who's to say? Perhaps they're just friends. Maybe their interest was in horses.'

'And perhaps not. You know, we have been looking at all this madness as though it was done under the cloak of politics. But what if it was of a religious nature.'

'I ...' began Martin, looking doubtful. 'I suppose ... I mean, the hidden reforming men would gain from the baby queen's death, I guess. Kill a Catholic heir, give support to a reformist governor – make him the new king. But ... I mean, who in their right mind would put their faith in Arran? Everyone knows that having his loyalty and friendship is like having an eel by the tail.'

'Pfft,' snorted Danforth. 'The heretics have no faith, and their minds are never right.'

'Should we suggest this to the dowager? About Forrest and that?'

Danforth took a deep breath, blew it out. It swirled in the cold air. 'No. Not yet. Not if she might stick fast by Forrest. *We* must stick to what we find for sure, not what we might suspect. I have told you before about dead alleys.' Danforth was determined not to let religious conviction cloud his judgement. That was the kind of thing a zealot might do, a blind fool like Guthrie. 'Still, I do not like it. Secret meetings with strangers in stables. Does her Grace know about those, I wonder? Does she know about his whispered curses against the true faith?'

'If he's a heretic, I'm sure she does. Perhaps she doesn't much care, if he's loyal. Perhaps she's tolerant.'

'Bah,' said Danforth. 'Womanish frailty, tolerance.' He jabbed a finger savagely at the pool of waste. 'That is where I should put heretics. That is the stinking pile that should house these reforming men. Why, if I had one finger tainted by heresy

I'd cut off my own hand. I'd sooner tolerate a fox troubling my chickens.'

'You keep chickens? Perhaps you and old Guthrie should start a feu-farm to raise them. You're sounding like him.'

'No, of course not. Do not try and jest.' Danforth did not care at all for the comparison. Unlike Guthrie, he fancied, his stance on religion was firm, but low-key. Respectable. He did not flaunt his medals like a goodwife on a Sunday. 'Yet I think I might draw out his opinions.'

'Whose, Guthrie's? I've had a gutful of those.'

'Forrest's, you young fool. I shall draw them out. By subtle acts, Arnaud,' said Danforth, a slight smile touching his lips. 'I fancy I am developing a talent for them.'

'Well, let me know if you do. I don't like it though, bringing Forrest into this. He's in charge of all our safety in there.'

'He may be wholly innocent. In which case, the real murderer would save his honour.'

'Or real murderers,' said Martin. 'What if there is more than one person in this thing?'

'No,' said Danforth, shaking his head. 'No, we must not chase notions. We have found the weapon – one of them, at any rate. One hand held it. Find whose hand it was and the rest will become clear.' He brushed aside Martin's suggestion. He needed the weapon to be significant. His mind fixed on it like a starving dog on a haunch. It was something – a hard, physical something. It was proof that the killer had breathed amongst them, was amongst them still, tangible and catchable. It was proof that he wasn't useless, that he might prove the value of his mind to the dowager.

'We should have questioned every man in the place when we first came here,' said Martin, interrupting his thoughts. 'We've played our hand wrong.'

'Pfft. The two of us? Taking in a hundred different stories, each with arms and legs attached? Forgive me,' he said, as Martin's face whitened. 'I did not mean that as a jest.' He could feel Fraser's ghost frowning. The man must now be sealed in his coffin, the flesh receding and puckering, mottling. Perhaps the journey to Edinburgh Gibb had mentioned had sped up the process, as the body was jounced about over rutted, half-frozen roads.

'So we now know how it was done, but not why it was done. Nor who did it. And one thing confuses me.'

'One thing?'

'Aye. Why this?' He raised his arm, wincing. 'Why me?'

'I cannot say. You and Mr Fraser, both victims.'

'It is some attack then on the cardinal?'

'Don't be foolish. If the cardinal's enemies wished him ill, they would have no better time to do so than in his prison.'

Martin shrugged. 'Another thing. Why show himself now? When we came he might have hidden. We would've thought he'd fled into the night. Some enemy of Fraser's, that's all. Why come out in the open by attacking me and Simms?'

Danforth looked around again. There was no one to hear them, no one to shoot from the dark. Still, it felt that they were being watched. It was a constant feeling, the product of living in close quarters with a gaggle of unknowns. He thought before answering, shifting possibilities. There were few. 'It might be two ways. Perhaps we are closer than we realise, and he had to chance silencing us.'

'Or?'

'Or perhaps his mission, whatever it is, is not yet complete. And so he presses on, thinking us irrelevant.'

'Bastard. So we are nowhere. No matter what scraps of knowledge we gather, the devil hides his face.'

'No. But ... have you ever seen a master painter at work, Arnaud?' Martin gave him a blank look. 'At first his work resembles nothing. Mere lines, splashes of colour. You have no notion what he is about. But the more lines, the more colours, are added, the more his subject becomes clear.

'Thus far we have the clothing. We have the weapon. We just need to find the man who wore one and wielded the other.'

18

Danforth set off for the lazar house early in the morning, leaving Martin snoring. A resolve had burned its way into him, a desire to find out more, to assemble enough pots of paint that he might make a clear picture. He checked the crate he had pushed against the door before sleeping. It was undisturbed.

He picked his way through the crowd of servants who rose early: maids to stoke up fires, grooms carrying bales of hay. He avoided contact with all of them, although they did bring a thought: of what rank might their murderer be? Could it be some unnamed domestic servant, one of those fresh-faced grooms, or a singing pot-boy? Ghosts were said to move about unseen when it suited them, but so too might lower servants, pressing themselves against walls when more important men and women chanced to appear in the same hall or room. If it were some servant, then the nebulous and taunting question of motive remained. So too did the disturbing idea that a chamber maid might at any time hide a dagger in his hammock, to pierce him as he slept, or a pot-boy might sprinkle ground glass on his trencher. Hitherto he would have cared nothing for danger, but when Martin had been shot at, something had come into his mind very clearly: he wanted to live – and to live with purpose. No, he decided. If it were a servant, he or she must have been guided. The lower orders, he assumed, were in language no less than barbarous and in wit no more than stupid. Had it been a servant, they would have left bloody footprints right to their bed. He clung to the thought like a blanket. There was some greater mind at work here. There had to be.

The sky above was a rich pink. He had always heard that that brought ill luck, and he crossed himself to banish it. There was something bracing about the chill morning. It was, he reasoned, the perfect time to visit a sick house. The air was fresh enough to blast away any evil vapours. It was the afternoon, when the sun was at its highest, that infection bred in the winds.

The burgh, when he reached it, was stirring too, the bakehouse already wafting sweet scents out and the other merchants setting up their displays. He caught the attention of a dull-eyed young woman carrying a basket and asked her where the lazar house was.

'Why do you want to go there?' She drew away from him as he spoke, as though he were diseased.

'My brother works there,' he invented. 'I seek only to see him'

'Oh, I see. You have to go by St Magdalene's Cross. The place sits out there. God go with you.'

'And with you, Mistress …'

'Muir.'

He followed the direction she had pointed in, wandering some way and asking for further directions from others. Eventually he found the place, a small collection of buildings with a cross denoting one as a chapel. He smiled at it, before taking the path to the largest one.

Inside, a masked man was sweeping the floor, his broom casting up feathers of dust and wood shavings. He set it against a large crate as Danforth closed the door behind him.

'Good day, sir,' said the attendant, his mask puffing. It gave his voice a thick, reverberating sound. 'What news?'

'Good day. I seek information on one of your patients. The fellow lately fallen ill at the palace.'

'Him again,' tutted the man. 'Auld Nick.'

Danforth started at the nickname more often used for the devil. 'Who?'

'Nicholas Kerr.'

'He was a Kerr?'

'Aye, from some bastard branch of them. I've nothin' tae tell I didnae tell the lad who came down here. Dunno who'd have wanted tae meet him up there, or why. Dunno what business he had taking letters from anyb'dy.'

'The letter,' said Danforth. 'That is what brought me. Can you tell me who delivered this letter to him?'

The man shrugged, grasping the broom again. 'Naw,' he said. 'Save nob'dy brought it here first. It must've got tae him some other way.'

'Did the fellow go out, then? Do your patients have liberty to leave?'

'Naw. Absolutely not. Cannae have diseased creatures out spreadin' their pestilence. Do you have some visor yoursel'?'

Danforth, rolling his eyes, removed a handkerchief from his pocket and tied it around his face. 'Are you saying,' he asked, 'that the fellow never left? How then did he get out? How did the letter get to him?'

'Dunno. This is a hospital, sir. We've a passel of sick men and women here. And at the alms-house next door. We can't keep them aw locked up aw the time.'

'And so he slipped out? You were derelict in your duties?'

The attendant's face clouded. 'Do you fancy this job, Mr? Working for the scraps we get from the diocese?'

'No,' frowned Danforth, unwilling to get into an argument about church revenue. 'No. I only mean … well, might he have slipped out by some other means? And might the letter have reached him by any others. His family perhaps, the Kerrs?'

'Ha! His family haven't come near in the months he's lain here. Would you want tae look at a face like that?'

'Perhaps not. Might I see his chamber?'

The man propped his broom against the crate again and moved towards a door. Over his shoulder he called, 'aye, well, are you comin' or no'?' Danforth followed, into a short hallway with doors on either side. From behind them came the muted sounds of sobbing, and some incomprehensible muttering, rising and falling in pitch. He watched his host's back, wondering what it might be like to work in such a place. It was good work, of course, but it must pluck at the soul, to be amongst the afflicted. Hearing the cries, he remembered the weeping mass of the diseased man – Kerr's – face. God commanded that his children show charity to such creatures, but he had never been able to do so properly. The thought of reaching out to comfort them disgusted him, as a spider or a snake might disgust some men.

Scrabbling at a key on a belt tied round his robes, the attendant unlocked the door to a long, thin cell, dominated by a coverless cot. A single cross hung on the wall, and a tall, wide window

156

admitted morning light. 'Here it is,' he said. 'Letter was lying on the bed. Didnae even know that old creature could read. Never spoke tae him save tae shove his food through the door. Cannae get too close tae them when they're that far gone.'

'I see,' said Danforth. He was looking past the bed, towards the window, its wooden shutters gaping. 'That window is fair.'

'They're all big here. Have tae be. Have tae let the good air in. Let the bad air out. Otherwise I'd be a patient mysel'. Don't fancy that. Most o' them go mad, locked up, the sickness eating away. Poor bastards.'

'I think,' said Danforth, 'there is no great mystery as to how he found escape. I wonder more of them don't.'

'Aye, well, they wouldnae get far. If the disease didnae bring them down, they'd be hanged first town they reached.'

'I see,' said Danforth again. 'Yet I think also the fellow had his letter by these means. Has anyone been seen around the …' he hesitated to use the word garden to describe the scrubby land around the hospital. He settled on, 'yards.'

'Naw,' said the attendant, scratching at his head. 'Just you and that wee lad yesterday.'

'And you said no one was interested in this Kerr?'

'Mr, nob'dy's interested in any of the poor souls here. Few ever get better. The only people who ever came were … well, the dowager used tae come down wi' divers of her household in better days. A few months back, before the king died. Used tae bring alms tae them. Hasn't been since the new queen was born.'

'You did say that Kerr had been here for months, did you not? How long?'

'I think,' he said, his eyes rolling up, 'Aye, I ken he came around the start of winter. He wasnae so eaten away then. The physicians don't bother wi' this place, so we rely on the apothecary fae the town. All he ever says is tae change whit they eat. So they rot. It was the smallpox or the French pox done for Kerr. A pox anyway. Who cares? God rest him.'

'Who cares, indeed,' said Danforth, thinking. A cry from one of the other rooms in the building tore him back – a hollow, weak yelp. 'I think I have seen enough. Her Highness the dowager wishes to do something for the family. I assume you have the names of his kin, and where they hail from?'

'Hmph. Aye. Doesnae seem right that they get looked after when they slung him on us. Should be this house that gets something, for the next poor bastard that gets his bed.'

The man had a point. Still, that was what Marie wanted, and it was hardly his place to counsel her otherwise. 'The names?'

'I'll write them out for you.'

'No,' said Danforth. 'Have them sent up.' A superstitious dread had come over him that taking anything from the place would breed infection in him. It was foolish, he knew, but now he had thought it, he could not un-ring the bell.

'Aye. Awright. When I've got time.'

'Thank you.' He cast one last look at the window. Something thrummed dimly in his brain, but it was too weak to make it out. Instead, he left the lazar house, snatching off the handkerchief. Before he left the grounds, he threw it away.

***

Martin slept late, waking with a rumbling stomach. He dressed himself awkwardly, flexing his arm to see how it fared. It was still raw, but the pain was less sharp. He stuck his head out the door and looked up and down the hall before leaving. He wasn't sure what he was looking for, exactly – someone with a gun trained, perhaps. He cast aside the paranoia. Living in fear was pointless. Instead he took himself up to the kitchens and scrounged some breakfast.

As he skipped back down the stairs, humming a tune, he was joined by a small army of craftsmen, who informed him that the revels were in readiness. They were being escorted out, barred from the palace so that only the invited guests would be within its walls for the afternoon's production. That, he guessed, should make him feel safer – it was a sign of good security. For some reason, though, the idea that he'd be trapped inside with people who had been present when Fraser had been murdered – never mind the panoply of other horrors – unsettled rather than comforted. He tried to shake off the gloom.

In the courtyard, he found Diane Beauterne rinsing what looked like a white sheet in the palace fountain. 'Haven't you got laundresses for that?' he asked her in French.

'Takes too long,' she said, grinning. 'If I do things myself, I know they're done right.'

'Do you like it, being a queen's lady?'

'I like helping people,' she said. What was it Danforth had called her? A Mistress Peaceweaver. It seemed apt. She smiled again, her cheeks like apples.

'What's your job this afternoon? A fair lady, to be won from a dragon? Or do you lead the dance?' He attempted a step in front of her, hissing as he jogged the little patch of skin over his armpit.

'You're foolish,' she laughed, drawing up the sheet and squeezing out the water. 'There haven't been any dragons in Scotland since … 1520!'

'Aye,' said Martin, impressed. 'Fraser of Glenvackie, 1520. Slew the last dragon.' He mimed thrusting a sword into her wet bundle. 'How did you know?'

'Long nights. There is nothing to do but share stories. In Scotland you had dragons to scare the children, in France we had the wolves of Paris. They came in 1450 during the great dearth and ate everybody up.' She made a claw of one hand and growled. Martin laughed again.

'But really, what is this for?'

'It is a dress. Opened up a little, I had to add a panel. I must dry it by the fire, and quickly.'

'Add a panel?' he asked. He considering making a pregnancy joke and thought better of it. This girl seemed anything but a bawd. 'Is it for this masque?'

'Yes. The ladies are to be dressed in white.'

'Are you taking part?'

'No,' she said, 'not really.' Martin half-turned his head, narrowing his eyes good-humouredly at her evasiveness. 'I have a friend,' was all she gave him, moving away with the bundle held out in front of her. He watched her go, pausing as she reached the entrance to the southwest tower. 'Someone,' she called back, still in French, 'is going to get the surprise of their life this afternoon!'.

'You look like a wolf carrying a sheep!' he called back. Something about her lightness had lifted his mood, albeit infinitesimally. Why, then, could he not shake the feeling of dread that seemed to be hanging over the place, mocking the men and women making ready to enjoy themselves beneath? As she disappeared, he wondered what on earth she was up to.

***

Danforth passed through the burgh and joined the Kirkgate, tensing his legs for the slog uphill to the palace. Windows, letters, households, it was all a jumble. He needed time to sort things through. There would be little enough in the afternoon unless he could find some way of avoiding the play. Even then, he supposed, the palace would be so full of noise and bustle that he would be unable to find peace. As he stomped up the cobbled street, a door opened to his left. He moved aside to let someone leave the low-roofed building he knew to be the Song School – that little educational institution used for teaching boys the basics of choral singing and any other knowledge they might need. He did a double take as a pair of piercing eyes met his. The man nodded curtly, before hurrying off in the direction of the town. It was the fellow, about his own age, who had been meeting in secret with Forrest. It was John Knox.

Danforth watched him go, his stride neat and determined. So too did the schoolmaster, standing in the doorway of the Song School. Danforth stepped towards him. 'Good day,' he hailed. 'I see you had words with my friend Knox.'

'Aye,' said the schoolmaster, looking him up and down. 'You're not come to harangue me too, are you, son?'

'Harangue? No, I have no mind to that. He was then pressing on you too? Oh, that Father John. A fine man, but he does … harangue good folk. I've said it myself to him often enough.' Danforth stopped, worried that he might go too far, say something that might be easily disproven. Or simply look like what he had suddenly become, his mind added with censure: a grubby, spying liar.

'Aye,' he laughed. 'For a deacon he has a right questioning sort of mind. Full of, uh, miscontentation.'

'I know it,' smiled Danforth. 'What were his lessons today? Not harping on' he lowered his voice, 'reform again, I hope?'

'What? No, no-no-no. Nothing like that. Och, just wanting to know what we teach the lads here. Why we don't teach them better things, their grammar and more Latin. I didn't know he was a reformer.' The old man's eyes twinkled with malicious glee. Panic struck Danforth: he might have just got the damned Knox fellow in trouble over something he had just invented as a tool to pry. If the schoolmaster ran off to the authorities, as well he might – and damned well should, now – he would have a lot of explaining to do to the cardinal.

'Well, he is a schoolmaster himself,' Danforth chanced. 'I fancy he wishes to share his own methods.'

'We have our own ways. Don't need some new man from out east who thinks he knows it all telling us how we ought to rear our bairns. Sorry, sir, if he's your friend. Who are you?'

'I am a gentleman of the lord cardinal,' said Danforth, throwing his shoulders back to let his cloak open.

'Oh, I see. How is his Grace?'

'On his way to Blackness, as I understand it.'

'Oh aye? It's a bad business, that. Those Hamiltons and Douglases keeping the Pope's own man kept close.'

'Aye,' agreed Danforth. 'It is that.'

'So his Grace's men are friends with thon serious fellow? Didn't know young Father John had other friends than old Forrest up yonder. Hmph. Suppose he's all about making friends. Odd ideas, that one. He'll grow out of them, I dare say.'

'Perhaps,' said Danforth. 'I shall keep an eye on him.'

'You do that, son.' He hesitated, tapping his forearm lightly on the doorframe, before adding, 'if your friend is hoping to move for reform whilst your master is kept out of the realm's affairs ... Ugh, like I said, a bad business. Watch your company, son.'

The schoolmaster bowed his head before stepping backwards and closing the door. Danforth looked again down the Kirkgate, but Knox had gone. There had been something unsettling about the man's stare. There was something even more unsettling about a 'questioning' man appearing in the burgh to meet his friend when that friend was in charge of security at a palace plagued by murders. If only, he thought again, he could have some quiet place to sort through matters.

***

There was no avoiding the dowager's masque. Or play, or interlude: from what Danforth could glean, the entertainment announced for the afternoon was to be some hodgepodge. Without a master of revels at her disposal, it seemed, Queen Marie would only be able to cobble together some poetry, music, and whatever the press-ganged players could recall from the entertainments staged in happier times. Danforth and Martin had picked up the news and a measure of the excitement when they washed at and drank from the fountain in the late-morning's crisp sun.

Again Danforth took the stairs in the northeast tower. This time the doors to the great hall were open, and already music was spilling from inside. In the short hall, men and women in Hamilton and Douglas colours were waiting to be shown to their places, Anthony Guthrie ushering them in pairs. Servants scooted out of the kitchen, ducking their way between the guests, their arms laden with silver trays of comfits.

'I met your little friend earlier,' said Martin.

'Is that so? Who might that be?'

'Mistress Peaceweaver.'

'Dia– Mistress Beauterne? The French lass?'

'Aye.'

'What had she to say for herself?'

'Nothing much. She said someone would get a great surprise at the masque. Dunno what she meant. I see what you mean about her.'

'What?' asked Danforth.

'All sweetness and light. My teeth were fair aching after talking to her.' Danforth murmured a dismissal. 'You know,' Martin, continued 'I didn't think you'd like plays.'

162

'They have their place.'

'All the larking about and that. Thought you'd hate it. You're just full of surprises, Simon.'

'I should hope so,' said Danforth, a dryness sharpening his tone. He had no desire to be thought of as a fuddy-duddy. It was a frustrating thing to imagine oneself through the eyes of others. Less and less he liked what they seemed to see.

'Aye, but I've never seen you at any of the cardinal's May Day revels. Fraser was the Abbot of Unreason at one of them, God rest him.'

'I prefer to read ballads and plays for the richness of their language, not for the general bawdry of the multitude.' He and Martin stepped forward as Guthrie welcomed the men in front of them, the three disappearing. In truth, Danforth had found the May revels too social, too likely to put him amongst his colleagues as a friend. For years he avoided abjured company, preferring to dedicate his life to work. Friendship had become part of his youth.

As they reached the front of the queue, a voice hissed behind them. 'A fair day for a farce.' Danforth turned to see Cam Hardie, a Douglas woman on his arm.

'What – how long have you been there? Why are you here?'

Hardie was wearing a black-and-grey suit, obviously expensive, with polished silver buttons. He eyed Martin's livery with a smirk, focusing on the amethyst-coloured faux gems he had had sewn on. 'Fair buttons,' he sniffed. The woman laughed, and Danforth could sense his friend's spine stiffen at his side. 'They match your eye.'

'I see,' said Danforth, 'that friend Forrest has not taken care with this palace's safety when he allows such a one as you into the place.'

'I am a Douglas,' said Hardie, straightening his cap and bouncing his head. 'I've more right to this place than some cardinal's imps.'

'Imps?' snarled Martin. 'If I had my dirk, I'd cut that tongue from your head.'

'Is that so? I fancy I could land my fist on your other eye before you might draw blade or breath.'

'How is your friend?' asked Danforth before Martin could speak. 'Not fallen on any more daggers?'

'You shut your mouth,' said Hardie, his voice lowered. 'You better watch what you say about the Douglases.'

Guthrie arrived then, preventing any further discussion. 'Mr Danforth,' he smiled. Then, 'Mr Martin. You're up and about? Splendid, you won't miss the revels. Heh. Will you be up to a dance? Heh. There's some ladies here special whom I reckon would take you up. One lady I know has her eye on you. Heh. She's married, but ...' He winked.

'Ladies?' asked Danforth. 'Dance?' But Guthrie had turned his back and was leading them into the great hall.

The ceiling soared above them, the voices of dozens – perhaps hundreds – of excited guests rising to meet it in a cheerful cloud. Dismal light poured in through the tall windows to their left, the biggest at the far end of the room. There sat Queen Marie, on her throne on its raised dais. The larger throne next to her was empty. She looked, thought Danforth, desperately lonely, smiling down at everyone like a graceful Madonna.

Benches lined the long walls on either side of the chamber, three deep. Guthrie showed them to seats in the middle row on the right, giving them a good view of various Hamilton backs, caps, and headdresses. The arrangement seemed clear: the front row on each side belonged to the titled guests, the middle row to those connected with the royal household, and the back row reserved for the menials belonging to palace itself. Danforth and Martin's view of the low stage – more an improvisation of wooden boards – was weak, but better than those behind them. It was a neat manner of doing things: it was orderly, hierarchical. Some attempt, Danforth noticed, had even been made at scenery, with painted clouds hanging from the ceiling and green splashes marking out lush fields on the stage-boards.

'What's it going to be about?' asked Martin. Danforth shrugged. Plays were usually about good and evil, or some mummery about Robin Hood. Much of the enjoyment came from seeing friends and colleagues humiliate themselves. 'I hope there's no clown.'

'What is that, Martin?' Danforth was drawn to the word.

164

'I hope there's no clown. Can't stick them.'

'I thought if there was one fellow you'd be drawn to, it would be a clown.'

'No. They're always tricksters. Always making you laugh and falling around. But they always turn out to be devils.'

Danforth nodded, thinking of Senat, the dowager's fool. She had not even made him laugh. A large figure pushed in front of him, and he drew in his knees, looking up. 'Good day to you, Danforth,' said Forrest, glowering down. The man's arm was stretched out behind him, leading a child. 'This is my son. His mother insisted on me bringing him up from the town for this flummery.' Danforth shifted to the left, causing Martin to do likewise, as Forrest lifted the boy, who could only have been about six, onto the bench.

'Good day,' he returned, ignoring the child. 'The place is secure for this?'

'Aye. As secure as it can be for this nonsense.'

'I ask only because there was a fellow in here earlier. You recall, the fellow who was with me when Martin here met with his accident. The yellow-haired one?' He spoke with one eye on the Hamilton men seated in front of him.

'A guest of the clan who sit on the other side,' said Forrest. 'My men are now protecting the queen in her nursery. The rest are at the gates of the palace. Both of 'em. No one comes in or goes out whilst the play and masque are being performed.'

'I wonder,' said Danforth, standing and cracking his back, 'if I might speak with you privately. Mr Martin here will watch your boy.'

They left Martin showing the boy tricks, and stood off to the side, between the dowager's dais and the benches, as the lower servants began to file in to the back row. 'What do you want, Danforth?'

'I noted your speech yesterday.' Danforth winked, he hoped conspiratorially. 'Your dislike of these fond capers and revels. I share it. I merely wondered if you should like to speak further on these–'

'I'll stop you there,' snapped Forrest, hooking his thumbs into his belt. 'Don't shame yourself any further, Master Cardinal's man. I'm no fool. I know what you're driving at.'

Danforth let his mask of friendliness slip, a wasted effort.

'My beliefs are my own,' went on Forrest. 'And known to her Grace. If you think to make trouble for me or mine, you'll be the worse for it. I'm no preacher, no converter. I think as my own conscience directs, with the help of Jesus Christ. Not with your Holy friends.'

'I saw a crossbow on your chamber floor,' hissed Danforth, hoping to regain the advantage. 'I saw it.'

'Is that so? So you men peep into cracks now?'

'Whatever it might take to catch a murderer.' He hoped there was an assured dignity to his tone.

'Keep your damn voice down. Aye, you saw the weapon. I found it there myself at the same time.'

'What? I am to believe that it was only just put there before I saw it?'

'Before you and I both saw it. It was cast there when I was without – dropped.'

'By whom?'

'That's what you're supposed to be finding out, sir,' said Forrest, his face expressionless but mirth twinkling his eyes.

'Her Grace,' said Danforth, chancing a look over at Marie, who was now watching them both. 'Does she know that you … found … this weapon on your chamber floor?'

'Naturally. I left the room almost immediately to inform her. You saw me.'

Danforth thought back. Yes, Forrest had burst past him before he went up to the kitchen. But he might have been going anywhere. 'Perhaps you would like to speak with the dowager,' said Forrest, half-turning, dragging him from his thoughts.

'No,' said Danforth grudgingly. 'I believe you. Or, at least, I shall trust in you. For the moment. And I suppose it was only the bow that was cast into your chamber? No sign yet of the missing wheellock?'

'No. Now, if you'll excuse me, I'm going to check on my boys.'

'Your son?'

'No, my lads at the gates. You and Martin can watch my boy.

These trifles are for bairns anyway, not grown people.'

'Wait, what?' spluttered Danforth. But Forrest was already striding away, past the stage without looking at it, and out the door. He had no choice but to take his seat, next to the little boy. He looked straight ahead, into the impenetrable square back in front of him. Still he could feel the irritating child's solemn gaze up at him. 'Martin,' he said, through clenched teeth. 'Entertain that whelp, can't you?'

Martin's nonsense talk filled the time until someone closed the curtains of the place, leaving only scattered wall sconce torches and some braziers lit around the stage to light the place. As his eyes accustomed to the darkness, Danforth heard the petulant voice of Guthrie fill the room from the dowager's dais.

'Good Christian people,' he intoned, 'lords and ladies, lairds and gentlemen, and you good serving men and women. We are come here together to laugh, to cry, to make merry, all. Yet it is meet and proper that first we remember in love our late sovereign lord, the right high and potent prince of imperial blood, King James.' A general murmur of approval sounded through the hall, rippling like a disturbed pond. 'And so our first reading comes from the lusty pen of our beloved makar.' He nodded briefly, and the musicians began to play from somewhere.

Then hastily I started out of my dream
Half in a fray, and speedily passed home
Lightly dined, with lust and appetite,
Then after passed into an oratory
And took my pen and there began to write
All the vision that I was shown before
But I beseech God for to send thee grace
To rule thy realm in unity and peace

'*The Dream*,' said Danforth, recognising the lyrics. 'He's reading from *The Dream*.' It was an old favourite by Sir David Lindsay, a copy of which the cardinal kept in his library. It was an allegory, crying out against misgovernment. Lindsay was a great lover of prophetic dreams and poetic visions. He wondered why Marie would have selected that – if, that was, she made her own choice of readings. Perhaps she liked to conquer her fears by confronting them. Whatever her purpose, it brought to mind the Finnart business, which Danforth had just about cast into the rubbish pile.

'Good people,' trilled Guthrie, 'before we begin our own vision to delight you, her Grace the queen dowager bids that you dance. Gentlemen, stay your hands. For the ladies shall have their pick of you lusty gallents.'

Danforth froze as a bevy of women emerged from some hidden passageway behind the dowager's dais. A hidden passage, he thought, right at her back. Was it being guarded?

Marie watched them go, one finger pressed against her lips. All were in flowing white gowns, their faces covered by silk masks. The line divided, some going towards the right-hand benches and some the left. The musicians had begun a slower tune, of the type favoured in French courtly exercises. As the women dispersed amongst the crowd, choosing partners, one came directly towards him. He felt the colour rise in his cheeks, hoping that this was the creature Guthrie had suggested had decided upon Martin. As she drew closer, though, the gait was unmistakable. Another, taller woman ambled behind her.

'Mr Danforth,' said the first lady. The flames of the torchlight sparkled yellow and orange in the depths of her eyes. 'I choose you.'

19

Ghosts and ghostly visions held no terrors comparable to those brought by having to dance before a great company. Especially, thought Danforth, when that company included Queen Marie of Guise and a host of high-ranking Hamilton and Douglas retainers.

'How did you get in here?' he asked his partner as they took their opening bows.

'Diane invited me,' said Rowan. 'Yesterday. I helped her put together some of her cloth after I left Mr Martin. She knew I fancied seeing all of this. Offered that I might take her place and dance.' She pressed a finger over her lips. 'Under this mask I might be anyone. Anyone in the world other than me.'

A heady perfume hung in the air, rich and vaporous. It was, Danforth felt, not unlike the scent one found in a good church or abbey, but somehow more delicate. Queen Marie had apparently abandoned the cinnamon scent she used in her bedchamber in favour of a thick amber. 'And why have you chosen to torture me thus?' he hissed. It was arrant foolishness – and for her and Diane, a gentlewoman, to concoct such a hare-brained scheme without their mistress's blessing was beyond the pale. He considered turning his back on her and storming back to his seat, but that would only invite further attention, spoiling everyone's good time. He had no wish to be confirmed as Simon Danforth, the cardinal's sad-eyed, miserable gentleman.

'You don't like to dance?'

'I have no call to do it. I'm a secretary of the cardinal, not some … courtly creature.'

'But his Grace keeps one of the greatest courts in the land,' said Rowan, pivoting under his raised arm and bobbing low. 'There was a muse of dance, was there not? In the nine muses?'

'Terpsichore,' said Danforth, as the music insisted he draw Rowan in close to him, his arm around her waist. Even in the gloom of torchlight, the whiteness of her dress contrasted starkly with the tan of her skin.

'What is your life like, Mr Danforth?' she asked.

'What?' It was an odd question.

'Are you happy? Doing what you do?'

'Aye, happy enough,' he said. Was he? He did not know.

'Can I tell you what I see?' When Danforth only frowned, she continued. 'I think you are afraid to feel. You should allow yourself.'

There was something uncanny in her dark glare. Intense. 'And you? Are you happy?'

'No. But I will be, one day, I hope.'

They spun together before separating to arm's length, each dipping, as they wound their way around the little stage. It was strange, thought Danforth, how easy it seemed. Ordinarily he was horrifically uncoordinated, muddling his right and his left. But the musicians were surprisingly subtle, keeping things slow enough to follow. They might not be poisoners, he smiled to himself, but they were certainly good performers.

As they moved with what Danforth hoped was a stately elegance, the next couple came close. Danforth saw Martin hesitantly touching his partner. Although her face was hidden, the headdress and build were familiar. It was Diane's mistress, and Queen Marie's chief gentlewoman, Madame LeBoeuf. She moved with surprising grace and agility, her arms stretching, like a great doyenne showing the youngsters how to do it. He felt Rowan laughing at the sight, her body vibrating. The lust-filled older woman, he thought, half-smiling. A mainstay of literature, the bawdy, ageing dame preying on young men: the wife of Bath. What others were there? The sweet virgin, pure and innocent. The duplicitous temptress, dark and beguiling. The shrew, full of vinegar. What was the woman with whom he was dancing, he wondered. As he let go, he could not be sure. She seemed to fit no script, with her hard exterior and eyes that seemed to melt from mockery to softness.

He let the thought dangle and then brushed it away. Distraction. There would be time enough to consider the merits of women after the grisly business at hand had been resolved. If then. He was in danger of becoming a dreamy-eyed fool, like

Martin. That was not how he had fashioned himself.

The swell of instruments signalled that the opening dance was reaching its climax and so, as he watched what the other couples were doing out of the corner of his eye, Danforth grasped Rowan lightly around the middle and hoisted her in the air. He could sense Martin struggling likewise with Madame LeBoeuf.

'Thank you, Mr Danforth,' said Rowan, 'for the dance.'

'Please, call me Simon.'

'Thank you, Simon,' she smiled. 'Now I must go.'

'Go? Where?'

'Home. I wanted one dance. Just one. To be part of everything, no one knowing what – who – I am. Now I must get back to my da', make sure he fares well.'

'A faithful Antigone.'

'Antig ... hopefully not making her end!' laughed Rowan. And then she was gone, a whirl of white. Only when she had departed did Danforth think to wonder whether or not she might be allowed to leave the palace. He supposed she would, a lone woman who was part of the revels.

***

The play followed, much as Danforth had suspected it would: a bizarre affair starring the spit-boys guised, somewhat badly, as Robin Hood and Little John, outwitting a cowardly Sheriff of Nottingham, played by another servant wearing, Danforth noticed, the colours of the Hamiltons. He capered around, falling and cowering, under the direction of a fourth, who was attired as King John, the padding and false red beard instead suggesting Henry VIII.

Queen Marie, thought Danforth, was a woman of not a little wit. The murmurings of the men in front of him, though, might have offered some doubt as to her judgement. The vagaries of politics!

Throughout the performance, Martin kept up a stream of chatter, sometimes to Forrest's boy, sometimes to no one in particular. 'See that!'; 'Behind you!'; 'Hisssss'; 'Halloooo!'; 'Look, here comes the fool!'

'I can do without the chorus, thank you,' whispered Danforth. There was little quite as irritating as someone who talked throughout a performance.

'Ugh,' said Martin, flopping back on the bench. 'I wish they'd decide if it's a comedy or a romance. I don't know what this is. We need a little tragedy.'

Danforth nodded tightly, turning his attention from the stage, where the sheriff's purse was being cut loose from behind by Robin Hood whilst Little John was talking to him. King John was at the same time spouting verse. It was impossible to follow, so much happening at the same time. 'Aye,' said Danforth, speaking over Forrest's boy, who had fallen asleep. 'No regard for unity of action or any other.'

'Woah, look there, sir!' Martin shouted, making Danforth jump. 'The sheriff gets it!' On the stage, one of the spit-boys had stabbed the Sheriff of Nottingham. The actor fell to the ground, ruining the effect by shifting to a more comfortable position. 'Finally we have some tragedy.'

Danforth chuckled. 'Aye, Arnaud. In his youth every boy wants a comedy. As he grows he fancies a touch of romance. And then, when he ages, he looks for tragedy.'

'Shhhh,' said Martin, putting a finger over his lips before laughing. 'I jest. You and Rowan danced well together. Looked good. What was she saying?'

'Oh, some womanish nonsense about happiness. What did your partner have to say?'

'Ha! That dame. You know what she said? That her husband was away. Alan doesn't mind what I do,' he mimicked.

'Shocking,' said Danforth, a slight smile playing over his lips.

The play stuttered its way towards its anti-climax, the young players seemingly improvising their lines, the audience shouting throughout for them to speak up. Still, the room seemed to Danforth to be good-natured, the people enjoying themselves. They enjoyed it more so when the performance ended with a group version of a song that seemed comprised entirely of the words, 'trip and go, hey' and 'hey trolly lolly love is jolly', joining in with the actors. That was the purpose of such entertainments. They relived the pressure on people, took their minds off of their own problems and focussed them elsewhere. Queen Marie had been wise to arrange it.

The actors retreated to their benches in the back rows of either side of the great hall, the domestic servants already seated there clapping their backs. Thereafter began another series of poetry readings from a number of the Hamilton and Douglas men, finally having their chance to take part in the festivities. One huge bearded man spoke in a high-pitched voice, reciting Dunbar.

Sweet rose of virtue and of gentleness,
delightful lily of youthful wantonness,
richest in bounty and in beauty clear
and in every virtue that is held most dear,
except only ... that you are merciless.

Into your garden, today, I followed you;
there I saw flowers of freshest hue,
both white and red, delightful to see,
and wholesome herbs, waving resplendently,
yet nowhere, one leaf or flower of rue.

I fear that March with his last arctic blast
has slain my fair rose of pallid and gentle cast,
whose piteous death does my heart such pain
that, if I could, I would compose her roots again,
so comforting her bowering leaves have been.

The words of love and beauty had their charmed effect. Danforth noticed immediately that men and women about the hall began to pair off and drift away, from the domestic servants in the back rows to the household staff in the middle and the Hamilton and Douglas notables at the front. The room did not empty immediately, but rather seemed to thin, as couples took advantage of the darkness to leave the great hall or to secrete themselves behind the curtained embrasures.

'Is that it?' asked Martin. 'Shouldn't a dance close the day?' Before Danforth could reply, the musicians did indeed strike up another tune, and some couples stood to dance. Before they could get into their steps, though, a blazing light filled the doorway of the great hall. Both he and Martin turned to it, shielding their eyes. Danforth had the fleeting impression of a small figure, all alight, waving its arms. Gasps rose from the assembled throats. 'Squibs?' asked Martin. 'Her Highness has squibs? I've heard of them, you can't put them up in–' Before he could finish, the gasps sounding from nearer the entrance had turned to screams. The entire company jumped to their feet, people standing on the benches, others pushing forward. Danforth chanced a glance towards the dais; Queen Marie was on her feet, trying to see what was happening whilst being hustled out of her private door by some ladies.

He launched himself upwards, pushing past the sleeping child, who murmured groggily at the commotion, past Martin. On, he pushed past the others in his row: the Master Cook, Marshall; Gibb, the jolly Horse Master. Still the light blazed, rose, was stifled, rose again. Still the screaming went on. At last he reached the doorway, just as the flames were pressed down and out. 'Jesus Christ,' he shouted. His words were drowned out. 'That's no squib. That's a man.'

He pushed his way through the ring of people encircling the figure. Some had removed their cloaks and used them to smother the flames, stamping and kicking. 'Is it dead?' a woman was shrieking. 'Becalm yourself, Bess, there's no fire now!' said her companion.

Reaching down, Danforth plucked at a singed cloak, pulling it up and casting it away. He squinted. At that moment someone opened curtains. Light spilled into the great hall. He found himself looking at a charred body, the skin burnt red and black. It was a small person. The remains of livery stood out, not totally burned away. It was a royal tabard, made for a page. It was Mathieu.

20

Martin was crouched on the floor, squeezing the boy's hand. 'Fetch someone,' he was screaming up at Danforth, at the whole assembled group. 'I don't care, get the fucking *physician*!'

'He's gone,' whispered Danforth, getting down on one knee himself. 'He's gone.' He cast one last look at the dead boy and then crossed himself, standing back up.

'Stay here, all of you,' he cried out into the hall. 'None leave.' A shocked muttering started up, and Danforth looked around at the ocean of faces. He turned his back on them, stepped away from Martin and Mathieu, and out into the short hall. It was clear. He crossed it and entered the kitchen. Inside, pandemonium reigned. The fire still blazed, the little room its usual furnace. His eyes followed the carnage as he attempted to work out what had happened. Some silver trays lay on the floor, comfits spilling jam and wine goblets leaving pools of claret. In the midst of them was a short knife. He chanced a look over at the wall cabinet, filled but for one. He leant to one of the claret puddles and dipped a finger, lifting it to his nostril. The sharp sting of metal. Mathieu, it appeared, had been stabbed, the force of the blow used to push him into the great open fire, no spit set up to block his path. Then he had staggered, aflame, out of the room and into the great hall, knocking at things as he went.

What monster could have done this?

'Mr Danforth, whit's it a' aboot?' barked a rough voice. He turned, to see the bulk of the cook, Marshall, filling the doorway.

'I said no one leave,' he barked, his voice hoarse. Marshall simply held up his hands.

'Someone is away to fetch guards.'

'Where were the guards?' rasped Danforth. But he knew. They were stationed around the queen and outside the palace. Stopping anyone getting in or out. If they were doing their jobs properly, that meant that the murderer walked amongst them. He was in the place when the play was being performed.

'Here, whit's this?'

'What?'

Marshall had come into the room and was staring down at the scarred wooden table. 'Something,' he shrugged. 'I didnae write this.'

Danforth turned and joined him. Part of the table was sheeted with a fine layer of flour. Into it, someone had traced the words, 'REMEMBER JANET GLAMIS SO END THE STEWART MURTHERERS ED'BURGH 1537'. Danforth shivered. Again, the murderer had left them with a note. Janet Douglas, Lady Glamis, had been burned to death by James V on the esplanade of Edinburgh Castle in 1537. She had been accused of witchcraft, but it had always been whispered that she had been a victim of the king's hatred of the Douglas clan. She was sister to the Douglas brothers who were now in the pay of King Henry, who were even now pulling the string's of the lord protector.

Danforth committed the message to memory and then wiped it away with one arm. 'Why did ye do that?' asked the cook. 'The depute will–'

'Say nothing of this,' said Danforth. 'The Douglas men out there might make trouble if it reaches their ears. If they think they are accused of some act of vengeance. Forget it.' Marshall gave him a doubtful look but rubbed his bald head and shrugged. Danforth stepped past him, intending to go back into the great hall, to wrench Martin away from the corpse of his young friend. His path was stopped by Diane, her face flushed.

'What are you doing out here?' he snapped.

'Men came down,' she panted. 'Saying someone had been in an accident.'

'Aye?'

'But … but … Mr Guthrie … the dowager's usher …'

'Spit it out, woman!'

'I think he's dead! Slain!'

Danforth put his head in his hands. A tide of weariness swept over him, sudden and strong. The weight of it pulled him down. The whole place was insane. The whole country. Too much was happening too quickly, and he felt his head swimming as he tried to make sense of it. 'What happened?'

'I don't know. He was pushed down the stairs, I think. Lying at the bottom. Some men were tending him as I came up.'

'And why were you downstairs?'

'I was taken down by a Douglas brute,' she cried. 'I didn't want to, but he dragged me. After the play. I am just after slapping his face and running off.'

'I … see. Go inside, mistress.' Danforth took her shoulders and steered her into the great hall. 'Don't look. The dowager's page has had an accident, young Mathieu. I fear … I fear he is dead.' Danforth felt the word catch in his throat, his eyes pricking. There had been too much death, but somehow it had all been abstract. Fraser, the infected man, even the attempt on Martin's life. This, though, was an affront, a monstrous abomination.

Colour had fled Diane's face and she stiffened under his grasp, entering the great hall ahead of him like a sleepwalker. Danforth released her into the room, and took up Martin, who was still hunched over the dead boy, now thankfully covered. He led him outside and turned to him. 'Be strong, Arnaud. Get the little Forrest boy tended to, have some woman look after him.' Tears had left twin furrow down the younger man's face, but when he spoke his voice was firm. 'I'm going to kill him,' he said. 'The hell with it, Simon. I'm going to kill the bastard myself.'

***

They cleared the great hall with difficulty but were eventually left alone with the boy's corpse. Danforth was intent on examining the body, but before doing so, he bid Martin wait outside for him, ostensibly to stop anyone from interrupting. His friend did so without objection.

The smell of burning flesh had mingled with the perfume in the air, souring it. The sudden silence in the great space was unsettling. Around the stage and the benches, dropped comfits and cakes splattered the rushes, and every movement he made echoed. He removed the white sheet from the lumpen form and immediately closed his eyes, steeling himself to look again.

All of the exposed skin was blistered and crackled. Most of the boy's hair had been blackened, his little cap fusing to it. Yet, if what it looked like in the kitchen were true, he should not have died so quickly. Danforth rolled up one of Mathieu's sleeves. It was still warm. The skin underneath it was still white – whiter even than usual. He lifted the front of the tabard, stiff from the heat but tarry. Underneath, a thin cut stood out on the chalky skin. The paleness, knew, was what sometimes came over the body during extreme moments of shock. The pupils of his eyes, startlingly blue in the craterous expanse of ravaged flesh, told the same story.

Danforth crossed himself – a thank you to God. Mathieu had not died the agonising death of burning. Rather, the short blow to his stomach and the shock of the sudden immolation had been too much for him. As he had staggered from the room, bleeding from the gut, his clothing and exposed skin torched, his little body had shut down. Still, though it was a mercy, the terror in those few minutes must have been unimaginable. Danforth thought of Hercules, burning on his pyre. Of Janet Douglas, whom he had been commanded to think about. Of the Forrest man who might have been kin to the depute of the guard. All must have felt the intense heat of the flames as it shrivelled their skin. None had been granted a swift exit, a punctured gut or the blessing of sudden shock.

Who could do this to a child?

Danforth felt around the boy's clothing, inside it, searching for pockets. His fingers closed on a piece of paper. Inhaling sharply – and then regretting it – he withdrew it. It had escaped unscathed, and he held it up.

Mathieu, I have a book on soldiery but it is stolen from the library and must be our secret meet me in the kitchen alone and I will give you the said book make sure you are not seen.

The lopsided script was identical to that written on the letter to Kerr. There was no signature. Danforth put the note in his own pocket. So, the boy had been lured to his death. It was no opportunistic killing, no selection based on bad luck, but a carefully-laid plan. But why the boy? What had he known? He reached again into the tabard, feeling a little lump. His heart leapt, but as he pulled it out, he realised it was only the little thistle badge Martin's mother had given the boy as a present. On impulse, he took the child's hand and squeezed it. A single tear rolled down his cheek and he blinked it away. It was foolish. He had seen death enough to know that tears solved nothing. He had barely known Mathieu. The boy was now speeded towards eternal life in a world free of sin. He covered him over again and stood up. Before leaving, he cast one last look at the great hall, from the abandoned stage and vanished audience to the rafters. Revels over indeed, he thought, before turning his back on the room to join Martin.

'What is it?' he asked as soon as Danforth closed the door. 'What did you see?'

'The boy did not suffer as he might have done. The end, when it came, was swift. God took him in His arms without … without the thing being prolonged. Yet … our killer took no chances. The boy was struck in the belly, a blow sure to kill. The fire … it … it was for display. Again.'

'Who did it?'

Danforth took a long look at Martin's face. A film of sweat glistened on his brow. His left eye was twitching, his jaw clenching and unclenching. 'That I cannot yet say.'

'But you will? I mean, don't you have – I don't know – some list of people who might be murderers? Some list of people who might have done this?' Martin's hands clutched at the jewelled buttons on his doublet. 'You must!' he spat, almost accusingly. 'You must have something, goddammit!'

'Such a list would perforce include every person in this place,' said Danforth, trying to keep his tone even. His friend, it was clear, was agitated beyond reason. Yet that did not excuse him. He himself had been the one to handle the corpse, to look upon it for evidence. The younger man's wild-eyed impatience, his lack of feeling, was pure selfishness. Again, Danforth had the odd feeling that he was viewed by others as a cold fish.

'Did you discover anything?' hissed Martin.

'Only that the boy died without pain, after the first shock.'

'Whoever gave him that first shock, Simon – I'm going to flay them alive. I've going to rip out their fingernails with red hot pincers.'

'Peace, now, Arnaud. We will find him.' Without speaking further, he passed over the thistle badge. It caught the light of the passage briefly before Martin gripped it, shoving it deep into his own pocket.

Danforth did not add that the finding of the note – something Martin need not know about – changed a great deal. In leaving it to be found, the killer had revealed himself as a strategist. If he had a plan, then that plan had a definite goal. Definite goals could always be found.

***

Guthrie was not, as Diane had worried, dead. Instead he was propped up on a bed in the wine cellar under the royal apartments, attended on by a number of people and seemingly enjoying himself as they hung on his every word. One arm was in a sling, like Martin's, and one foot was heavily bound. His face lit up further when Danforth entered the room. Dozens of candles gave him the appearance of a religious figure, surrounded by acolytes, and crosses and medals of various sizes were dotted around the bed and walls. He and Martin joined the throng. 'Go out, all of you. On the queen dowager's command,' said Danforth.

Dirty looks were thrown in his direction as the folk filed out. Guthrie sank back on the bed, disappointment flooding his ruddy features. 'What happened to you?' asked Martin.

'I was assaulted,' said Guthrie, 'by an evil spirit.' He paused as though letting the drama of the words sink in.

'What happened,' echoed Danforth without expression.

'I was coming upstairs.'

'Why were you downstairs?'

'I was checking on the apartments above us,' said Guthrie, frowning. 'You can't leave the royal rooms unattended, leastways I can't, play or no play, not for long anyway. The young lasses will tempt the lads into all kinds. By the saints, some of the young lads will tempt some of the older ones. Devilry, I've told you. I've told everyone, and none listen. Anyway, I was coming back up, back to the great hall, and there it was, right in front of me. A demon all in blue. Right before me. I just saw little white shoes and the skirl of blue, well, you know they say that the devil dances mad jigs in hell, and before I could cry out it shoved me. Hard. Right back down the stairs. And I fainted away dead in fright. Wouldn't you?'

'You seem,' said Martin, 'well enough.' Danforth was barely listening to the man's rambling, his eyes turned to a stitched embroidery of the virgin nailed up on the wall.

'You reckon? That demon near broke my arm and my ankle. But the physician says they're sprained, so I can be up and helping you fellows fight the devil as soon as I can put weight on my foot.' He raised his sling proudly, before his features darkened. 'Touched me, it did, and I've been all day trying to ward off the evils of it. And the scare of it, the terror, you know thon way? I've had some claret from over there, though. Fair revived me. Heh. One good thing about being forced to dwell in this pit. Tell me is it true that someone was killed?'

'Mathieu,' said Martin, putting a hand to his forehead. 'The queen's page.'

'No.' Guthrie sank even further into his cushions. 'No. It must have been an accident.'

'No accident,' said Danforth. 'The boy was pushed into the fire. In the kitchen. And it was not a devil, not a ghost, but a man that did it.'

At this, Guthrie turned white. And then tears formed in his eyes. 'You mean the creature who attacked me was the murderer? The possessed creature who killed your friend? Oh, Jesus Christ preserve us. Mr Danforth, Mr Martin, I … that poor boy. He was a good boy. You see what's happening?' Hysteria tinged his voice. 'You see? You need to get your master to reinstate the mass. This whole country is going to the devil, snatching folk up in his claws!'

'Hold your peace,' said Martin. 'He was a good boy, that's right enough. And I'll be revenged on him.'

'Not,' said Guthrie, 'if I'm first. This bastard has thrust now not just at your household, but at mine. That bairn was one of mine, one of ours in her Highness' care.'

'How do you propose on doing that?' asked Danforth.

'Oh, I have my ways,' said Guthrie. He had grasped his crucifix. Alongside it he had hung wooden rosary beads. With his other hand he gestured around the dank room at the candles and charms. 'When the devil comes into a place, he must be fought. If I lay hands on this possessed creature, I'll flay Satan out of him. With this, and these.'

A thought had struck Danforth, though. 'Do you recall, Mr Guthrie, when I was speeding from the dowager's chamber yesterday? You said you wished a word with me.' He had forgotten his own golden rule: that tiresome gossips had big mouths but bigger ears. 'What was that about, sir?'

Guthrie's brow knitted. 'Oh aye! I was going to ask if you'd read today, at the close of the interlude, you know, after the play had finished. Doesn't seem important now, I guess, not with this madman running loose, killing and bringing terror. Have you spoken with the dowager yet, gentlemen? What is she saying to it?'

Shaking his head in frustration, Danforth left the man, Martin following. Into the vacuum, the waiting curiosity-seekers flocked back.

***

Queen Marie did not offer either Danforth or Martin cushions. Instead, she paced her chamber, muttering in French, before addressing them. Her eyes, Danforth noticed, were red-rimmed, but the tears had been staunched. 'It must be that it was some accident. Oui, I shall write his parents in France, poor souls, that he has met with an accident. And pray that they do not wish to come here to this madness, this realm of spirits and devils. That is what you must say, it is what we must frame ourselves to. If it is known what goes on … my child will be taken from me by force, for her protection. And,' she added, 'I wonder now if that might not be best!'

'Your Highness,' chanced Danforth, 'we know the weapon used on Mr Fraser. We know that the boy was slain in the fire, the murderer fleeing downstairs.'

'And out,' she cried, 'out into the great blue sky! Mr Forrest tells me that no one saw him enter the courtyard. He fled downstairs and disappeared, like a ghost indeed! This spirit kills my page and assaults my usher and no one sees anything. It may be that it passes through walls, passes up to where my child sleeps.'

Danforth cleared his throat. 'No one confesses to having seen where he went, madam. Men and women went downstairs and upstairs to find places to kiss and ... lord knows what else.'

'Ha! You sound like Forrest. Passions inflamed by all that lewd bawdry, he said. No man or woman willing to admit what they have seen lest they be caught in some tryst.' He kept his head down, determined to endure the royal displeasure with equanimity. He had no choice. 'And my boy, my boy ... if one is struck belonging to my household, then all is lost. None safe.'

'There was a message, my lady,' Danforth half-whispered. 'I ... it warned of the dangers of Edinburgh. It spoke of Lady Glamis. Burned to death back in the year–'

'1537,' she snapped. 'The year before I was wed. And so my daughter and I pay for the misdeeds of my husband.' She sat down, making a fist and putting her forehead to it. 'A Douglas plot, perhaps?'

'Madam, I think not,' said Danforth.

She looked up sharply. 'Why not? The message is clear enough.'

'Too clear, I think. It might be that it was to make us think that the Douglas men – or even their friends the Hamilton men – were behind this.'

'If not, then who? Either the devil himself or one he has taken in thrall. *Who*?'

'I cannot say. Not yet.'

'You can never say.' She threw her head back. 'I have charged you with bringing this man to good Christian justice, and you have failed to deliver him. You have been – *what* have you been doing – whilst this monster of nature stalks my halls and kills my people, frightens and bedevils them?'

'We have been,' started Martin, but she cut him off.

'You have been eating from my table and finding his bloody footprints. Still you cannot tell me who he is or why he acts!'

'We shall,' said Danforth, looking up, his face shining. 'His bloody footprints cannot last. They shall lead to him We shall find him.'

'And then,' Martin added, 'I shall kill him.'

A knock at the door made them all start. Forrest entered, dragging a half-dressed priest. 'Found him, your Highness. He didn't want to come.'

'Good day, father,' she said. The emotional outpour had ceased, and her voice had taken on a light, almost serene sound. 'I thank you for coming.' The priest dropped to his knees, mumbling obeisance. 'We have,' she went on, 'had a most unfortunate accident in this place. One of our most beloved servants has been taken to God. We would have him buried straightaway, with all proper honours.'

At this, the priest looked up, and drew air through his teeth. 'Cannae, yer Highness. Cannae be daein that. No services until the cardinal's at liberty. We've the ordnances fae Rome, and we–'

'Listen to me, father,' said Marie. The serenity had been replaced with a thin blade of steel. 'Our boy – *my* boy – was a good and faithful Christian. He died ... he died a good and faithful Catholic child. Whether Rome, or these men's master', she gestured towards Danforth and Martin, 'says otherwise, I will have my boy laid to his eternal rest with the full honours and glory of God. Do you understand me? I advise you to understand it well, father. Or else you will repent of it.'

The priest's mouth fell open. He looked towards Martin and Danforth for support, but they kept their heads bent. 'There,' she said. 'You see? The lord cardinal's men have no objection. You will say mass for my boy's soul. You will speed him on his way with all godliness. Now go and prepare. I wish him at his rest forthwith. Go!'

He fled, nodding and mumbling again. If a little of the gilding of the royal presence had been tarnished by the dowager's displeasure, she restored it with her show of steel. If there was one thing that Frenchwomen could not be faulted for, thought Danforth, it was their mastery of elegant, imperious anger.

'Now, gentlemen,' said Marie. 'My little Mathieu shall be put to bed forever on the morrow. And on the morrow I shall decide what is to be done. Come to me again tomorrow evening. I shall give you no longer before I act. Use the time well. You have my leave.'

They left her presence. Martin's face was shining with determination. Danforth was wondering exactly what the dowager had meant by 'deciding what is to be done'.

21

They sat inside St Michael's church, listening to the harsh bark of Latin from the unwilling priest. A fresh grave had been dug outside, the sexton presumably working throughout the cold night. After their meeting with Queen Marie the previous evening, Martin had been eager to be out, to spend the evening hunting their prey, to be searching. Danforth, however, had refused him. He insisted that Martin must rest his injured arm, despite the time limit given them. His friend had refused, and eventually went off to join the dirge in the dowager's rooms, that grotesque outpouring of grief that presaged the requiem mass. That worked for Danforth too. Privately, he had needed time to think.

He had counted the bodies that had thus far piled up. Fraser, killed in approximation of the deaths of Margaret of Denmark and Sir James Hamilton of Finnart, victims of James III and James V. Mathieu, killed in approximation of Janet Douglas, Lady Glamis, victim of James V. Though they had survived, Martin and Geordie Simms, wounded in approximation of James IV, whom many said was the victim of his own great folly, his desire to be at the foremost of any fighting.

And the perpetrator. What was known about him? He favoured stalking and killing in the garb of a well-known spirit of the palace. He clearly knew his history. He was motivated by some vengeance against the Stewart family, and directly threatened the life of the baby queen. He had just proven that he would kill a child. Their man liked spectacle, he liked show. If only he would show himself.

Something in this case was different from every other that he had seen. Even living in London, working under the coroner, the bodies had been beaten, stabbed, strangled – but ultimately they had been either hidden or left where they fell. In Scotland, too, killers would either seek to hide their victims or leave them where they dropped, hiding themselves instead. Here, though, this creature wanted the poor, slain folk seen. He advertised.

There was something in that. For the first time, Danforth let the possibility of devilry enter his mind. He did not doubt for a moment that the devil existed. In fact, he had long contemplated writing a treatise on the existence of evil, theorising that the world was a great tapestry spun by God, stretching into eternity. Devils were outside that tapestry, outside God, but they could pull and tear at the men and women stitched into it. If the devil did have a role to play in this, and he must, as surely as God must direct them in solving it, he was twitching at someone's string, making them dance to his wicked tune.

As he had lain in his hammock, thinking, he had watched the candle in his and Martin's chamber burn down. The darkness, when it came, was absolute.

The dark thought brought him back to the church. How bare it looked, in the wintry morning light. Stark. To think he had been desperate to see inside, to cast his eyes over the famed twenty-four altars. But not like this. He chanced a glimpse over to the wall, where was painted a vivid image of sinners being tormented in hell flames, their eyes rolled back in their heads, the demons at their feet grinning. Yes, he thought, listening to the words of the requiem. Satan was somewhere out there. The priest droned on.

Lux aeterna luceat eis, Domine,
 cum sanctis tuis in aeternum,
 quia pius es.
 Requiem aeternam dona eis Domine,
 et lux perpetua luceat eis,
 quia pius es.

The words sunk in like healing water, as though he was bathing. Yet they could not wash away the feeling of dread. Since coming to Linlithgow, the whole matter had seemed a jape, a grand puzzle. A political murder of a man he detested. Even Martin's shooting, whilst making things more dangerous, had turned out to be of little consequence. The infected man was vile, an affront, but it was never likely to have been successful – it was a stunt. But, hearing the words of death intoned over a child's corpse: this was too dark. He let his gaze slide towards Martin, sitting stiffly at his side. What is it he had said at the masque? We need a tragedy. Well, he had one. He wondered at what the words were doing to his friend. Martin, he knew, had a soft spot for the young. In other circumstances it was almost endearing, but in the present, it might lead to a lapse in judgement. Hopefully his mind was not truly turned to vengeance; he had cured him of that vice in Stirling.

If Martin was focused on violent retribution, well … sensing that, a devil might pull his thread yet.

**

Martin, for his part, had stopped listening to the words of the mass midway through the *Dies Irae*. There, his mind had leapt on the words, translated rapidly, as 'when the judge takes his seat

all that is hidden shall appear. Nothing will remain unavenged'. There was a beautiful, deadly assuredness about them. He had no doubt now that Danforth would find the killer. He had always done so before. This time, though, he would not balk at the idea of the murderer being slain. This was different. The little boy's death had changed everything.

The night before, as he had stood in the dowager's inner chamber, amidst a sea of crying men and women, he had sensed it. Certainly, he thought, some of their grief was feigned. What did they care for a royal servant, a faceless page? But his own was not. Mathieu had been an innocent. He had hoped to be a soldier, much as Martin himself had once done. The murderer had taken that away from him, robbed a family, still ignorant of the fact, of their boy. There could be no forgiveness this time, nor even a turning away whilst proper justice was done. When Danforth pulled off the blue cloak, he was going to be there with his dagger. As he had walked away from the dirge, back through the silent halls of the palace, down the dark stairs, each step had brought fewer angry tears and more determination. He had been almost willing the murderer to appear with his gun, to grapple with him. It was no longer time for tears – the dirge had done its work and released them.

The priest had reached his crescendo. He had, Martin noticed, finally begun to inject some vibrance into the Latin, as he intoned, 'let everlasting light shine upon them, Lord, with Thy saints for ever, for Thou art merciful. Grant them eternal rest, Lord, and let perpetual light shine upon them,

for Thou art merciful.'

But there could be no mercy. Not after this. At the dirge, dozens of voices had cried out against mercy. They had cried out for retribution. Because this time, the enemy was not some corrupted doctor, not a mad person, not a shiftless criminal.

This time, it was the devil.

***

There had been no time for the carpenters to fashion a coffin for the child, not with the dowager's insistence that he be put to the ground honourably and immediately. Thus it was that Mathieu's corpse had been forced into an old chest, one that had been used for storing cloth for the masque. There was something obscene about the cheap little wooden crate. There was something obscene about life in the palace going on without the boy. But it must. To Danforth, it seemed impossible that that had only taken place the day before; less than twenty-four hours ago, he had danced with Rowan Allen, watched a couple of boys not much younger than Mathieu caper around a stage.

The dowager did not stay for the burial but was escorted back into the palace after the requiem mass, a towering figure veiled from head to foot in black. Danforth and Martin, however, remained to watch the tiny makeshift casket be lowered into the grave. The digging had brought up the rich, wet scent of earth. Nearby some bluebells were shooting out, despite the odd clump of hard frozen snow that had clung on in the shade of the trees. Spring really was making its presence known. When it truly flowered, Mathieu would not be there to see it. He would be just a memory of the people for whom he had run around, each year dumping a greater weight of forgetting on his grave.

Not for the first time, Danforth wondered what became of the dead, particularly those brought to their end by violence. The poor souls had no time to be shriven, no time to make heir peace with God. Instead, they must arrive in Purgatory in horror, amazed at their new surroundings. He hoped that the innocent, especially, would be understood, forgiven, welcomed quickly into Heaven. The thought of Mathieu, his oversized tabard flying out behind him, racing up to the clouds brought him back to the cold graveyard.

Had the boy known something? Seen something? That could be the only reason for his being lured to death. The note on his body proved that he was not simply in the wrong place at the wrong time. Unless, of course, it was an old note – but he brushed that potential away. The boy had been attacked in the kitchen after being invited to the kitchen. Still, the questions rang in Danforth's head as the group began to mill away. Already, he thought, they were turning their minds to their own lives: to what they were going to do with the rest of their day; to what they were going to eat and drink; to what they might do the next day and the next and the next.

Eventually, only Martin and himself were left. Danforth tentatively put a hand on the younger man's good shoulder. 'We have seen the lad off,' he said. 'We can do no more.'

'What? No more? We can catch the bastard who did this and rip him open.'

Danforth's lips curled downwards. He hoped that Martin was speaking only from the passion of the moment. 'Catch him. Aye, we can catch him. And we have little time. By tonight we must produce something to take before the dowager.'

'Aye, aye – where do we start? What to we do?' Martin was hopping about from foot to foot, eyes blazing.

'I shall go back to the palace. I have some–' Before he could finish, a tumult of noise sounded from the entrance to the palace. A small wave of men and women in the Douglas colours poured out, heading towards the burgh, the odd horse dotted amongst them.

'Where are they going?' asked Martin, peering over Danforth's shoulder.

'I cannot say. To the town, by the look of it. It might be worth taking a walk down there, Arnaud. Follow them. Find out where

190

they are heading and why.'

'What about you?'

'As I said, I wish to go back into the palace. I have some things I wish to follow up.'

Martin smiled, but there was no humour in it. 'Being a riddle again, Simon? It's fine. I trust your mind. Will I get you back up there, or in the burgh?'

'I cannot be certain yet. It will depend on what I discover. At any rate, I shall see you later.'

They parted, Martin joining the throng of Douglas folk beating a path to the town. Danforth sent a silent thanks to God. He did have something he wished to investigate in the palace, but it was a slim chance. And it was one that Martin, in his present euphoria of grief, might compromise.

Once certain his friend had gone, he took one last look at the grave, already having dirt shovelled onto it, crossed himself, and turned his back on the dead boy.

22

Danforth reeled his way up the turnpike stairs, this time in the northwest tower. As ever, the spiral upwards dizzied him, giving him an impression of what it must be like to be at sea. However, he was not bound for the royal apartments. Instead, he had been directed upwards by a limping Guthrie, who was busy lecturing a servant in the courtyard. All he could make out was 'Old Nick himself, the very devil, done up in the garb of St Andrew! I've said it time and again, the heretics bring devils amongst us! Saw it myself!' He offered a silent look of sympathy to the servant, tempered with thanks. It did not surprise him to see Guthrie already on his feet; not when there appeared to be so much activity caused by the flight of some of the dowager's guests.

He found Mathieu's chamber with ease. Someone had hung a black cloth over the lintel. Ignoring it, he pushed his way in. He was unsure what he expected to find. Some note, hastily scribbled, perhaps. Or more likely nothing.

The little cell was barren save for a hammock and box – it was like a smaller version of Danforth and Martin's own chamber. Yet, Danforth recalled, the boy had said something about 'hidey-holes', about keeping his things under his bed. Danforth inspected the hammock, but there was nothing in or under it. As he ducked to look under, though, he felt the floor under him rock slightly. Edging his foot around it, he felt how loose it was, and, prying, he was able to lift up one of the flat stones. Beneath it was a hollowed-out space, a thin manual on soldiering laid out in it. The manual's cushion, though, was not hard-packed earth. Danforth drew breath. It was a folded blue cloak.

***

Martin hovered around the posse of Douglases, all of them chattering animatedly, none of them paying him the slightest attention. As he hurried along down the slope to the town, he caught snatches here and there of conversation. 'Bloody madness'; 'say nothing'; 'I told you it was a cursed place, cursed since Flodden'; 'breathe not a word to anyone outside – don't want the blame of any of this, let the Hamilton lot suffer it'.

He waited around the market cross. For the first time, he had no thought at all of meeting Marion Muir, by accident or otherwise. Instead, his eyes were trained on what the various Douglases were doing. Some disappeared to reappear with horses, and gradually they drew together in knots, embracing and breaking up. It was clear to him that they were fleeing Linlithgow, palace and town. Something had spooked them. Whether it was the stories of ghouls and demons or the possibility of being implicated in some shady business aimed at the life of Queen Mary, he could not say. He purchased an apple from a street vendor and, as he munched, he saw Cam Hardie peep out of the door of an inn, call for news, and then disappear back inside. Tossing the core into the open sewer channel, he crossed to the inn.

Ignoring the questions of the innkeeper, Martin barrelled up the rickety wooden stairs two at a time and battered on the first door he reached. To his disgust, the priest who had conducted the funeral service opened it, stripped to the waist. A woman's voice drifted out. 'Tell them to bugger off.' Ordinarily, Martin would have been amused, but not today. Before he could exchange a word with the priest, Hardie's sneering voice reached him from further down the hall. He turned towards it, letting the priest close the door on his shame.

'Mr Martin. How's the eye?' As Martin turned, he added, 'Oh – I see it's turned yellow. Well, remind me one day to give your other eye a matching colour.'

'It'll be a cold day in hell when you lay hands on me, Hardie. If you want to fight, I'll fight you, I swear to God. Wound or no wound, I'm in just the mood.'

'Well I'm not,' yawned Hardie. 'You'll have to wait until next we meet.'

Martin had stepped down the hall, to where Hardie was lounging against the frame. His blonde hair was squashed down

193

by a great feathered hat, and a travelling cloak was draped over his shoulders. 'Oh? And where are you going?'

Hardie shrugged. 'Away from this dump. The Douglases,' he said with a flourish, 'are moving out. You and the Hamiltons are welcome to this cursed town and that cursed palace. If you lot wish to consort with demons and tangle with sorcery, that's up to you. It's not for us. And I tell you this for free – if those Hamiltons up there are double-crossing us, we shall know of it. If that madness in the palace is some, some scheme to slander and dishonour our noble house … well, they'll be sorry.'

'So,' said Martin. 'You're fleeing right enough. Cowards.' His lip curled in a smile. If the two factions of political men were ready to turn on one another through suspicion, that was fine with him. It would please the cardinal too.

Expecting – hoping for – anger, Martin was disappointed when Hardie barked out jagged laughter. 'Cowards? What have I got to fear? What do any of us have to fear? We're Douglases, of that ancient and noble House. If I'm threatened, I'll have twenty men at my back, daggers drawn and blood up. Who's at your back, Martin? Yon useless English pish-stain?'

'I can fight my own battles.'

'Aye? Aye, looks like it. Don't forget, I've seen you struck down and led away crying like a lassie.'

'I did not cry,' said Martin. 'I … your friend has no honour. He struck me without call, without warning. It was done dishonourably.'

'Is that so? Let's see what he thinks of that. Here, Geordie – Martin here is looking for another square go.' He stepped back, letting the squat Simms fill the doorway.

'Fuck off,' he growled. 'When I'm at myself, that's when I'll come back and finish you. You'll see us again.' With that, he slammed the door in Martin's face.

***

Danforth had hidden the blue cloak under his own robe and furtively made it back to his own chamber. There he had stowed it under Martin's pillow, unsure what to do next. It made no sense. At first, he wondered if Mathieu had somehow been

194

involved, throwing himself into the fire, or even really falling in by accident. Reason intervened. Whoever was wearing the thing had bolted downstairs, past Guthrie, and presumably taken it off *en route*. He might have hidden it amongst Mathieu's things at any point afterwards. The boy had made no secret of his hiding place.

Before burying under the pillow, Danforth had felt the thing, stretching it, stroking it. He had considered putting it on to try out the size, but something about it repulsed him. It had been in this that the murderer had slain a child. It might have been in this that he had shot Martin. It might also have been in this that he had butchered Fraser's corpse.

But had it? The infected man had been in a blue cloak too, sent care of 'St Andrew'. Was it the same one? No, thought Danforth, kneading his temple. Forrest had stabbed that man through the heart, killing him. Then servants had covered up the corpse and removed it to be slung into the loch or burned. True, he had not seen that done. Yet no one would dive into a loch to strip a diseased corpse or be able to spirit it away before the flames touched it. No one human, anyway. He killed off that thought before it could grow. No, this was a different robe. The murderer must have had more than one. That meant … what did that mean? He reached under the pillow again and ran a finger along the cloth. He had felt similar material before. Recently.

He left the room, going immediately to the fountain to wash his hands. He heard a shrill voice call his name and cursed at the thought of Guthrie getting hold of him. It was almost a pleasure to find Diane saluting him.

She crossed to him, still in the sombre dress she had worn when she accompanied the dowager to the funeral. 'A sad day,' she was saying. 'A truly day.'

'Aye, mistress. It is that. How does the dowager fare?'

'Not well, I fear. This news has come near to breaking her, on top of everything else. And now the Douglases are fleeing.' She lowered her voice. 'We're all of us glad to see that rabble gone. Spies, they were, reporting on her Highness to their wicked old masters. Yet it looks bad. They might say anything. That the dowager has lost control of her house. That her daughter must be taken from her by force. She is scared. Bad.'

It was bad. If the dowager was getting to breaking point, she really would have no patience left. Danforth felt the urge to spit at the name Douglas – an action he deplored. Worthless, spying lackies – it made giving service to a master … dishonourable. Ugly. Hitherto he had thought there no higher station than giving loyalty to one's betters. These men – and women – made a mockery of that. Made a mockery of him, and all he had ever stood for.

He would have to move quickly. He gave Diane a long look, before smiling. It was almost like she had been sent from God. He had remembered where he had felt the material used in the blue cloak before. 'I wonder, mistress, if you would like to walk into the burgh?'

'Yes,' she said, without hesitation. 'Oui, indeed. I … this place, Mr Danforth. It has become so … I do not know how you say it. I cannot think of a word bad enough.'

'Haunted.'

'Worse than that. That little boy, our Mathieu. He was no hazard to anyone. To have made such an end.'

'It is truly horrible.' He touched her shoulder lightly and, to his surprise, she hugged him briefly before drawing back.

'I have said, I try always to look for good in the world. And always I find bad. Will it ever end?'

'As long as there are good people to fight it, yes. Yes, Mistress Beauterne, I think it will end.'

Together they walked away from the fountain. The sun had broken through the clouds, sending spears of light into the courtyard, turning the yellowed walls and flagstones a glinting gold. Danforth walked with Diane on his arm, his heavy boot-treads slowed to accommodate the lighter step of her slippers.

***

It was the sound of weeping that drew Martin to the house. He didn't know the source, didn't know the house, and yet felt compelled, in his present mood, to join it. An elderly couple were leaving a fine-looking half-timbered house in a street leading off the market cross. Each embraced Rowan Allen before stumbling off, clutching handkerchiefs to their eyes. He crossed to her, holding up his good hand.

'Mistress Allen,' he said. 'What news? Are you well?' Reading the expression on her face, he felt his heart sink. 'Your father,' he said.

'Aye,' she said, all trace of her usual sardonic humour gone. 'He's gone.'

Martin followed her into the house. A short hall opened into a parlour, and her father was laid out on a large side-table, candles surrounding him. Martin tried not to look, but the waxen face drew him irresistibly, the spiderlike hands crossed over his chest seeming to beckon. 'It happened yesterday,' said Rowan, tears falling again. 'When I was at that foolish masque. When I was out making merry, he was dying in his bed. I wasn't here. I should've been here. I wasn't here.'

Martin took her hands, but didn't know what to say, other than, 'I'm sorry.' As though she were a sleepwalker, she poured him wine and pushed him into a seat. He let her, still at loss. Eventually she began to talk, still weeping: about her father, about all that he had done for her, all that he had given her when her real parents, whoever they were, had cast her out. It felt odd, her discussing the dead man in his presence. Martin recalled his own father's body, laid out in his mother's hall, whilst neighbours stopped by to condole. Perhaps, he mused, it had been then that he had developed an aversion towards corpses, a disgust. 'Maman – my mother – she always says it's a world to be out of.' He said when she paused to blow her nose. 'I don't think I agree with that.'

'Me neither.'

'If you don't mind my asking, what will you do now?'

'What will I do now?' she echoed. 'What indeed. I've no idea. I can't think about that now.'

'Do you want to stay in Linlithgow?'

'No,' she said immediately.

'Do you like to travel?'

'I don't know,' she said, looking up into nothing. 'I haven't travelled. But I've no wish to stay here, not without my parents.

So I suppose it doesn't matter whether I like to travel or not.'

'Has he … I mean, will you be …'

'Do you mean have I been left a great fortune? Will I live?' A trace of her smile reappeared, but there was little humour in it. 'Aye, I've been left enough. I knew this was coming, of course, he'd been so ill for so long. But you … even when you know, you just never expect it will be this day or that day.'

'I know,' said Martin. He thought of his own father, who had simply dropped dead whilst riding back from Stirling one day. There had been no warning of that. One day he was there, rosy-cheeked and full of Gallic life and charm, and the next day the entire family simply had to get along without him. 'It is never an easy thing, losing someone you love.'

'I did love him,' said Rowan, her voice catching. 'I loved both of them. I'm alone in the world now. Can you imagine, Arnaud – I'm near twenty-six and I feel like an orphan child. No one warns you of that.'

'I'm truly sorry, mistress.'

'Call me Rowan, please.'

'Yes. I'm sorry. But this will pass. I've lost my father too. It … each day, each week, you know, it gets easier. You start to be able to joke about them even – the things the might've said if they were still around at any time. Remembering the daft things they did. The grief passes. The dolour.'

'Aye, I know. It did with my ma'. But not tomorrow, or the day after. I don't even know – I've no idea what to do about the funeral or anything. With the mass off still. Who do I talk to?'

Martin was about to say, 'the parish priest', but suddenly remembered the lecherous man cavorting with a slattern in the inn. Instead, he said, 'Mr Danforth and I, we'll write the cardinal. He'll be able to do something. He can do anything. Even in prison.'

'Thank you. Lord, but I've bent your ear. It's just … death is a cruel thing. It helps to talk. As if talking about it takes away its terrors.'

'Aye,' said Martin. Then, on impulse, 'the little boy died. Up at the palace. Did you know Mathieu, the page?'

'What?' Rowan leant forward, her hands clutching at the

material of her dress. 'What happened?'

'It was ... I can't say – an accident.'

'Another accident,' she said drily. 'I see. Mr Martin – Arnaud – why don't you tell me the truth? Tell me what in God's name has really been going on in that, that Olympus up there. What are you and Danforth looking for? What have you found?'

Martin smiled at the interest on her face. Perhaps, he thought, it would take her mind off her present troubles. He told her. When he had finished, she tilted her head back and exhaled. 'Jesus. Jesus. It sounds to me like you are in some very troubled waters. If I were you I would gather my things and go. Get away from it all.'

'Aye right. Run like cowards, like those Douglas creatures. No. We'll see it through. We'll unmask whoever or whatever is working its evil up there. Mr Danforth is a sharp man at these things. He hasn't failed yet, never lost his head.'

'Then I wish you luck. Both of you. I think you'll need it.'

Martin shook his head dismissively. 'You know ...' he chanced. He had been going to suggest she now speak to Danforth, let him know that she was now free to leave Linlithgow, to marry. With a dowry. Instead, he said, 'if ever you need to talk again, Simon is full of wisdom. About all kinds of things.'

Finally, a real smile broke out on her face.

23

Linlithgow's combination draper and tailor shop was run by a widowed woman. Her white hair was swept up into an outrageous coif with a neat cap slicing through it like a ship parting waves. He had asked Diane to buy them some refreshments, asking casually where she had done business the day before the masque. When her back was turned, he had taken himself into the little place, not far along the street from the apothecary.

Inside, the little woman had introduced herself as Mistress Lithgow. He had bitten his tongue at the obviously false name – a jejune attempt at giving her establishment an air of civic style and class. Still, the woman herself was impressive in her brusque manner. 'What do you want?'

'Only some information, mistress.'

'We don't sell that,' she said, turning to snap at a woman working under her. In one corded hand she held a little wooden mannequin, of the type affectionately known as a 'baby', a miniature purple dress fitted neatly onto it.

'It concerns the royal household,' said Danforth. 'I'm a gentleman and secretary to the lord cardinal. I am at present engaged on the business of Queen Marie.'

At this, Lithgow's expression softened minutely. 'A good customer. Pays on time. Used to come in here herself, Queen Marie, can you believe that? Right into this shop, when she was giving out alms in the burgh.'

'I can believe it.'

'Yet her Highness can't be after more material. I've given her near all I've got. It's not another masque already, is it?' She set down the baby and leant forward on the counter on her elbows.

'No, it concerns the order already filled.'

'Nothing wrong with it,' she said without hesitation. 'I measured that cloth myself. Made sure it was of the highest quality.'

Danforth shook his head. 'Nothing like that. I don't doubt

your work for a moment. No, it was only that … her Highness is concerned that there is some irregularity in the order. A mistake made by some servant or other. You understand, she must keep an orderly house.'

'Can't have servants pinching things, eh? What, have they been adding their own stuff to her orders? Seen that sort of thing before, and not just from the royal household.'

'Something like that. Perhaps. If you have the order, the list?'

Without a word, Lithgow nodded and disappeared into the back of the shop, returning quickly with a small silver casket. She drew a key from a chain around her neck and opened it. A young woman, presumably one of her servants, had followed her, and tried to peek. 'Do you want a sherrackin', lass? Get away with you. Do some work.' Pouting, the girl disappeared, Lithgow looking up at him apologetically.

With deft, practiced movements, she sorted through the papers in the casket, her eyes flitting down one of them before she handed it over. 'This is the order,' she said. 'Looked fair to me. Unusual, maybe, but I'd heard she had a masque getting put on from her lassie. Beauterne, her name was.'

Danforth scanned the document, reading the contents allowed. He had no idea what he was reading. The handwriting alone was a difficult to penetrate. 'Why do you say unusual, mistress?' he asked at last.

'Just like a man,' she said. 'Well, it's not so strange in itself. Her Highness, she often orders material from here. Purple, violet, pink, white. Black, too, the expensive stuff, French black. But in this order and,' she flipped again through her casket, producing another note, 'this one, from the week before last, there were requests for blue. No particular shade, just blue. I've never known her to want so many ells of blue. Rarely even carry it. Had to order it in. I assumed she was putting on some sea play – you know, making up false waves.' She raised an arm and motioned waves with her hand. 'But, well – look – the blue was to be run up as cloaks. With hoods, specified, see. Were they capering about as mermaids up there, or dolphins?'

'No, mistress,' said Danforth quietly. She shrugged. 'The blue, I see, is written at the bottom of the notes. Added in. I think the handwriting is a wee thing different.' She took back the notes and peered closely, comparing them.

'Aye. Like I said, everyone in the household can add what they need to these notes before they come down to me. It's a foolish thing – it breeds corruption in servants.'

'Who brings the notes to you? You said Mistress Beauterne?'

'I said she collected the material. Carried it up to the palace the other day. No, usually it's someone else.'

'Who?' asked Danforth, leaning in eagerly. 'I must know, mistress. It is important.'

'The boy,' she said. 'The little page boy, Mathieu.'

***

He found Diane in the market cross, a crust of bread in either hand. She rushed towards him, petulance making a comical mask of her pretty features. 'Where did you go?' she asked him. 'You just left me.'

'I apologise, mistress,' he said. 'I had to … nature called.' He essayed a blush. In truth, he felt he was getting better at dissembling.

'I see,' she said, a warm smile spreading again. 'Sorry. I did not mean to pry. Here, I got you this. You can have the bigger one.'

They ate in silence, Danforth watching as Cam Hardie and Geordie Simms exited the inn and retrieved their horses. Thankfully they did not notice him, and cantered out of the town, shouting, 'A Douglas! A Douglas!' as townspeople cleared a path, throwing up aggrieved and wearied looks.

'That's the fellow who sought to trifle with me at the masque,' said Diane. 'The fair young man, who was not so fair in manner.'

'Is that so, mistress?' asked Danforth, after swallowing some of the dry bread. 'Perhaps you have learned not to be taken in by fair looks and fair words. They can mask dark hearts. You must learn to be less trusting. No all handsome gallants are all innocence.'

'I prefer to trust and be sometimes wrong than distrust and be hardened.'

'Then I wish you luck in this dark world.' She shifted. So, thought Danforth. Mr Hardie was out of the great hall when the boy was killed. It might be nothing – it probably was nothing. Still, it was a shame the fool was riding away when he might question him about his whereabouts – and about Diane's tale, of course. Nothing should be taken as read.

'Simon, Diane,' said Martin, joining them. 'I didn't think to see you here.'

'Good morrow, Mr Martin,' said Danforth, frowning and laying emphasis on the surname. They were in public, after all. 'Mistress Beauterne and I felt the sudden need to be out of the palace. You can imagine, after this morning. And yesterday.'

'Aye,' said Martin, fists balling. 'I understand.' Danforth was pleased to see that Martin had the wit not to question him any further, that the younger man did not automatically ask why he was not in the palace investigating, in front of the girl. He was learning. A chill ran through him. There had been opportunities enough to learn lately. Perhaps Scotland really was cursed. Not only the parade of deaths at the hands of the Stewart kings conjured up by their killer, but all the murders he had seen in the country lately. The realm had run mad.

'But now I fear we must return.'

'Wait,' said Martin. 'Rowan – Mistress Allen – her father has passed away.'

'What? Oh no,' Diane half-shrieked, raising her hands to her mouth. 'What is happening, gentlemen? He wasn't murdered?'

'Peace, no. He was ill, had been ill. He went peacefully in his sleep. Mr Danforth, I think she'd like to see you. If you would go to her, perhaps, Mistress Beauterne and I can go up to the palace.'

'There is no time for that,' said Danforth. The image of Rowan danced into his mind, his hands on her waist, her laughing smile as she dipped. He did not want to see her crying. 'Perhaps some other time.' He could handle no more death, not at that moment. It almost felt as though he himself were cursed, as though knowledge of him carried death in it.

He began stomping away from the cross, leaving a crestfallen

Martin and a disappointed-looking Diane in his wake.

***

The palace courtyard, when they reached it, was in uproar. What now? wondered Danforth. Perhaps the Hamilton flunkies were now leaving. But when he saw the cause of the uproar, he cursed. Swarming about were servants, their expressions mutinous. Some were armed with the tools of their trade: brooms, brushes – one woman was even waving a wet cloth in the air. Anthony Guthrie hobbled before them, waving him own stave of office like a baton, a general leading his troops. Had the man gone mad, wondered Danforth, before pushing his way through the crowd.

'Mr Guthrie, what is going on here?' he shouted.

Guthrie ignored him. The man's eyes had gone wild, and though he was shouting himself, it was not directed at Danforth. 'I have seen it! I have seen the devil! He walks among us, invited here by foul practices of sorcery! Friends, friends, we must leave this place! Will we tarry here to be slain as our young Mathieu was slain? No, I say!' Finally he caught Danforth's eye. 'There! Those men – look what they have brought upon us. You must bring our masses back! Your master must be free!' He looked back at his wild mob. 'And those Hamilton men – it is they who brought the wrath of Rome, who made the Holy Father turn his back on us, deprive us. Will we suffer it? No, I say! The cardinal must go free, and the mass restored! Freedom! Freedom from evil!'

The group of rampaging servants waved their tools in the air and cried out in approbation. At that moment, Forrest appeared, leading his own battalion: the household musicians, Rab Gibb, the cook, Marshall, and a handful of guards, their hands resting uneasily on their weapons. They ranged themselves opposite the marauding servants. 'Stop this nonsense at once,' cried Forrest. 'In the name of her Grace Queen Mary, go back to your business. Stop this madness!'

Danforth led Diane and Martin through the disgruntled crowd. 'Help us, Mr Danforth,' shrieked Guthrie. 'You know that the dark arts are at work here. You know it!' Danforth ignored him, leading his troupe towards Forrest, who looked him up and down.

'Forrest, what is all this wild scrimmage?'

'Are you men for us or against us?' the depute asked.

'I am for order. Not chaos,' answered Danforth.

'Right. This lot might turn ugly. Guthrie's been winding them up, they're all half-mad with fear.'

'Go easy,' said Martin. 'You can't blame them.'

'I can keep this house in order. You two men are wanted upstairs anyway. The dowager demanded your presence earlier. I couldn't find you.' Danforth sensed a note of criticism, but Forrest had already turned back to Guthrie and his followers. 'Listen, folk,' he shouted. 'There will be no need for violence if you return to your work. Her Highness understands your concerns and is acting on them even as I speak.'

Wondering what he meant, Danforth led Martin and Diane away from the rebellion and up through the tower to the queen's rooms.

They left Diane in the outer chamber, where she joined some gossiping, wide-eyed women, and passed through the inner one. Knots of Hamiltons stood around, their heads down, speaking in hushed tones. Danforth ignored them and headed directly into Queen Marie's bedchamber, knocking before slipping through.

'Good morrow, gentlemen,' she said. She was standing over Madame LaBoeuf, directing the woman as she carefully laid various bits of clothing in trunks.

'Good morrow, your Highness,' they said in unison. 'You called for us?' added Danforth.

'Yes,' she said, collapsing wearily into a chair. It was not, he noticed, her usual chair of estate, but a little sitting chair by the great bed. 'C'est fini. I release you from your duty.'

The men exchanged looks. 'But … your Highness said that we had until tonight.'

'Ah. So then you have found nothing yet.'

'I … I found another blue cloak. In young Mathieu's chamber.' He hurried on, ignoring Martin's gaping mouth. 'It is further evidence. It came from the tailor, a Madame Lithgow. Someone in your household added it to the list.'

Marie raised an eyebrow. 'And?'

'Well, if we discover who has been adding to the orders sent to the tailor, we have the man behind all of this.'

'Yet you do not know who it was who did this.'

'I thought,' said Danforth, raising a hand to loosen his collar, 'that you might know. Who might have access to these order lists, who might add to them.'

'Anyone might add to them,' said Madame LeBoeuf, shutting a trunk with a reverberating bang. 'Anyone. You would have to ask Mathieu.'

Danforth bowed his head. 'My lady is quite right,' said Marie. 'Such lists are open to anyone before my boy took them to the tradespeople. I cannot concern myself with all accounts. I trust my people.'

'Might anyone else gain access? Outside the household?' asked Danforth.

Marie shrugged. 'Forget it, Mr Danforth. You had your time to discover the truth of this affair. There is no more. You have seen the mad affray out there?'

'We have,' said Martin. 'Your usher is leading it.'

'He will be dealt with,' she said. 'When we have reached some place of safety. I told you, it is over. You are released. I am sure you did your best.' It was unclear from her tone if she was angry, disappointed, or weary. To Danforth, the bluntness somehow made it worse.

'What,' he asked, his mouth drying, 'can you mean, your Highness?'

'I mean that I am leaving this place, with or without the blessing of that man Arran. He cannot keep me here, nor my daughter.'

'But where will you go, where will you take her?' asked Martin.

'I …' Marie raised a hand to her forehead. 'I have lost. I will throw myself on the mercy of Henry of England. He shall have my daughter. Arran cannot speak against that. At least she shall be safe in England. I hear that the man, Sadler, has already crossed Berwick – I shall go to meet him if I must, deliver the child into his hands. Me, I shall seek protection in France. Or stay here. I do not greatly care what becomes of me, provided my child is safe.'

'Not England,' croaked Danforth. 'Please, your Highness. Things cannot have got so far.'

She gave him a half-smile. 'No love for your former realm? I understand. No, Mr Danforth, things have gone so far. Nowhere in Scotland is safe, every place holds terror. Every place holds violent death. A thirst for vengeance against my daughter's progenitors. Only in England are the Stewarts not despised by some faction or other.'

'Have you announced this?' asked Danforth, his mind turning quickly.

'Not yet.'

'Madam, might I speak with you alone?'

'It will do no good. My mind is clear and I wish matters to move apace. We leave for Holyroodhouse tomorrow. And I will have letters sent under my own hand to King Henry.'

'Please, your Highness.'

She sighed, saying nothing. In the fire, a log crackled and fell. Eventually she looked up. 'Very well, Mr Danforth. If you are quick. Madame, Mr Martin, pray wait outside for a moment.'

'Wait,' protested Martin, casting an appealing look at Danforth. 'He meant us both.'

'No, Martin. Do as her Highness commands.'

'Like hell, I–' Martin, seemingly remembering where he was, slammed his mouth shut. 'Aye, your Highness,' he said. Danforth absorbed his look of anger as he and the waiting woman filed out. He waited until the door was closed before he spoke.

'Please, your Highness, I think I might be on the brink of discovering our murderer. Of discovering what has been behind the foul events in the palace since before our coming here.'

'It is too late,' she said, irritation threatening. 'I have told you this.'

'No,' he said, matching her firmness. 'I need only one chance. It … it shall involve some pretence on both our parts. All I ask is … might you delay announcing your intention to give your child to the English king until tonight? Then you might assemble the whole household. And when you do so, might I see you privately in this room before you go out there and speak?'

She looked at him, a hint of amusement playing on her lips. 'What is this, sir? Some game? Some farce?'

'I confess it is something like that. And if I might press further, would you happen to have some token? A ring, or some such, that might be taken for a strong royal pledge? If it looks like it is of English design, so much the better.'

At this, she laughed, and stood, crossing the room to a cabinet. She pulled open a door in it, and rifled, producing a ruby and gold ring. 'This is not only of English design, Mr Danforth. It comes from England's king. It was sent me years ago by Mr Cromwell, when he sought me for King Henry's bed. A mark of his Majesty's favour and esteem, the letter said. I did not take the husband, but I did keep the ring.' She held it out, and Danforth rose from his knee, crossing to take it. It was heavy, cold. He slipped it into a pocket. 'You will return it?'

'Of course, your Highness,' he said, and she laughed at the look on his face.

'I trust you. Yes, Mr Danforth. I wish to see what scheme you have concocted. I will see you here tonight. Until then I will say nothing. But I warn you, this is your last throw of the dice. My mind is quite made up, as sorry as I am to be brought to this pass.'

'Becalm yourself, your Highness,' said Danforth. 'I trust that this evening all will be revealed.'

24

Martin lay on his cot, staring up at the ceiling. Although burning with curiosity, he had not waited on Danforth. If his friend did not trust him to share the dowager's confidences, then to hell with him. He had instead stormed downstairs and back across the courtyard, where a kind of order had been restored. The servants, led by Guthrie, had put down their weapons, and were now chanting doggerel Latin verses about staving off evil. Forrest and his fellow adherents of order ringed the fountain, watching the odd little spectacle moodily. Martin had ignored both groups, slamming the door of his and Danforth's chambers behind them. He had not bothered to greet the older man when he returned, but rolled over and stared at the wall, only returning to his back when his arm ached.

'I had no choice, Arnaud.' Martin ignored him. 'Yet now I need to ask a favour.' Still Martin said nothing, hoping to annoy him. 'We have to return to the dowager's apartments tonight.'

Unable to hold out, Martin spat, 'I'm not going anywhere with someone who doesn't trust me.'

'Very well, remain here, then.'

'Oh, you'd like that, would you? Then I will come.' Martin pounded his pillow, finally turning to Danforth. He had spoken now, and so there was little sense in lapsing back into silence. 'What are you doing?'

Danforth had scraped open the wooden shutters and was leaning out. For a moment, Danforth thought he was vomiting. Then he stepped back into the room, yanking the shutters closed. He opened and closed them one more time. 'What are you doing?' repeated Martin.

'I am trying to get some air into this room. It reeks of a sickroom.'

'Oh, does it? I am so sorry. I am so sorry I was shot at and struck in the eye. I'm so sorry I have to rub reeking ointments into a hole in my arm, Mr Danforth.'

'I forgive you.' Danforth's face was without expression. That

209

STEVEN VEERAPEN

annoyed Martin even more. 'Your little friend Mathieu ...'

'You leave him out of this. Aye,' he said, sitting up and swinging his legs off the cot. 'You never said anything about him, about a cloak in his room, or lists, either. Making me look like a gawping fish in front of the dowager like that.'

'There was no time. I only learned of it before meeting you in the burgh. I had no opportunity to speak with you properly before we were drawn into her Highness' presence.'

'I still say it's rotten. You know, Mr Danforth, I thought you'd changed. I thought you had given up being a secretive man, keeping every little thing to yourself. Stewing like a ...' he struggled to finish the simile, and so substituted a proverb. 'A leopard doesn't change its spots.' He smiled savagely at the look of genuine hurt that crept over Danforth's face, and then felt guilty. 'Anyway, what is it about Mathieu?'

'I think he knew his killer. And I think he was slain because he knew something. He knew who had ordered blue cloth.'

'Well we can't ask him, the poor little lad.'

'No,' agreed Danforth, his lip curling in a grimace. In Paisley, he recalled, a draper had given him critical information. Here it had led in an infuriating circle, like a bad joke. 'But we can avenge him. I have been thinking,' said Danforth, his voice turning low, 'on the nature of stories. We have seen a good many of them brought to ... well, I cannot say life. But we have seen them acted out before our eyes since coming into this palace. King James' dream, Queen Margaret's poisoning, the other Margaret's vision, James IV's warning – all of it and more. But what do stories do?' Martin shrugged. 'Really, Arnaud, I'm asking – what do they do? Think even of that play we saw acted.'

Martin, unwilling to be drawn into Danforth's riddles, mumbled. 'Dunno. Make us laugh. Cry. Think about ourselves.'

'Aye, all of that. But they can also bring fear. You saw that rabble out there as well as I did, all driven by fear. Queen Marie herself is now in a great terror – so scared she would send her daughter into the care of that fat boar in England.'

'Aye. I s'pose.'

'I think our murderer is a storyteller, Arnaud. A craftsman.

210

This killer is using hoary old bricks, though – constructing a story to bring fear out of the thrice-heated tales of this country's past.'

'Why?'

'I have an idea. But it must be tested. Tonight.'

'Oh? Is this the great thing between you and the old queen?'

Danforth smiled. Martin didn't like the look of it. 'So you're going to discover the killer tonight?' In spite of his irritation – justified though he knew it was – his interest was piqued. 'Who is it, do you think? A Hamilton? The Douglases are gone. Or is it the reformists?'

'I cannot say.' Danforth folded his arms over his chest. 'Tell me, have you ever heard of the eighth Earl of Douglas?'

'No. I mean, I suppose there was one.' Riddles again. 'Why, what is it?'

'The eighth earl,' said Danforth, 'was slain by King James II. Stabbed to death. His brains beaten out with a poleax.'

'That's pretty.'

'Indeed. It's what happened to the body that interests me. It is one thing that I suspect our murderer does not wish attention drawn to.' Danforth reached out a hand to help Martin up.

'What? Are you saying there's going to be another murder?' he asked, ignoring the proffered arm and awkwardly shifting himself.

'No. It may be nothing. It may be everything. That is why I must test my theory. But I will say this, Arnaud. Forget the politics. Forget, for the moment, religion. We have been led a merry dance, I think, around and around the stage. Forget even those poor dead souls, old and new. This whole mess is about one person's ambition. Tonight they might admit to it, whether willing or not.'

***

It was only a couple of hours later that Martin waited in the inner chamber, his livery brushed, Diane keeping him company. The number of Hamilton retainers, he noticed, had dwindled. Some of them, too, must have decided that the palace was too dangerous a place to be. Occasionally Madame LaBoeuf swept over to him, patting his arm and asking him how he fared, before doing her rounds of the room. The dowager had seemingly gathered the entire household, even Guthrie, without his band of domestic servants. Every eye and ear were alert, the air heavy with the expectation that something was to be announced. Martin sipped at a cup of claret, after waiting to see that the rest of the guests had had their own cups filled from the same vessel.

He felt a little stab at his heart when the door opened and an older page crossed the room, entered the bedchamber, and then emerged to blow on his horn. Out stepped Danforth. Behind him came the dowager, nearly a head taller, with a hand resting on his arm. Immediately the room hushed, people falling to their knees or dropping curtsies.

'Me thank you for coming hither,' said Marie, her heavy accent back. 'All mine guests. Me wish to let it be known … that mine daughter the Queen should be to go to England. It be mine own wish as dearest mother to her that she live in England as the most illustrious Prince Edward's own betrothed wife. Me must thank Mr Danforth for bringing letters from King Henry.' Breaths were drawn in around the room as Danforth fell to one knee.

Forgetting himself again, Martin spoke aloud. 'What the hell, Simon? Letters?'

Danforth stood, brushing down the front of his livery in a fussy little gesture. 'Aye,' he said. 'Martin, I return now to England. Your master is no longer my own.'

'What the actual–' began Martin, as realisation dawned. 'You traitor,' he snapped. 'You bloody traitor to his Grace.'

'I am a faithful man and true to King Henry,' Danforth added. 'And I seek nothing more than amity between his Majesty's realm and this one. That might only be achieved by marriage between the kingdoms. It is to my own regret that I have been unable to convince the lord cardinal of the wisdom of this course. He has remained deaf to my pleas on behalf of my sovereign lord in England. And thus I take my leave of both him and you.'

Danforth turned with a flourish, dropping again to one knee

before taking Marie's hand and kissing it. 'Madam,' he said, 'I shall take your letters forthwith to his Majesty. He shall then instruct the governor of Scotland, his vassal, to convey your child out of this realm, whose subjects shall soon learn to be loyal and faithful.'

Marie nodded placidly, saying nothing, as Danforth walked backwards, head bowed, towards the outer chamber. Mouth hanging open, Guthrie stood to open it for him, and then he was gone.

Martin and the rest of the company regained their feet. His mind whirred. So this little piece of acting had been Danforth's plan, then. What had its purpose been? And where was he really going? As Queen Marie returned to his private prison, the assembly of household staff and Hamilton guests broke into excited, confused gabble.

***

Danforth raced downstairs and across the courtyard. The gauntlet had been thrown down. All that remained was to see who picked it up. Gibb was not in the stable – he had, Danforth had been sure, saw the man in the inner chamber. Instead, one of his underlings passed Woebegone's reins to him and helped him mount. For the hundredth time, he patted his breast to make sure the ring was still present. He smiled at the reassuring hard lump, kicked the stirrup, and trotted out of the main entrance. 'Farewell,' he shouted, 'farewell, you wretched palace. May England's verdant fields never see such bloodshed.'

He slowed Woebegone down as they processed along the path past St Michael's. When he reached the stone arch of the outer gait, he pulled in to the side to wait. It had turned cold again, and the occasional star twinkled from behind a shred of cloud. His performance, he thought, had been particularly strong. So had the dowager's. No one present could doubt that he had been Henry's man, that he was now claiming responsibility for the dowager's desire for the infant queen to be brought up in England. It had been a shame that he could not tell Martin, but he had worried that the younger man would insist on some foppish display of his own, overdoing it, like a snarling image of vice in morality play. No, the little scene called for his own, restrained, behaviour.

He wondered how long he would have to wait. Not long, surely. His heart began to race with anticipation. All that remained was this final piece of the puzzle – this final unmasking. He knew, or thought he knew, what face lurked under that damned blue hood, but now was the time to pull it back.

But what if nothing happened? He had not allowed himself to consider that possibility. Then he had announced himself before the household, before the Hamiltons, before the world, to be a double-dealing trickster. He shuddered. It would be possible that the cardinal would let him go, unwilling to keep such a loose cannon in his employ. Had there been any other way, he would have taken it. Time was simply too pressing. The die had to be cast. But what if nothing happened?

The answer came clopping towards him in the form of light hoofbeats. A hunched figure, silhouetted against the lights of the palace, descended towards him. Again he shivered. 'Mr Danforth,' a voice whispered into the night. 'Danforth, are you there? Is that you?'

Danforth shook Woebegone awake and rode him a step or two forward, out of the archway and back towards the palace. He recognised the voice. It was exactly as he had suspected. He chanced another look at the church, thanking God. Now, how to play it.

He cleared his throat, before assuming a tone of disinterested irritation. 'What kept you?' he asked. 'King Henry is not a patient man, and nor am I. It is too cold a night to be lurking in shadows.' His voice caught in his throat. He wondered if the figure now sitting opposite him noticed it. What Danforth had noticed was the glimmer of metal. The missing wheellock was pointed at him. 'I think,' he drawled, 'that you can put that away. I am quite true in my loyalty to England's king, Mr Guthrie.'

25

'You see?' Slowly, holding up his empty hands, Danforth drew the dowager's ring out of the breast of his doublet. He held it up. Guthrie took it in one hand and drew it to his eyes, his lips mumbling. 'It is my pledge, my proof, from King Henry. You see, engraved within are the roses, white and red together. His Majesty bid me use this as proof of loyalty were I ever to meet any Scots who might incline to his service.'

'Aye, is that so?' asked Guthrie, stretching to hand the ring back. 'So you're truly no cardinal's man?'

'Bah! Beaton is finished. Spying on him and his minions is no use to King Henry any longer. Now that the old man is done, I might return to my true master. My loyalty need no longer be cloaked.'

'Loyalty, eh? So loyal you'd be taking credit for my work?'

'I assure you,' said Danforth, his eyes not leaving the gun, 'that my master has been well informed of your … assiduous … labour in bringing the dowager to see reason. I have sent him secret communications of what has been done here.'

'What do you mean? How did you know?'

'I have known all along, sir,' lied Danforth. Woebegone raised a leg, shifting, and he cursed the old brute. It was almost as if the horse could sense him lying.

'I haven't told anyone. I've been careful. They all,' said Guthrie, waving the gun briefly before retraining it on Danforth, 'think I'm just holy old Mr Guthrie, wedded to the true church and like to talk their ears off.'

'I give credit to your playing,' said Danforth. 'Yet, from the first, it was clear that you were otherwise.'

'How so?' Guthrie sounded almost annoyed, and Danforth wondered whether to continue. The man was obviously mad and had killed before. Antagonising him was not a good idea.

'When first we met, I asked you if you had heard of the tale of Hamilton of Finnart haunting the late king. You said you had not. I thought that odd at the time. That story is as old as the hills and warmed every hearth in Scotland a few years back. Even King Henry knows of it.'

'Pfft. You didn't get it from that.'

'No. Not just that. I counted you as a friend to we English when I understood what had happened to that old fool Fraser.' Guthrie said nothing, but still he did not lower the gun. Danforth had been hoping the 'we English' would have an effect. He went on, 'At first I could not understand how it had been done. But then I realised that the old fool was not drawn outside the palace. He was drugged and died in his chamber. Drugs stolen from that French physician, I imagine. I heard him ranting about thieves. And you told me, after all, that you shared that chamber with Fraser. Then you forced the corpse out the window and let it roll towards the loch, only going out later to mark him in the manner of the king's dream. Yet tell me – why him?'

Guthrie chuckled. 'Aye, I shouldn't have doubted one of King Henry's men. You lot brought down More and Fisher – there's little you can't devise. Why Fraser? You knew him, did you not? I've never known a man take so long to give in to poison. I gave him enough to kill ten men, too, according to the book I was told to look at. You have been busy, sir.'

'I am used to discovery. Found all sorts in the old monasteries in England, uncovered much,' said Danforth. That was a risk; he had not been in England when the monasteries fell.

'Tsk. That was a bad business that, all those great buildings torn down. Still, it gives a man with the skill to build opportunity, all those new grand houses going up in their place. Oh, I picked up more from old Finnart than just how to haunt. Christ, but what a curse it was getting that daft old goat out that window. Had to crawl out after him and push him.'

'Aye,' said Danforth, forcing a wry smile. 'I saw that he had been through the bushes under the window. Some jagged little skelves of wood from those damned shutters had lodged in his clothing too.'

'And mine, the jaggy little bastards. Well, the job was done, wasn't it? Shame I couldn't get the head off. Dunno how the headsmen do it – filthy business. But it worked out in the end. Heh. That stupid French cow up there thought it was a threat to the bairn right enough.'

'Not enough to bring her to move the child, though.'

'No. Not with those Hamiltons and Douglases around. More interested in keeping everything quiet, so she was.'

'And so,' Danforth went on, 'you had to put her off sending the child to Stirling.'

'And Edinburgh, and France. In the end, it was England or death. Ah,' he added quickly, 'not that I ever would have harmed the bairn. She was never to be hurt.'

'Of course not,' said Danforth. 'It was all a great game to frighten the dowager enough to send the child southwards. Not west or east or to France, but southwards, to my master's gentle nursery. Yet ... King Henry knew nothing of this plot. Leastways, he mentioned nothing to me, or I might have helped you.' He could almost feel the earth shift and sway beneath Woebegone's hooves. Another gamble. But he had to know if Henry VIII had been directing events, sitting like a swollen-bellied spider at the centre of England's web, whilst his swarming minions did his work.

'No. No, it was a plot of my own devising. But after his wishes, I fancied.'

'Indeed, sir. His Majesty will be most pleased at all you have done here.'

'Aye,' said Guthrie. 'You'll tell King Henry about it, confirm that I've done his work? You'll take me south to meet him, to tell him myself. Christ, I can't go back up there. I've wound up the idiot servants enough to be dismissed.' Neediness crept into his tone, and Danforth felt like striking him himself. The great killer he had sought, the mastermind, was nothing but a crawling little murderous weasel, trying to ingratiate himself with the island's most notorious man.

'I have already written letters informing his Majesty of your work in England's interests. He is always keen to reward good service. I might recommend you yet for some work on one of his palaces. Your interest in building works was, I assume, not feigned?'

'No, Danforth, no. You think you can get me that?'

'I have the king's ear,' said Danforth. 'I feel sure that I can. I would know, though, why did you not make an end of that fool Martin? He stuck by me such that I could never meet privately with you.'

'I tried,' said Guthrie, spittle flying, 'I tried, but those goddamn Douglas fools stopped me. I got one of them in the gut, but still. And then I thought I might smother the young wretch, but that black bitch flower-seller was on her way to service him.'

'I see.'

'But I did try, sir. Since I heard you say at dinner that you would be quit of him, I read your meaning and tried.'

'Well, King Henry shall not hold one slight failure against your many good works. It is a shame you had to kill the boy, though. His Majesty will not like that.'

'I ...' Guthrie wiped at his mouth. When he spoke, his voice was low. 'I would've had that otherwise. He knew too much, though, ranting about hidey-holes. He knew I'd added blue cloaks to the list of things from that old bitch down in the burgh. He had to go. But I'd have preferred a woman for that one – a woman to be thrown in the flames. That's what the old king actually did.'

'Well ... perhaps in my report to King Henry, we can have it that a woman was burned rather than a boy. An adulterous woman,' he added, putting a finger thoughtfully to his lips. 'Aye, that should please him more.'

'You'll do that then? Thank you, Mr Danforth, thank you. I'll be shriven for it by King Henry's priests, forgiven for all I've been forced to do. Henry's a good Catholic still, from what I hear, Pope or no. I'll be forgiven. Sending a few more to eternal life before they expected it – it's what was needed. And then I can meet my true calling. Good service in building up the greatest palaces ever seen in England. Not much chance for that kind of advancement under a useless governor or a child, eh? Heh. And you won't let those goddamn Douglases or Hamiltons take the credit for delivering the little brat into Henry's hands?'

'Of course,' said Danforth. He was running out of ways to stall for time.

'Well we must go,' snapped Guthrie. 'It will take long enough for me to move with this bloody arm and ankle. Had to make it look real, you know, once the boy was dead. Remind me,' he said, an ugly peal of laughter in his voice, 'never to toss myself down King Henry's palace stairs.'

Slowly, Danforth turned Woebegone back towards the dark archway. 'Aye, there was no need to try and distract me with nonsense about a demon in white slippers.'

'I didn't know,' shrugged Guthrie, 'who and what you were. If you were not King Henry's man, I'd have had you chasing after one of the women as the … person who brought all this about.'

'And you'd have had to have made your service known to King Henry yourself.'

'Aye, I didn't like that. That's why I was so pleased when a good Englishman appeared. I knew you must still be loyal to the old boy.'

'We might make as much speed as we can,' said Danforth, chancing, raising his voice.

'Halt,' cried Forrest, stepping into the archway from the town side. 'You're both under arrest.'

Danforth tensed.

'We're betrayed,' cried Guthrie.

'Becalm yourself,' hissed Danforth. 'He cannot arrest me. I am not a subject of this realm.'

'Take him,' screeched Guthrie. 'It was him, Forrest. You know me – it was this English bastard all along. Kill him. I'll do it! I'll save us all!'

Forrest fired first, the arrow shooting from his crossbow and piercing Guthrie in the stomach. As he fell from his horse the wheellock discharged. The entire archway lit up, as though lightning had struck. Danforth felt like he had been punched in the side, the left of his body going numb. As he began to fall himself, he felt the pain spread, claws sinking into his flesh. The ground came racing towards him.

***

Martin heard the explosion. He had been drinking from the

219

fountain, trying to clear the rich, vinegary taste out of his mouth. Leaving Diane, he raced immediately out of the palace and came upon the scene. Forrest was standing over Danforth, who was on the ground beside Woebegone. A torch had been lit in the archway, illuminating also the writhing figure of Guthrie. From somewhere came the sound of another horse's terrified wails, its hoofbeats receding as it ran free.

'What happened,' shouted Martin. 'Danforth, is he hurt?'

'He's been shot,' said Forrest. 'I can't tell how bad. I can't get enough light.'

'And Guthrie?' asked Martin. He was unsure what he was seeing. His suspicion had fallen immediately on Forrest. Had he attacked both men? He looked to the ground. Not far from Guthrie's hand was an old pistol. 'Guthrie?' he repeated stupidly.

'Aye,' said Forrest. 'Your man here warned me to watch this gate. Before he went up to the dowager's rooms. He said that he'd deliver the murderer of your friend, and the boy. He did, by God.'

On the ground, Danforth stirred. Martin looked to Guthrie, who was clutching his stomach. In the torchlight, the blood pouring appeared a rich burgundy, occasionally lightening to ruby as the flames twitched. 'Lying,' he coughed. 'Lying. It was Forrest. Don't listen.' Little bubbles of blood blossomed from his red-stained lips.

'It … was Guthrie. All along,' said Danforth. 'Guthrie.'

'Simon! You're alive.'

'Don't … stupid questions. Get me up.' Before Martin could, Forrest was helping him to his feet. Instead, he turned again to Guthrie.

'This … this old bastard killed that wee boy? Truly?'

'Aye,' said Forrest. 'He's dead anyway.'

'Well,' said Martin, his heart pounding. 'Not before he feels a little of what the child did.' Leaning over, he grasped the end of the arrow protruding from Guthrie's gut. His arm trembling, he twisted it, stirring, before wrenching it out. Guthrie choked out what sounded like a mixture of laughter and pain. Martin raised the arrow and poised to drive it into his heart. Not for the first time, fingers clenched around his wrist. They were Forrest's.

'Leave him,' croaked Danforth, who was leaning on his horse, clutching his side. His skin, Martin noticed, had turned the colour of paper, yellowy-white. 'He is done for. His insides are torn. There's no saving him. Let him … let him suffer.'

Martin dropped the arrow, and Forrest released him. Still Guthrie writhed. 'I want you to suffer,' he hissed at the dying man. Again, he pictured the boy, his skin burned, his tousled hair scorched away.

'We have to get your friend up to the palace,' said Forrest. 'Lead the way, please, Mr Martin.'

'Aye … right,' said Martin. 'You are sure this thing can't get back up, get away?'

'He's going nowhere. I'll send some men down forthwith.'

'Right,' said Martin. He made to move off back up the path. As one final insult, he stepped lightly on Guthrie's stomach, mashing his foot into the gore. The usher managed only weak grunts. Martin was pleased to see that tears were pouring down the side of his head. 'Now you will meet the devil,' he said, wiping his foot on the grass by the path before leading Danforth and Forrest away.

26

When Danforth came to, he was in Martin's cot. It was pain that brought him round, but he considered that a good thing. If he could feel pain, he wasn't done for. He tried moving and felt pressure on his torso. 'Cease moving,' said Rowan.

'Mistress Allen,' he said. His voice sounded loud in his ears.

'It seems I'm always attending on you lads,' she smiled. 'Like Acaste, to the children of Adrastus.'

He smiled. 'What time is it? How long have I been asleep?' He tried to read the light in the room, but spring light was secretive.

'You slept all night. As I hear, Mr Forrest and Arnaud helped you in to the palace and you fell into a deep sleep. Arnaud refused to let the physician attend on you. Said it had to be me, and so he fetched me up this morning. What does that boy have against physicians anyway?'

'It is too long a tale,' said Danforth. 'Am I grievous hurt?' He poked at his side, drawing his hand away sharply.

'I think not. The bullet grazed you. It drew up a lot of blood, but your body will make more. It was more a wound of the flesh than the insides. Not like that other.'

'Guthrie?' asked Danforth, trying to rise and falling back. 'He's dead?'

'What did I say about moving? Aye, he's dead. I saw him carried away. I understand it's the dowager's pleasure that his corpse be torn apart and burned.'

'I think his soul already feeds the flames.'

'If what Arnaud tells me, I agree.'

'What has he told you, mistress?'

'Oh,' she said airily, rising from the box she sat on and gathering her things together, 'everything. Every rotten thing that's been going on in this palace. Mr Martin told me yesterday you thought it was some attempt on the life of the new queen. It isn't, then?'

'No. No, it never was. It was all designed to make us think it

222

was. To make the dowager think it was. So that she'd send the child to that heretic king in England and reward the architect of the foul design. It was greed that moved Guthrie. Like the man he wished to serve. A monster of ambition.'

'A traitorous murdering bastard, from what I hear.'

'Aye, and that. And worse. He led us all to suspect it was otherwise.'

'Very interesting,' said Rowan, but her voice did not betray much interest. 'Politics,' she shrugged. 'All it brings is death.'

The word struck a chord with Danforth. 'Mr Martin told me about your father. I am very sorry for it.'

'Thank you, Simon.'

'If there is anything you need ...'

'Arnaud said you would both see what the cardinal might say about burial. That his Grace might order some priest to do it, regardless of this suspension of services.'

'I will do all I can.'

'Thank you,' she repeated. Danforth read something else in her face, but he couldn't quite place it. He wasn't sure if he wanted to.

'It is I who owe you thanks,' he said. 'It seems you have saved my life.'

'Oh, it was never in danger. Not if infection can be warded off.'

'Still, I thank you.' She waited, expectantly. 'If ever you need anything that is in my gift, Rowan,' he went on, 'I wish that you would come to me and ask it. It is my will – no, it is my desire – that you consider me your friend. Your very great friend.'

'Friend,' she whispered. Then her tone became clipped again. 'Yes, thank you. I shall bid you good day and wish you good health.' Gathering her little pack of medicines, she made for the door. Paused. Turned. 'I have a desire too. I wish that you would come around some time and visit. I'm finishing up my father's estate. Some friends who have visited have offered to get things in order. And so I am quite free and alone, with time to spare. It would be a good thing to see a friend.' She gave a quick, curt nod, as though satisfied with her piece, and left, her black waves bouncing.

Danforth smiled up to the ceiling. Another friend, he thought. His re-entry to the world was coming along well, as though it had all been ordained. What else, he wondered, might it entail? It was right that a man had friends. It was right that a man had work. It was right that a man had a wife. All of these things were not just acceptable to God but encouraged. He slipped Queen Marie's ring out of his doublet and twisted it in his fingers. Pale light reflected off its silvery-golden surface, picking out the engraving. A ring …

Before he could complete the thought, Martin came in. Hastily, he hid the heavy sliver of gold. 'Simon, how do you fare? Rowan said you were well, that there was no danger.'

'Quite well,' said Danforth. This time he did sit up, gritting his teeth against the pain. 'Look at us both, shot and wounded.'

'Both alive,' smiled Martin.

'Aye. I hear Guthrie is dead.' Martin spat on the floor. 'Kindly do not spit,' said Danforth. 'I thought you considered yourself fit for a Court.'

'They spit at Court,' he shrugged. 'I'm glad you're well, Simon. Aye, that's Guthrie in hell. He got off too easily, if you ask me. Forrest's already tearing down all his images, all his charms.'

'Is he indeed? There is a job I think he shall enjoy.'

'Anyway, I see Rowan has patched you up. We match. Sort of. What were you talking about, you two?'

'Nothing of any import. She is a good friend.' He laid emphasis on the word.

Martin tutted. 'Since you're become a great player, why not play at being a man of flesh and blood?'

In the past, Danforth's anger would have flared at that. It did not. Instead he said, 'I have in mind to do just that.' He enjoyed the look of confusion on Martin's face, half-excited, half-curious.

'What, you have some secret communication with her? I like her, Simon – she's a good girl. A good serious girl. She'd fit a good serious man, I reckon. Did she say anything to you, like give you some sign, or – what? I mean it's fitting that a gentleman like you should start to think of taking a girl on.'

'Arnaud,' said Danforth, shaking his head. 'Contrary to your manner of thinking, there are some parts of a man's life that belong to him alone.' Eager to stifle any more babble, he hurried on. 'But enough of this fond talk. What news?'

'Oh, her Highness wishes to see you. The post rider has just been – I heard his horn. So I guess she shall have news to tell you. Another meeting alone, eh?'

'You might come if you wish. Here, help me up.'

'Oh really, I'm being invited into the royal presence with the new pet?'

'Hold your peace,' smiled Danforth. 'Let us see what her Highness has to say about the suffering of those in her service. By the mass, I'm not looking forward to those stairs'

Together they tottered off, each bound and bandaged, to see what reward awaited them.

***

The dowager was in her bedchamber, back in her chair of estate. Danforth noticed that the trunks had been unpacked. In fact, several new ones were in place, their contents spewing out. 'My things return from Stirling,' she said, waving an arm at them. 'It seems I am going nowhere again.'

'You have announced this,' asked Danforth. 'That the race to England is off?'

'Oui, yes. Mr Forrest has told me of all that has truly been going on in this place. The palace itself is now made safe, no ghosts, nor wicked men feigning their presence. And if those Hamilton creatures out there report it to the governor ... well, I think it might do me no hurt to be seen as a weak-willed woman, bending in the wind. Your part, Mr Danforth, might require more explanation.'

Danforth bowed his head. He had wondered about that himself. If word got around that he was an agent of King Henry's, who knew what he might expect, lie or not. Still, there was nothing he could do about that, other than to continue in Cardinal Beaton's service, proving his loyalty by good work, as he always had.

'What did you wish further of us, your Highness?' asked Martin.

'Nothing to trouble you,' she said. 'No, no. You gentleman have done – and suffered – enough. For the sake of a sickness lodged within my own household.' She spat into a little silver salver to the side of the chair. Danforth felt Martin's eyes roll towards him. 'No, I wish to thank you. And to provide for you.' She paused before continuing. 'It is my will that you might join my service as your permanent occupation. Come, gentlemen, and work for me. I can have the bonds written up. You will be queen's men. What do you think of that? And with that dratted English ambassador coming you shall not lack honest work.' She seemed to misread their silence for awe. 'I want men of keen minds and stout courage. I want you in my service. And my daughter's.'

Danforth and Martin both looked up. She was smiling. 'Leave the cardinal?' asked Martin. Danforth said nothing. Royal service … the words were emblazoned in his mind, written in red and gold. There was no greater earthly honour, save papal service. Simon Danforth, gentlemen to the Queen and the Queen Dowager of Scotland.

'I regret I cannot,' he said.

'Nor I,' added Martin. 'Not yet.'

'What?' she asked. 'But … it is our will that you should.'

'Not at this present time, your Highness,' Danforth qualified. 'Whilst his Grace is in such difficult straits.'

Marie clucked her tongue, thudding one hand down on the arm of her chair. 'I see. I am a patient woman, gentlemen, but you understand that I cannot keep places for you forever.'

'No, your Highness,' said Martin. 'May … may I let you know of my decision later?'

'Of course, yes. I think I shall be at this palace for some time yet. I wish that I might be able to enjoy its beauty now. But not much later. I need my faith restored in my servants as soon as can be.' She relaxed in her chair, staring into space. Neither Danforth nor Martin moved. 'Then,' she said, sitting forward again, her eyes suddenly bright, 'I have another gift for you. You shall meet your sovereign lady.' She laughed, high and clear, no trace of anxiety. 'Yes, you shall have an audience with the Queen of Scots.' She rose. 'Come, gentlemen. Follow me.'

Marie led them through a door in the back of the room, stooping as she went through it. The three of them trooped up a narrower spiral staircase which ended in another door, a guard outside glittering in polished steel. He moved aside to let them emerge into a small room directly above the dowager's bedchamber. Every surface was gilded, the carpets alternating red and yellow. Tapestries showing scenes from antiquity lined the walls: Athena with an owl on her arm; Venus rising from the waves; Helen standing on the walls of Troy whilst a battle raged. Two more guards stood by the open windows, the sunlight turning their helmets white.

On a chair in the corner sat a large woman, the baby in her arms. She rose and curtsied when she saw the dowager. 'Good morrow, mistress, and how does her Grace?' asked Marie.

'Bonny and lusty as always. Just been fed.'

'Good. Pray show these gentlemen their queen.'

The wet nurse placed the child in a huge wooden cradle in the corner of the room, and slowly unwrapped her. Marie nodded encouragement. 'Go, go. Meet my daughter. Meet Mary, Queen of Scots.'

Danforth and Martin stepped towards the cradle and looked down. The child was milky white, its eyes closed. 'She favours you,' said Martin, grinning.

'Yes,' smiled Marie. 'She has my eyes. And I doubt not that she shall grow to be as tall.'

Danforth felt his heart stir. But it was not because of the presence of a sovereign child. The sight of any child might have done it. 'God save your Grace,' he whispered.

'Well, have you ever seen so good a child?' asked Marie. There was a little note of challenge in her voice.

'Never,' said Martin.

'I only pray that she is served in her time by better men than I have been. Soon she shall meet the English ambassador. Letters have come telling me he is even now in Edinburgh, and will soon be upon us here. Still I must feign that she will go to Henry as a bride for his son. But, thanks to you gentlemen, it will be a false hope. Your unmasking that, that false murdering knave Guthrie has stiffened my resolve that England will never have my little queen.' Danforth bit his lip, hoping she was right. What King Henry was not given willingly, he suspected, me might try to take by force. 'Never,' she repeated with finality. 'The French king is sending the Earl of Lennox to join me and your master in resisting any attempts by that man Arran and his Douglas masters. Or Henry of England. This child is the chief jewel of Scotland. She is mine. Not theirs.'

Bowing to the cradle, the men stepped away, following Marie back to her bedchamber. The windows were open, and birds were squawking outside. Fresh air and sunlight filled the room. Danforth's could feel his heartbeat. He wanted to ask to speak to Marie alone again but was wary of offending Martin. He cleared his throat. 'Your ring, your Highness. I must return to you your ring.'

'Keep it,' she said, throwing a hand up. 'I have no use for it. I seldom wear it.'

'Thank you. There is one more thing I feel I must ask your permission for, as I am still under your service.' She raised an eyebrow, amusement kindling her features. 'You might write the cardinal and ask him likewise. You see, I ... I have it in my head to marry, and beget children of my own...'

Epilogue

Few women could boast that their wedding rings had once been given by a king in pursuit of one of the most beautiful and eligible noblewomen in France. Diane Beauterne could. She smiled her open, guileless smile at Danforth as he slipped it onto her finger.

They were married in the chapel of St Andrews castle, on a bright summer morning in June. Cardinal Beaton himself presided. After being shunted around the country, Danforth's master had been finally set at liberty, to return behind the forbidding walls of his own great ecclesiastical abode. He had offered to wed Danforth to Diane before going off to await a French fleet, which was supposed to arrive to help resist the marriage between Queen Mary and Prince Edward, even then being debated. As the politics rumbled on, Danforth had only smiled, at his bride to be, and at the assured words of Queen Marie: England would never have Mary Queen of Scots. The much-vaunted parliament of March had indeed made the Bible available in the vernacular, but Danforth had courtship to turn his mind from the spread of dangerous new ideas. He hoped only that the decision, once made and enacted, would shut the hot gospellers up. Besides, he been busy otherwise. He had improved his French and learned about the orchards and flat lands of France, of the peasants and the wolves and the wild forests. In turn he had told Diane everything, of his life in London, of his flight northwards, of the loss of his first wife and their child. She had been like a smiling nursemaid, listening and applying the salve of her smile.

As he looked at her, he recalled his proposal, in the bare little library at Linlithgow. For a moment he was back there again.

***

Dust hung in the air, making its way languidly nowhere. She entered, her passage disturbing it, making it dance and spin. His heart began racing, just as it had when he had sought his meeting with Guthrie, knowing he had tipped off Forrest to be ready with a weapon. It was absurd to think of that, he knew. His bandaged side testified to the end of those horrors. Besides, he had spoken with the dowager, who had in turn spoken to Madame LaBoeuf. All had been done properly. All was correct. No reason to fear.

Still his heart hummed.

'You wished to see me, sir?'

'Yes, mistress. Oui,' he added, trying to smile. It felt ugly. He relaxed his face. 'Do you – have you been told on what matter?'

'Oui,' she said. He thought he saw a blush as she looked downwards, into the little bouquet of flowers clutched at the front of her bodice.

'Good. Please … do not think me forward in asking for your hand. It is … these past days, amidst such horror. I find you have become a bright jewel. Though I am not a rich man, I have space enough for a bride. After a proper space of courtship of course. You … you will never be poor in love.' The words seemed almost to be spoken by someone else. He did not know if he meant them. It was too early for love; that came after marriage. But he could love this woman. Something about her made him want to reach out and protect her goodness from the savagery of the world. 'If you would consent. I ask your consent.'

'It is,' she said, looking up – and yes, there was a blush, 'my father you must ask.'

'Your mistress has written,' he said. 'It is the dowager's will.' That came out wrong, and he bit his tongue. He did not wish her forced to marry him. 'It is your will I hope for. Will you marry me?'

'Have I your heart, sir?'

'Yes.'

'Then yes. I will marry you, and gladly. You're a good man, I think. My friend, she told me so.' Danforth barely had time to consider who she meant before she plucked a flower and held it out to him. It was lilac. He took it, the brief touch of their fingers warming him like good wine, and slid it into his doublet, over his heart. 'My parents will send the dowry – the tocher they call it here, I think. Then I should be glad to find some place in the world away from … from all of the world of madness and cruelty.'

He shook his head minutely, disinterested in dowries. She was bringing him something he had been grasping at only weakly for months. A key. A key that might open a door and let him out of himself, and back into the world.

***

She looked up at him now, and he smiled. Her dress was violet, a gift from Marie. It did not fit well, but custom dictated, of course, that it could not be altered. Her blonde hair cascaded down it, curled and waved. Danforth reached out and brushed it, his own suit hanging loosely. Helping him dress that morning, Martin had told him that it was bad luck for the groom to have the knots and latchets on his clothing tied on his wedding day. It would not do to court misfortune.

When he had finished reading the sacraments, Beaton smiled at them, Danforth last. 'Well,' he said in Scots, 'I thought you might have taken a Scottish lass to bed and board many years since. Mr Danforth! Well, in the eyes of God, it's better late than never. And Mistress Beauterne, wife to Danforth … take care of my lad here. He won't take care of himself.'

They parted after the ceremony, Diane going off to change for the dinner and masque that the cardinal had arranged for the afternoon. They were bound for Danforth's – for their – home in Edinburgh the next day. Beaton had given him a month off, joking that he had no need for an English secretary unless he exchanged his pens for guns. It was strange – even just the previous year, enforced time away from his work would have been a curse, not a blessing.

Danforth left the chapel for his own chamber in the castle. He found Martin waiting outside. He smiled at his friend, but the smile was hesitant. Martin had entertained some foolish notion about his marrying Rowan Allen. It was absurd – he would have thought Martin delighted to see him married to a French girl. He would never had imagined such a fate for himself. Yet when he had realised, back in Linlithgow, that it was Diane he favoured, the younger man had nearly collapsed, cursing him for all the fools on earth. Well, it was done now. Diane was his wife.

'Congratulations, Simon.' Martin held up his hands. 'You've beaten me to the altar. I never would have thought it.'

'Aye,' smiled Danforth. 'Though she was all for us being hand-fasted only. It would not do, of course. I insisted that a good ceremony, in the grace and presence of God, was necessary.'

'Of course you did. How does it feel?'

'Feel?'

'To be married, I mean.'

They were walking along the hall of the servants quarters, crunching over rushes. Danforth sensed an edge again in Martin's voice. 'It feels good, Martin. I … it feels right. Her goodness, it is … well, it is like a shining candle in a dark world.'

'Have you told her that?'

'I think that she must know.'

'You should tell her. Here, go and change and then come and have a bite with me, before dinner. I have something to tell you.'

Danforth changed into his livery and walked downstairs with Martin. The younger man had stolen from the kitchen, and together they skirted the bustling servants preparing for the cardinal's military expedition and passed out into the bright sunlight. A stiff ocean breeze whipped at them, their light cloaks flapping.

'Well,' he asked, 'what is it so urgent that you must tell me on this of all days?' A sudden dark thought crossed his mind: surely not another murder.

'I … in a minute, Simon. I meant to ask you first, what brought you to this?'

'To here? You did.'

'No, no – you know fine well what I mean. What brought you round to the idea of marriage, all of a sudden? I thought you were a confirmed widower.'

'She is a good woman,' said Danforth. Then, feeling as though he ought to say more, 'I found I have no wish to go on alone. To end up like one of those Douglas creatures, Simms or Hardie. Mindless servants, bound to their master like bees to their queen.'

'Is that all?'

'Life, Arnaud. It is a short thing. I thought mine ended when my wife and child passed away in England. Yet here I stand still. What is that for? Why was I spared, if not to go on to something else? God commands that we go forth and multiply, not put our hands over our chests and wait for the grave. So ... so many of us have our time on this earth cut short. Painfully short. It seemed to me a great selfishness that I should be given such a stretch of life only to squander it in misery, never thinking. God gave us minds too, the better to serve him.'

'Good for you. I mean it,' said Martin.

'Was that all? You wished to interrogate me?'

'No. There is something else. I ... I'm going to Linlithgow,' He gnawed on a chunk of bread and then threw the rest to the ground. Immediately a seagull came down and barked at it before snatching it up and tearing off.

'What, has his Grace some message for the dowager? You might ride south with us – we are leaving tomorrow.'

'I want to see Mathieu's grave,' said Martin, his eyes still on the ground. One hand wandered up to his breast, where he had pinned the little thistle badge. Danforth fell silent, crossing himself at the boy's name.

'He was a good child. I am sure he will be missed by all who knew him.'

'Aye. But ... it's not just that. I've decided ... I'm leaving his Grace's service.'

'What?' Danforth jerked forward, putting out a hand to him.

'Don't try and convince me otherwise, Simon. I'm going over to the dowager. I've let him know.' He looked up, a crooked grin on his face. 'The cardinal says it's better to have a man on the inside anyway.'

'What?' Danforth repeated, cursing the stupidity of it. 'You are going to spy on her?'

'Of course not. No. He was just jesting. But I am going. I'm going to be a queen's man. Thought you'd be pleased at the

233

sound of that – me working for the royal household, can you imagine?'

'But … are you not happy in his Grace's service?'

'I'm not happy at all, Simon. I'm … I don't know. But not happy. Maybe I will be working for the dowager. Or maybe everything will be the same. But I want something else in life. I … I want to be married, to be like you.'

Danforth paused, his mouth falling open. No one had ever been envious of him before. He had not imagined it possible. 'But … but … you are a young man yet. Younger than me, past thirty now. There is time.'

'I hope so. I certainly don't want to wait until I'm at your great age before I take a wife!'

'Pah – better to wait and be sure she is a good woman. You – you are likely to end up with some toothless old dame with more money than sense. A kept man.'

Martin chuckled. 'Perhaps. Who knows.' They walked on a little in silence, veering around loaded and covered wagons, towards the gate of the palace. 'Let's take a look at the sea.'

The path led out, grassy stretches on either side curving round the high, whitewashed walls. They approached the edge of the cliffs on which the castle stood. The rhythmic roar and crash of the tide swept up to them, the screeching of seabirds occasionally drowned out by it. Ahead, the iron sheet stretched into the distance, broken here and there by white rollers. 'Well, there it is,' said Danforth. 'You have seen it? It looks to be at peace today,' he said. 'A good sight.' The salt picked its way into his nostrils, fresh and clean.

'It wouldn't dare be otherwise. Not on the day of your wedding.'

Danforth strained to detect a note of bitterness beneath the bonhomie. 'Let us hope it stays that way.

Martin was looking out intently. 'Aye. The great ocean. We're all like little fishes in that ocean.'

'All Neptune's minnows, to be sure.'

'Jesus,' said Martin, brushing a few crumbs from his doublet. 'I hope your new wife can stomach all of that pish. Rowan would have.'

234

'I think you will find, sir, that my wife has a stout heart and mind.'

'Do you love her?'

'I … I will do,' he said, taken aback by the bluntness of the question. 'At any rate, I shall enjoy greatly coming to know a woman's love again. Mistress … My wife – she makes me smile.' That, at least, had the benefit of unvarnished honesty.

'Should've been Rowan,' Martin muttered.

'Enough! Arrant nonsense. To speak of another woman on my wedding day, have you no shame?' He turned, crossing his arms, and beginning a march back the way they had come. Martin joined him, plucking at his sleeve.

'She'll need a stout mind as husband to a man who spends all day carping on Greek Gods! Unless you've just been after a cloth-eared nurse to wipe your arse and feed you soup with a spoon.'

'Neptune is the Roman name,' snapped Danforth. 'Not Greek. Any schoolboy might know that. And I should think you would want to learn while you can, for you will find few stout minds and fewer books in the library at Linlithgow!'

Together they made their way back to the castle, bickering contentedly.

Author's Note

From February to July 1543, Marie de Guise was indeed a virtual prisoner in the palace of Linlithgow, having been chased out of that other great Stewart palace, Holyroodhouse, by the lord governor and protector of Scotland, James Hamilton, Earl of Arran. In the ensuing months and years of political wilderness, Marie (I've rendered the spelling of her name in this way to avoid confusion with her infant daughter) was under scrutiny from the governor, whilst being courted by Cardinal Beaton. In March 1543, Beaton was moved from Dalkeith to Blackness before being released to his own castle. In that same month, the Scottish parliament legislated in favour of making the Bible available in Scots and English, and the queen dowager and Beaton joined forces with the newly-returned Matthew Stuart, Earl of Lennox (who was later to court Marie, be disappointed, and defect to the English, marrying Margaret Douglas and producing the infamous Lord Darnley, later husband to Mary Queen of Scots). Marie never gave up her attempts to secure her daughter's future, eventually sending her to France and finally managing to wrest governorship of Scotland from Arran. She became the country's regent in 1554 and held it until her death in 1560.

For those interested in Marie de Guise's life, I recommend Rosalind Marshall's masterful biography, *Mary of Guise* (Collins, 1977). In addition to covering the details of her life in France and Scotland, it recounts her serious and unspotted reputation, her occasional impatience, and, of course, her famous quip when Henry VIII sought her as a bride. Knowing that she was tall, the uxorious English king is said to have stated that, being big in person, he was in need of a big wife. Marie responded that although she might be a big woman, she had a little neck. If you are interested in her life beyond the period covered in the novel, her political ascent is covered in Pamela Ritchie's *Mary of Guise in Scotland, 1548 – 1560: A Political Study* (Tuckwell Press, 2002).

It was from Marshall's book that I also learned about the influx of Hamilton spies to Marie's household in the crucial days of 1543 on which the novel focuses. The inclusion of their allies, the Douglases, is my own invention. Real figures in Marie's household include Robert Gibb, her master of horse, and Thomas Marshall, her master cook. Gibb, who went on to be rewarded for his faithful service to the Stewarts with significant property and land grants, had his story told by his descendant, Sir George Duncan Gibb, in *The Life and Times of Robert Gib, Lord of Carribber* (1874, Longmans, Green, and Co.).

In charge of Scotland were not only Governor Arran, who was assured this position due to his being a grandson of James II, but the nefarious Douglas brothers, Archibald, Earl of Angus, and Sir George. This pair of rogues had long been exiled from Scotland, having fallen foul of James V, and as refugees in England, had been bought by Henry VIII. As a result, their goal during the period depicted in *The Cradle Queen* was to convince the Scottish governor and parliament (then known as 'the estates') to grant the infant Mary Queen of Scots to Henry VIII for marriage to his son, Prince Edward. However, as they were veteran turncoats, it is unclear exactly how committed they were to doing Henry's bidding (Angus, for example, was to fight against the English during the war known as the Rough Wooing). Marcus Merriman's *The Rough Wooings of Mary Queen of Scots* (Tuckwell Press, 2000) is invaluable in making sense of this time in Scottish and English history.

After the execution of Sir James Hamilton of Finnart, James V really is reported to have been haunted by dreams of his former friend. In those dreams, as the novel depicts, Finnart's ghost is said to have struck off the king's arms and threatened his head. This was interpreted as relating to the twin deaths of the king's sons, Albany and Ross. The tale can be found in George Buchanan's *History of Scotland* (Blackie and Fullerton, 1827), and is related in more modern biographies of James, such as Caroline Bingham's *James V, King of Scots* (Harper Collins, 1971). Bingham's and Merriman's books also record the gruesome legends of Finnart carving his initials into the faces of his victims.

In addition to Finnart's ethereal dream-haunting, the following stories depicted in the novel all have their genesis in sixteenth-century accounts: Margaret of Denmark's alleged poisoning; the burning of Janet Douglas; a wizened, blue-robed ghost warning James IV not to fight the English in 1513; Margaret Tudor's vision of her husband's body pierced with arrows; and the death of the tubercular Madeleine de Valois shortly after her arrival in Scotland. Needless to say, none of these events, whether the factual deaths or the ghostly tales, were recreated in 1543! Interesting reading here includes George Goodwin's *Fatal Rivalry* (Hachette, 2013), Caroline Bingham's *The Stewart Kingdom of Scotland, 1371 – 1603* (Weidenfeld & Nicolson, 1974), and John Ferguson's *Linlithgow Palace, Its History and Traditions* (Oxford University Press, 1910).

The subject of dreams in the early modern period is a fascinating one. For those who would like to know more about it, I would recommend Janine Rivière's unpublished PhD thesis, 'Dreams in Early Modern England: Frameworks of Interpretation' (University of Toronto, 2013). Valuable too is *Reading the Early Modern Dream: The Terrors of the Night* (Routledge, 2008) by Katharine Hodgkin, Michelle O'Callaghan, and S. J. Wiseman. For ghosts and similarly spooky matters, I strongly recommend Jane P. Davidson's *Early Modern Supernatural: The Dark Side of European Culture, 1400–1700* (Praeger, 2012), and Julian Goodare, Lauren Martin, and Joyce Miller's *Witchcraft and belief in Early Modern Scotland* (Palgrave Macmillan, 2008). As Goodare notes in the latter, ghosts in early modern Scottish culture are under researched.

That chief architect of the Reformation in Scotland, John Knox, was, during the events of the novel, an ordained Catholic priest and schoolmaster, as depicted. However, there is no evidence that he visited Linlithgow during Marie and Mary's pseudo-captivity there. He was, though, interested in reform, and it was in 1543, according to his personal history, that he was enjoying contact with like-minded men, notably George

Wishart (whom Cardinal Beaton was later to send to the stake). I enjoyed Roderick Graham's lively account of Knox's life, *John Knox: Democrat* (Hale, 2001), and it was in this fascinating biography I learnt that, to quote Graham, it was in 1543 'the first shoots of his reforming spirit broke through'. Those interested in seeing him beyond the stereotype of the ranting misogynist should enjoy Marie Macpherson's superb series of novels, *The First* and *Second Blast of the Trumpet* (Knox Robinson Publishing, 2013, 2016). *The Last Blast* is thankfully forthcoming. Knox's own *History of the Reformation in Scotland* (Wentworth Press, 2016) is also a (highly partisan) goldmine of information.

Linlithgow Palace is now a remarkably well-kept ruin, its roof lost to fire centuries ago. Still open to the public, it does not take much imagination to recreate its Renaissance splendour. I had the pleasure of visiting whilst researching the novel and must thank the local schoolchildren who served as tour guides. They were able to teach me much I did not know (and could not find in books) and I commend their ability to learn and recite massive amounts of information. I could not do that at their (or any) age. One liberty I have taken is with the stable block. For the purposes of the story, I have added one to the palace. However, the docent Frances at Linlithgow Palace very helpfully pointed out that in the early-sixteenth-century, treasurer's accounts indicate that horses were stabled in the burgh rather than within the palace walls. For matters relating to horses' behaviour and care, I must thank my friend – and expert horsewoman – Samantha Laing.

A useful guide to the palace of Linlithgow can be found in David and Judy Steel's beautifully-illustrated *Mary Stuart's Scotland* (Harmony Books, 1987). Information on furnishing and architecture is also available in John Dunbar's seminal *Scottish Royal Palaces* (Tuckwell Press, 1999), in which I was able to find information on Marie's tapestries, and the National Trust's *Scottish Renaissance Interiors* (1987, Mowbray House Press). Also incredibly helpful was *Stewart Style* (Tuckwell Press, 1996), edited by Janet Hadley Williams and *The History of the Town and Palace of Linlithgow* by George Waldie (A.

Waldie, 1868), from which I drew the information about one Henry Forrest being dismissed by James V as town provost. This Henry Forrest, who was provost of Linlithgow until the king replaced with Robert Wutherspoon, should not be confused with his namesake, the Henry Forrest, also apparently from Linlithgow, who was burned for heresy in the early 1530s. The reasons behind his dismissal are obscure. Alexander Forrest is fictional, but the brother mentioned in the novel is not.

Plays, interludes, and masques were performed in early modern Scotland, and in depicting one, I drew on a number of sources. These include A. J. Mill's *Mediaeval Plays in Scotland* (Blom, 1969), *Ballatis of Luve: The Courtly Love Lyric 1400 – 1570* (Edinburgh University Press, 1970), edited by John MacQueen, and *Scottish Poetry of the Sixteenth Century* (Sands & Company, 1892), edited by George Eyre-Todd. Danforth's speech about the Douglas brothers being akin to two fruit trees is adapted from Daniel de Bosola's lines in one of my favourite Renaissance plays, *The Duchess of Malfi*, by one of my favourite early modern playwrights, John Ford's. In keeping with the theme of Renaissance drama, it felt right to end the story with a wedding. Whether or not Simon Danforth ended up with the right woman, I don't know. What do you think? Let me know on Twitter @ScrutinEye.

*

Printed in Poland
by Amazon Fulfillment
Poland Sp. z o.o., Wrocław

54475959R00148